The Urchin Heiress

by

Cheryl A. Cornell

This is a work of fiction. Names, characters, places, and incidents are either the product of the author's imagination or are used fictitiously, and any resemblance to actual persons living or dead, business establishments, events, or locales, is entirely coincidental.

The Urchin Heiress

Contact Information: info@thewildrosepress.com

Cover Art by *Tina Lynn Stout*

The Wild Rose Press, Inc.
PO Box 708
Adams Basin, NY 14410-0708
Visit us at www.thewildrosepress.com

Publishing History
First Edition, 2023
Trade Paperback ISBN 978-1-5092-4971-8
Digital ISBN 978-1-5092-4972-5

Published in the United States of America

"I don't scream and yell unless it's my choice to prove a point. I prefer to lean in and speak very softly so the person has no choice but to give me their full attention."

Dodd burst out laughing. "Damn, girl, are you sure you never met Old Adley?"

"I got better. I was raised by his daughter. She was his original student."

"What do you want, Lark? Where do we start?" Greg pushed his plate away and brought his coffee forward.

"For today, I'd like to drop the animosity, get some true information, and take a tour of the offices."

"I'm not sure that would be such a good idea. Will thinks having you around the office might make some employees antsy." He glanced at her.

She knew it was a good call to keep her appearance the same. Jeans, boots, and a blazer, with minimal makeup and her hair pulled back in a braid.

"Antsy? That's what Mr. Dodd thinks I'll make the employees?" She sat back and smiled at the corporate lawyer. "My plan is to make the employees a bit antsy. I plan on making the board downright frightened." She reined in her smile. "If Mr. Dodd thinks my presence will be disruptive, he has no idea." She turned to stare at Dodd. "Does the entire board feel the same?"

Neither man answered.

"Well?"

"They generally keep to themselves, and Greg and I keep to our jobs."

"Which are?" she asked.

Greg stood and glared at her. "I won't be questioned or scrutinized like this." He left the dining room, avoiding Spike.

From her perspective, his tantrum was a major overreaction to her question.

Praise for Cheryl A. Cornell

Another Man's Love 5 Books from Long and Short Reviews

The Proxy Wife "You Gotta Read" from yougottareadreviews.com

Dedication

To anyone who has been underestimated and prevailed.

Acknowledgments

My thanks to everyone at The Wild Rose Press for their continued support, especially my very patient editors Roseann Armstrong and Josette Arthur and Tina Lynn Stout for the beautiful cover art.

Chapter One

Urchin—a mischievous young unkempt child.

Greg hated the required social events that went with giving money to charity, even if it was in a palatial historical music school. Hell, in his mind just writing the check should have been enough. Why spend so much of the profits to have a party to prove…what? That they needed contributions to put on affairs so they could get dressed up and rub elbows with their contributors. They'd have a lot more money to spend on programs if they skipped these arduous receptions. If he hadn't felt a kinship to this particular charity, he would have just sent the check and forgotten all about the party. Since he had been in California on vacation, his company's board members had impressed upon him the need to show the Braylin face in society.

He let out a sigh. He used to hate when Adley reminded him of his duties to the family and company. Now the company had taken to reminding him too, although they believed blatant worked best. After listening to their rants, he missed Adley. At least the old guy had a bit of finesse.

Business was business. So he'd pulled on a black suit sans tie and made his appearance.

Musicians played on a rotating basis in different areas of the main level of the school. After an hour of subpar champagne and wilted canapés being passed by waitstaff looking to impress some Hollywood bigwigs, he'd hit his limit. He'd dealt with too many handshakes with long-ago contemporaries of his and his family's conglomerate to stand another minute. The few people he'd figured he'd see had been seen, quick pleasantries passed, and he was on his way out.

Since his arrival, his photo had been snapped for the tabloids, websites, blogs, and private collections. Winding through the crowd toward the front door, he was sidetracked too many times. He turned on his heel and headed to the side entrance. That was when he saw her.

She was stunning in her simplicity. Even a distance away, he saw she was tall and lean with breasts too many women paid for. No way could she be wearing a bra under the dress. The outline of her protruding raspberry nipples proved her breasts were natural. His fingers flexed at his sides, aching to feel their fullness. The front was deceiving, almost modest because of the draped neckline. She'd pushed back the long sleeves of the silky material, an antique diamond watch on her left wrist catching the light.

Her dark brunette hair was pulled back in some fancy twist, revealing the nape of her neck. Ornate clips brought attention to the style with their glint. She wore no rings or necklace. Dangling diamond earrings in an ornate design defined her long, slim neck. His breath caught in his throat when she turned away. The back of her dress was all but nonexistent. The material draped slightly at the base of her spine, mimicking the neckline. Her bare back and no visible inner construction was how he knew she wasn't wearing a bra. She stood steady in high heels the same color as the dress. In this light, the color looked like a ripe peach. She held a small clutch bag in the same hue.

Normally, Greg didn't chase a woman. He spent most of the evening trying to avoid women. Some he knew, some he'd met, and even more wanted introductions or were bold enough to introduce themselves. His jacket pocket held several business cards he'd taken to be polite. Two more had been tucked into his handkerchief pocket by women who had wandering hands.

Years earlier he would have joked with his frat brothers about how many women's phone numbers they'd come home with after each party. But tonight, in this moment, he would do just about anything to find out who the statuesque brunette was and why he'd never seen or met her before. Just watching her could be habit forming. When she turned in his direction, he flashed her his best smile with a nod. She looked past him or through him. Either way, she didn't acknowledge his existence. With an intense realization, he knew the extra draw was that she'd shut down his glance without consideration. His worldly smile hadn't garnered her attention; rather, she seemed bored by the move. Now meeting her became a matter of pride.

Weaving through the crowd, he wanted to reach her quickly. Who knew if he'd see her again. The lobby of the concert hall had several areas set up with students still performing. The event was supposed to expose him to new talent and allow him to see where his money was going. Maybe this woman was a student.

As he approached, he caught her throaty laughter filtering through the crowd at something an older gentleman said. He knew the man and held back a grimace when the guy let his hand drop to her waist and then her butt. He didn't hold back a laugh when she deliberately used her hand to pick his up and drop it at his side. Whatever she said to the man, he looked as white as a ghost. The woman disappeared into the crowd. Seeing the woman put the old codger in his place made his evening worthwhile.

Only the color of her dress allowed him to find her among the throngs of people. She was heading toward the side exit, which had been his destination too. With a bit of gentle maneuvering, he caught up with her or rather made it to the area just before she did.

He wasn't often speechless. But this woman took his voice away and gave him an instant erection. She was stunning up close. She had dark brown eyes and wore minimal makeup.

"Don't you just hate these fundraiser appearances? I could think of other things I'd rather be doing tonight." He looked directly at her and waited for a response. Under different circumstances, he might have continued with something along the lines of "join me for a fire and brandy back at my place." Not tonight, not with this woman.

"I dislike any required appearances. It makes me feel like chattel being displayed for the cause." She looked directly at him.

Greg had no idea what she was thinking, only that her gaze was intense. He had to wonder if she did everything with the same intensity. The image of her on her knees before him with his cock between her lips made him shift his hips to accommodate his growing erection. He'd been hard at the first sight of her. Now he was about to lose his composure. He had a fleeting image of a woman he'd met long ago at an outdoor rock concert. The memory was hazy, but it brought a smile to his lips.

"I've not seen you at any of these fundraisers before. Are you new to the cause?"

She threw back her head and gave him a throaty laugh. "No, I usually avoid them. But tonight, an old friend was playing piano in the other room. I came for moral support."

"Is he any good?"

"She. I think so, but music is subjective to the listener."

"I'm…" He reached his hand to her, and she took a step back. He didn't finish his introduction. Had they met in the past and he'd forgotten her? But that wouldn't happen. She was a woman he would remember.

"I'm not interested," she finished for him, switching the wineglass to her right hand, effectively shutting down any handshake or contact.

"Not interested in me or any of the men here tonight?"

"I've met more strangers, mostly men, tonight than I care to remember. Right about now, I'm thinking I've done my duty. My friend saw I attended *her* performance, the charity got their check, and I'm sick of plastering on this fake smile for the cameras that seem to be everywhere."

"That I can relate to. I sometimes think people go out of their way to use a poor photograph for their posts just to annoy me."

"I'll agree with you on that. Which is another reason I try to avoid this type of party."

"So we're both bored. How about accompanying me to a small, dark restaurant for a real drink?" He gave her one of his best smiles.

She shook her head. "If you had said burgers and fries, I might have been tempted."

"I could arrange that too," he offered a bit too quickly. They were facing each other, glancing to the side at the crowd occasionally. "I liked the way you handled that old fool feeling you up. I have to wonder what you told him that made him pale."

She smiled at him. "A gal can't give away all her secrets. You never know. I might need to use the same line on you one day."

"I'm crushed, Ms.?" He waited for her to answer, but she just looked him up and down, the way he would size up a woman. He didn't like the move and suddenly realized how callous he'd been in the past.

Her look was an obvious check of his overall being. His erection pushing the limits of his zipper didn't help his situation. This intense scrutiny was going to get him in trouble. Just when he was afraid he'd get a similar brush-off as the old dude, she curled her lips into a smile.

"Your cock is hard," she said.

"I know."

"How long have you been holding that back tonight?"

"About ten minutes, since I saw you across the room."

She laughed openly at him. "I guess I deserved that one. Too bad. If I truly thought I'd inspired your hard-on, I might have wanted to help you do something about it."

"What?" His voice squeaked that single word, and

he glanced around to see if anyone had turned to look at him. Then he added, “Do I get to know your name?”

She laughed at him again. “Look, I don’t want to know your name, your story, or anything about you. I don’t live around here, so I doubt we’d run into each other. You are a stunning specimen of the male being. Besides, I have a thing for blond-haired men with green eyes.”

Greg swallowed hard. “You’re blunt.”

“Yes, it helps thin the herd. Are you discreet?”

“To a fault,” he told this engaging brunette. That was what he decided she was, simply engaging. No small talk, no mixed messages. Just lust.

“Are you interested in a quick moment in time that doesn’t exist after it’s over? Can you screw and not be clingy after?”

He nodded.

She studied him to the point he began to fidget. “I never figured I’d see you again,” she said with a sly smile.

“Excuse me?” he asked, suddenly on alert. Her laugh wove its way into his brain before her answer struck him. “I assume this means you like all kinds of music.” If she didn’t acknowledge his comment, he’d forget that passing memory of years earlier and just enjoy the moment.

“Never assume, especially when it comes to me.”

“No assumptions, just clarifications. And I never thought I’d see you again either. Only in my dreams on occasion.” He let his lips curl into a smile. “You’ve grown up since then.”

“I’m not the same woman you met at that rock concert. But you’ve matured and cleaned up nicely.”

"Thank you, but you win that category. This is quite a change in appearance and attitude from the jeans and T-shirt of that first night."

The expression on her face changed as she glanced past him. Her smile was gone, and she looked visibly annoyed, her hand clutching her purse tighter.

"Are you okay?"

"Yes, just a bit disgusted." She nodded to a man across the room who was heading in their direction. "My attitude is appropriate with him."

"Is he a problem?" he asked, not wanting to get involved in a lover's quarrel.

"Only in his mind. He didn't take rejection well." She stood tall and stared at the other man.

If Greg were on the receiving end of that look, he'd turn around. He was fascinated that she could change from this sensual woman to someone he wouldn't ever want to cross. Again, he asked, "Is he a problem?"

The man paused to talk with another woman, and she seemed relieved. "No. Our parents were in the same social circle years ago. He always made assumptions because of that association. I remember him bullying me in junior high school. I was too tall, too thin, and the braces didn't help."

"Somehow I don't picture you allowing anyone to bully you. How did you handle it?" He shifted his weight to his other hip, hoping his erection would settle.

Her smile gave him pause. He wasn't sure how to read it, only that he wouldn't want to be the one to cross her.

"We didn't allow it for long. My mom took me to self-defense classes when I turned twelve, and I surprised him at school. Laid him out twice." She didn't hold back a laugh but didn't share the details. She only said, "The first time he said I caught him off guard. The second time he took the hint."

Now it was Greg's turn to let out a hearty laugh. "What happened after that?"

"It was a slight problem at the time. His parents weren't happy I'd embarrassed their son. My mom told them bluntly he and boys like him were the reason I took those classes. It didn't hurt that she added they should be thankful I laid him out because she'd have embarrassed him worse if she'd had to step in. She mentioned a lawyer in the family that would take over if necessary."

"How did they react to that?"

"They kept away from my mother and me. The only reason Mom had anything to do with them was because of a few charities they had in common. It was easy enough to take a step back from those functions."

"Your mom let them chase her away from the charities?"

"No, she'd never allowed anyone to run her off something she was truly invested in. The parents had the same problem as the son, overprivileged and overgrown egos. It was simpler to just ignore them and move on. She continued to support her interests." Again, she smiled but didn't share the memory. "They gave her a wide berth after that incident. And trust me, if my mother gave you a look of disgust, you didn't take it lightly."

"I'm getting the feeling you developed the same 'look.' "

"Don't cross me, and it won't be a problem. Besides, I'm more inclined to send a check and skip these functions. Dread comes to mind with this type of party."

"What other charities do you support? Maybe we'll

meet at another function one day."

"Music and the arts and animal rescue. I doubt we'd meet again. I'm only in town for business."

"Those are all good causes. I'm only here to support the music program." He sipped his flat champagne just to wet his lips. "And to represent my family. And I don't live here either. Just a side stop on my way home from a vacation."

"So neither of us prefers to spend our evenings at these functions. I still prefer rock concerts." She gave him a slight smile.

"So do I, but family duty prevailed. This crowd is too snooty for my liking. Half of them don't know me. The other half only want new gossip for their rumor mills."

"Neither of those are my preference. They have my money, and I've been seen. I can leave now with a clear conscience."

He glanced around the room. They were garnering too much attention. "It seems people are curious about both of us tonight."

"Imagine if they knew how we really met and what we did that last time." Her laugh was natural.

"Let's not tell them. I have enough problems with the tabloids and gossip sites when they don't have the truth." His thought slipped out before he could censor the content.

"So far, I've kept off the radar. I'll drop out of sight after tonight and go back to my quiet, staid life."

"You? Staid and quiet? I don't think I believe that." He shook his head.

"I like my life, my friends, and my work. I just don't like an audience." She surveyed the room and nodded to someone in the group. "Look, you might be an interesting aside on this trip, and I'd like to finish what we started years back. But there are too many prying eyes."

"Agreed. Maybe we could meet someplace later?"

"No, it's now or never. I'm leaving." She looked at her watch. "My flight is in a few hours."

"Then I take now. Can you find us a place?" The worst that could happen was she'd refuse.

"Yes. There are private practice rooms on the second floor." Her voice never wavered.

Was she calling his bluff? If he went upstairs, would she be there, or would the room be empty? "You go ahead. I'll circle the crowd one more time and meet you up there." He paused and looked at her. "Have you used the rooms for privacy before?"

"No, I just found them when I was here a few years ago. I wanted a quiet place to slip away…alone for a bit." She looked at her watch. "I've got fifteen minutes before my car is due. Are you interested?"

"Yes." It was all he could verbalize.

She glanced at the side staircase and headed in that direction. When she reached the top landing, she turned right. He put his glass on the tray of a passing waiter, skirted the room, and headed upstairs. At the top, he turned right. She was standing beside an open door. No light was on inside. The door had a small window high up. She crooked her finger at him and disappeared inside. He wavered for one blinding moment. Was this a setup? He just didn't care.

The room was small, maybe eight by ten, with an upright piano on the far wall and a small wooden bench before it.

She sat on the bench, waiting for him with her legs crossed, a long length of toned thigh visible. As he closed the door, he automatically looked to the corners for an obvious camera.

"I didn't spot any recording devices in here." She uncrossed her legs. "Can you do this with no regrets and no chance of ever seeing me again?"

"Yes, I can. One time with you would be better than none. I'd wondered what happened to you after that night."

"No names. I don't want to know anything about you, just about your erection." She hitched up her skirt a bit and widened her legs, revealing more of her toned thighs. "One last question—are you married, engaged, or otherwise entangled with another male or female right now?"

"No," he said, still not sure this was really happening.

"Good." She reached to the piano and grabbed her clutch purse. Then she pulled a condom package from it and placed it on the wooden surface. She turned back to him. "Come here."

He didn't stagger, but his erection made it difficult to walk the few steps to her. She stood and grasped his cock with her right hand. She used minimal pressure to stroke him up and back. Her other hand wrapped around his neck, her fingers filtering through his hair as she nipped at his bottom lip.

She squeezed her hand a bit tighter, and he wrapped one arm around her waist and the other behind her head. With a slight shift, he had her pressed to him. This was his moment, and he took it, using his hand to move her head into position, his lips covering hers immediately.

He didn't force his tongue into her mouth. He simply kissed her. And she kissed back. It was a sensual kiss, not a vapid, saliva-dripping, slobbering kiss like others he'd experienced and abhorred.

This woman knew the art of kissing, of how sensual and erotic a kiss could be. He throbbed in her palm. He had to change the dynamic of the situation, or he would lose his control.

She must have sensed his predicament because she took her hand from his erection and repositioned her hips so her core rubbed against his length. Greg didn't know how long they stayed that way in the small, dark room with her rubbing against him and their hands roaming. She managed to unbutton his shirt and pulled it from his pants. He pushed the shoulder of her dress, and it slipped down her arm, baring her breast to his sight and touch.

"Your nipple is hard. I love raspberry nipples. Yours are so responsive." He rolled her skin between his fingers, and she pushed harder against his touch. When she groaned at his move, he figured he was on the right track. He wrapped his lips around the hardened nub and sucked lightly.

"Harder. You won't hurt me," she told him as she twitched her hips against his length.

He went with her want and pulled her deeper between his lips. Her hand rose behind his head, gently giving him permission to take more. He did, sucking harder and taking a bit of the surrounding flesh. That groan was different from the last. She was the one to pull his lips from her breast.

At first, he figured he'd gone too far, but she was pushing the other shoulder of her dress down, baring her other breast to him. He switched sides, and she continued to rub against him, dropping her hand to press against both of them. If he didn't stop this, it would end here. Then she froze, her body quivering and her breath becoming uneven. For several seconds, he stayed where they were, still sucking her nipple while her body shook against him.

****

Her body quaked, and she closed her eyes to see the flecks of pinpoint colored light reflect on her eyelids. With several deep breaths, she composed herself.

"I need you inside me to really come." It was a flat statement. She carefully released his belt and, even slower, the zipper on his pants. "Wouldn't want to hurt that before I got to use it."

His laughing lightened her mood and the moment. She pushed his pants down his hips, and he sprang to life before her. She grabbed him and held his base. "You're hot to my touch."

"You knew that," he told her.

She liked that he was almost breathless. With her fingers still wrapped around him, she went back to his mouth, kissing him boldly but not with her tongue, just her lips. When she drew back, she released him and snaked her hands under her dress to remove her peach-colored silk panties. She didn't make a show of the move. It was just a necessity.

With two steps back to the piano and two back to this hot, horny man, she tore open the package and unrolled the condom over his length. She looked at him as she covered him, and he groaned.

"Change your mind?" she questioned.

"No, but if you keep handling me like that, this will be over before it starts."

"That's a yes to continuing?"

"A definite yes."

"Good." She gathered the skirt of her dress and lifted it high. Immediately, his hand dropped to stroke her lips.

"God, you're hot and slick. Let me lick you."

"Not now. I'm too close," she told him. "Hold me up."

He did by grasping her waist and lifting her. She wrapped her legs around his thighs and used one hand around his neck to balance herself. She used the other hand to steady his base and lower onto his condom-clad length. When she thought to take him slowly, in small increments to feel how he stretched her when the moment came, she couldn't resist. Holding his erection, she dropped her full weight onto him, accepting him into her body. She squirmed over him until he was just where she wanted him. She rose slightly and let her weight fall back.

He switched his hands to under her butt, guiding her movements and holding her tight. He took a staggering step back against the wall and braced his weight as they continued the slow up-and-back slide. She shifted from side to side to keep him off-kilter and loved the exasperated look on his face and the way his green eyes watched her in the darkened room.

"You're trying to drive me crazy," he whispered and latched onto her left nipple. Immediately, her hand went to his neck, pushing him harder against her skin. He'd leave her breast for a beat, kiss her hard on the lips, and take her other nipple between his lips.

"Harder. Bite me hard. Suck me harder." She didn't care about a pattern. She used her inner muscles to taunt him, to pull him deeper inside her. She shifted her weight, rising just a bit, until he hit her spot. "Please don't move," she whispered into his ear before she bit his lobe.

"You're throbbing against me, drawing me deeper. You're like a warm velvet vise around me. It's like I'm a prisoner inside you."

"Mine until I come." With a light hand, she lifted his chin and kissed him firmly on the lips. "You're good." She let her head fall back as she released her hold on him.

He caught on quickly, taking her nipple and sucking hard.

Her words were almost a whisper. "Make me come."

"The lady has a wish." With a sly grin, he went back to sucking her harder.

She liked that he understood her terse commands. With more pressure, he sucked her nipple deeper, taking more of the surrounding tissue between his lips. That was when it happened, when it all lined up for her. With this stranger's lips suckling her nipple and his fingers biting into her buttocks, his erection throbbed at the exact spot she needed.

Grasping him tighter, she let her body ride out her orgasm. She held his head tight to her and felt him throb deep within her walls. Still clutching him, she used her hips to taunt him a bit more, feeling those same stirrings. Lighter but still a stir that had her inner muscles flexing around him.

If she wanted to, she could keep him inside her and most likely get him hard again, but that could be dangerous. So she did the last thing she wanted to. She relaxed over him. He licked at her nipple, but it was a soothing lick, not a sucking nip. He held her tight to him, and his breath was as out of sync as hers.

Eventually, his legs shook, and her thighs cried out from the position. Carefully and slowly, she used her hands on his shoulders to balance herself and rose, letting him slide from her body. Allowing one leg to drop changed the ache in her thighs. She kept the other one wrapped around his hip a bit longer, not relinquishing him completely. Reaching her hands to his head and directing him to her lips was too easy. Even then, he seemed to sense kissing her was different. Moments later he released her leg and shifted to stand straight.

He grasped her waist until she was steady. "You okay?"

"I got what I wanted, twice. How about you?"

"Do you know how tight you felt around me? Christ, at one point I was afraid you'd snap me in two."

"I swim for recreation," she told him with a laugh.

"Hell, you must be an Olympic swimmer."

"No, just a hobby, but it does help muscle control all over."

"I'll have to try it sometime." He stood where she'd left him.

She should have been embarrassed, but she couldn't muster the emotion. Instead, she just felt sated. Pulling her skirt down and pushing the sleeves of her dress back up her shoulders was easy enough. She was aware of how fiercely he studied her as she shifted inside the silky fabric. She walked to the piano and plucked a tissue from her purse. Then she reached down, picked up the condom wrapper, and handed that to him along with the tissue. He used the tissue to cover the used condom and crushed it in his hand. She dipped to pick up her panties. Those she folded over several times before she tucked them inside her purse.

"What color do you call your dress?" He shifted from the wall and hiked his pants up his hips. Then he buttoned his shirt and tucked it in before zippering himself up.

"I'd call it apricot, but it might look pink or peach depending on the light."

"Apricot," he said as he finished putting his clothes to rights. "To my eyes, it looks peach."

A phone dinged in the background, and she went back to her purse. With a quick look, she turned to him. "My car is here. My fifteen minutes are up. Am I reasonably put back together?"

"Unfortunately, yes. I'd much rather muss you again."

"If that happened, one of us might become attached to the other, and then what would happen? One of us would want a relationship, and the other not so much. Let's just let this be what it was."

"Just what was it?" He looked at her and reached forward.

She didn't hesitate to push her breast into the palm of his hand. "Just a moment in time to remember and smile about one day." She held her hand over his. "A moment to think about when I'm old and gray. A moment when I didn't walk away from something I wanted to experience." She looked at him, and his green eyes glistened. "What did you think that was?"

"Like you said, just a moment in time to remember fondly."

"Good. Thank you for ending this evening a lot more interesting than it started."

"I'd say I'd be willing to oblige anytime, but I don't think you'd want that."

"Smart man." She took the final step to close the space between them before she rose and kissed him hard on the lips. "Don't forget to get rid of the condom. I don't want some student or the janitorial staff finding it."

"Got you covered," he told her. "Can I walk you out to your car?"

"No, I'd prefer you didn't. And so you don't have to worry, I won't be coming back here for any more fundraisers this season. I'm heading north."

"Maybe one day we'll run into each other."

"I hope not. I'd rather keep you as a memory."

"A great memory?" he asked.

"See? There you go getting all needy." She laughed and reached for her purse. "Please give me a few minutes to slip out before going back down to the party."

"I can do that for you." He leaned back against the wall.

"Goodbye," she said as she checked her dress one last time. With a quick move, she smoothed her hair back in place. "Bright light when I open the door."

She steadied herself and closed her eyes when she opened the door. The bright fluorescent light from the hall would have been blinding in the first second. She squared her shoulders and headed downstairs and straight out the front door. Her car was there as expected. Slipping into the back seat of the darkened vehicle, she got lost in her thoughts.

Thankfully, this guy had realized it was her scene and let her make the major moves. She liked the control factor, especially on a night like this.

On occasion, she took a total stranger to use for her

satisfaction. To never see again, just to use his body, as many men had tried to use hers over the years. Tonight she'd picked an amazing man. He was tall, with blond hair that brushed his collar. She couldn't miss his piercing green eyes. His cock was long, thick, and hot to her touch. She liked how he kissed her and how he seemed to sense the limits she put on it.

She wondered what might have been if they weren't interrupted the first time they met. Then again, they had both been young, and she'd never know how it might have turned out. Best to let that stay where it was, to keep the memory of kissing and fondling a stranger who had made her feel sexual and sensual.

Chapter Two

Five Years Later

Lark was annoyed. In her mind, she had plenty of reasons. As the private plane took off from San Francisco to the East Coast, she settled the dogs. At first, she'd thought a private flight was a waste of money. But since this would be a permanent move, or maybe a semipermanent move, she needed the extra space. The dogs had never been on a plane. Hell, she'd never cared for the experience on the past flights she'd taken. She did not like being out of control. At least this way, she had the dogs with her in the cabin, not in cages in the cargo hold. She only crated the dogs if she was driving alone. If they whined and barked, she didn't care. Two pilots were at the controls, and a steward fussed around her to distraction.

"I'd appreciate a bowl of water for the dogs, and I'll just take coffee for now."

She had to remember the Braylin board members wouldn't have resorted to bringing her there if they had any other means. Now it seemed they had a use for her. Of course, they hadn't summoned her with that excuse. Rather, the contact had been made through a sleazy lawyer who showed up at her door with an invitation to visit her adopted cousin. He'd made it apparent she and her cousin were to share the Long Island estate. The wording had made her feel like the poor relation he had no other way to deal with. The toady little man had told her that she should be "honored by their acceptance of her into their family."

She smiled when she remembered him shuffling his feet on the top step of her house. She hadn't allowed him to bully his way into her home. "You're a complete stranger, sir. What do you want?" What she had done was take the papers from him and briskly send him away after listening to only a few of his demands. She had watched him through the curtained window while he stood on her front porch after she'd closed the door in his face.

The confused expression on his face suggested nobody had ever dared do something like that before. After all, he was counsel for the Braylins. Lark didn't give a fuck who he was. What she wanted to know was why, after all these years, did they suddenly want to acknowledge her as Adley's granddaughter.

That had led her to the computer and days of research on the family and their holdings. With the help of a friend from college, she managed deeper research than the few pages the lawyer had given her. Steve's mind worked in different directions than hers. With his searches, they found a stunning amount of information in unprotected files. That would be the first thing she changed. Only corporate employees should be able to access corporate files.

Then she hired an attorney she'd worked with on a few bankruptcy cases while practicing as a CPA. He managed to break the different firewalls and codes in place and gave her access to a plethora of information not meant for public viewing. The amount of information both her friends gathered was too much to comprehend.

Braylin Industries board members had spent the last five years using the corporate and family money as they pleased. And they neglected to inform her she was the major recipient in Adley Braylin's will. Only after it was explained to them by the lawyers that she was necessary to make certain funds available was she contacted. Suddenly, she had value, monetary value they needed. As a certified accountant, she'd done her due diligence, and the research had turned up a distressing situation. Lark would now be responsible for every employee's job and future long term. None of the board would be happy with the restructuring she planned to accomplish.

As Adley's letter to her stated, he hoped that, as the only living true-blood heir, she'd have more business sense. One thing she wanted was to find out if the resealed envelope containing the letter from her grandfather to her was the original. It was dated a few months before his death.

It's my greatest hope that you can teach your "adopted cousin" the value of a true day's work. I believe Greg will accept the board members' advice without doing any research of his own. This oversight on his part may have led the board to consider some of their financial crimes wouldn't be discovered. Once brought to light, the information would create chaos for the company, stockholders, employees, and those board members involved.

I fear I've waited too long and will not live long enough to use the information I've collected against the board members and hidden. I've protected the files because once revealed, the company will never be the same.

Greg just wanted to cash checks and have a lavish lifestyle without actually working. From your school and work history, I hope you'll not be taken in by the board members' platitudes and pats on the head. My greatest hope is you'll set Braylin back to rights and keep it prospering into the future.

There was more in the letter. Apparently, Adley had kept a watch on his daughter and granddaughter. He'd hoped his daughter would fail and come back to the family for monetary and moral support. He never considered Maureen wouldn't follow his missives and come back to Long Island. For now, until she got to know the players better, she'd let them think she was a shy woman with no business drive.

After reviewing the files for the umpteenth time, she closed the laptop and rubbed her temples. She smiled at the steward, who put a fresh cup of coffee before her and paused to pet the dog he'd just stepped over. While Spike let out a low growl, she slipped her finger through his collar and patted his head, assuring him it was okay. The dog stood, stretched, and circled before lying back down across her lap, facing the aisle. He was on alert, and that was fine with her.

When she couldn't drink any more coffee, she asked for sparkling water and opened the paper files. There she studied the family and Greg Braylin's bio yet again, committing it to memory. Her grandfather, Adley Braylin, had been a railroad engineer when he met his wife, Nancy. She was taken with him at first sight. Nancy's family had other ideas for her future and who she would marry until Adley made a stand.

He proposed to Nancy, and they eloped. Needless to say, her family wasn't happy. They cut the couple off for three years. When they learned Adley was prospering and making a decent living, he and Nancy were accepted back into the family, albeit with strained and staid views and morals.

Nancy went on to have a son, Roderick, and then a daughter, Maureen. From what her mother had told her, Nancy became a wilting violet after their births, weak willed and prone to health issues, real and imaginary. Adley pushed on to make his mark and prove worthy of Nancy's choice. Her family had defined ideas of how a society wife was supposed to behave. Hands-on parenting had horrified and embarrassed her family.

Lark remembered her mother would admit that she always knew when Nancy's parents were about to visit by the distinct change of attitude in the household. Nancy would be nervous before and physically and emotionally drained after for days that turned into weeks. Maureen hadn't made the correlation until she was an adult.

Maureen had relayed memories of a few visits to her grandparents' stately mansion. Church clothes and manners were expected. She and Rod were supposed to be seen and not heard.

When Nancy's parents died, her core family moved from their middle-class ranch home she had fond memories of to Nancy's family mansion that came with rules and harsh memories. Even so, in the first years they lived there, she remembered laughter and affection. But when Nancy's extended family visited, the old mores and attitudes returned.

Apparently, Nancy's cousins were beyond annoyed they didn't inherit any of her parents' money. Adley had gone on to make all the decisions for the business and family. Nancy inherited the estate, as Maureen had described it, on Long Island. That was when Adley truly flourished. All Nancy had to do was make occasional social appearances and not question her husband.

Adley must have been a hard old guy. Rod was expected to excel in school and athletics. Maureen excelled in swimming and tennis. Rod was also groomed to do business on the golf course.

Their dates were carefully chosen for each of them. While Roderick—or Rod, as her mother had referred to him—accepted his father's choices for possible future spouses, Maureen rebelled. She dated artists and musicians. After all, it was the 1990s.

At college, which was chosen for her, Maureen managed to keep her grades up and hide her artistic draw to ceramics and eventually glass designs.

From what Lark remembered of her mother's stories of young adulthood, the first time her mother showed her works, they'd been widely received as colorful and abstract. Adley, however, had not seen the value in her works. He'd only seen the wasted time.

Maureen and Lark discussed his total lack of realization when issuing his orders. After all, his wife Nancy had gone against her parents' wishes to marry him. He should have realized his actions all but forced her and her brother to avoid his determination to make his family respectable for public consumption.

Her brother, Rod, had stuck to the plan, somewhat. The right college, the right business degree, and on to the family business. He was the golden boy, while Maureen was considered the throwback hippie child with no future.

Rod got away from marriage by spending a year abroad studying with other corporations that worked with or depended on the Braylin corporation. Maureen escaped by spending her gap year in Europe too. But she wasn't learning the family business; she was studying the art and architecture of the foreign lands.

When their mother Nancy took ill, both were recalled home. Rod came home with a woman he'd met and married in England. Margaret Maden was considered acceptable because she was a widow with a small son, Greg Maden. Adley made it clear that Greg would never inherit the Braylin fortune or business. Rather, the children of Rod and Margaret would receive the benefits of the name and fortune.

Rod, in a moment of defiance, legally adopted Greg and gave him the Braylin name. Unfortunately, Margaret never had another child, and when she died suddenly of an aneurism, everyone thought it very sad.

While Maureen was in France studying, she met a man whose name was never uttered, even by Maureen. To this day, Lark only knew her father's first name was Jacques from letters she'd found after her mother died. When he found out Maureen was pregnant with his child, he'd simply left. Maureen had never looked for him and refused to let Lark start a search, refusing to give names and details.

Lark would change that eventually, out of curiosity and anger. She'd find Jacques and show him what he lost, namely her, when he'd abandoned her and her mother. Returning home, Maureen had kept her pregnancy private until Nancy passed away. Maureen was then shunned by Adley. He cut her off just as his wife, Nancy, had been cut off years before by her family.

But Maureen was no shrinking-violet personality. She packed her bag and left, eventually settling in San

Francisco where she had her daughter. Her name was chosen because Adley called the relationship and pregnancy a lark that should be terminated so she could find a suitable husband. When she was born, her mother named her Lark Braylin. They lived on the West Coast and never had contact with the East Coast side of the family.

From her research, Lark knew Rod had gone on to disobey his father a second time and married a divorcée, Linda. While they stayed married, Linda never produced a proper Braylin heir either. Later, at Adley's insistence and arduous tests, Rod discovered he didn't have a high sperm count and would most likely never father any children.

Lark found that information in a letter from one of Maureen's childhood friends. They quietly kept in contact, and Maureen learned what was going on in the family.

Adley's one concession to the information was to send Rod and Linda to Europe where test-tube babies were being conceived. Still, it didn't work. Linda never got pregnant.

But from what Lark learned, she made Rod and his adopted son happy. Both Rod and Linda were killed in an auto accident on a rainy night on the back roads of Long Island. Thankfully, by then Greg was in college and slightly out of Adley's reach. Maureen was never notified of her brother's death; rather, she found out in the business section of the daily newspaper. The same information was in the last letter from her East Coast friend. That last letter also mentioned her friend's illness. There were no letters after that one.

Her grandfather had died five years ago. Maureen

was never notified. Again, she read about it in the business section of the newspaper. The other thing that nobody, even Greg, was notified of was the changes Adley made to his will when Rod and Linda passed. It was kept quiet by a staff of lawyers who were assigned with keeping the estates and businesses afloat.

Her friend Steve had recovered in-house memos to that regard. The "boy," as Adley referred to him in all correspondence, had a figurehead position. He seemed to never truly care about the inheritance. He just presumed. He was told it was being handled, and he never looked further. From her research, she assumed taking on a real job would interfere with his social life.

Yet, the bottom was about to fall out. When Greg wanted to remortgage the Long Island estate for cash on hand to keep up his lifestyle, assumptions and illusions had been destroyed. How she would have liked to have been a fly on the wall during that meeting.

From further in-house emails, Lark concluded he was crushed and then angered that Adley had made her a seventy-percent shareholder in all the businesses and all assets. Suddenly she had value. While she could see the "boy's" side of the issue, the will having been written with clauses wasn't her fault. She let her lips curl into a smile. She would have to be careful to call him Greg, not the "boy."

She sent up yet another small prayer of thanks to her West Coast friends who'd found out all this information she was now armed with. She made a point of keeping her personal lawyer on a retainer, one she paid privately to keep him and his name out of the impending battle. That was how she saw her immediate future, as a war brewing within the company. If she needed his help again, she would have his full attention to her plight.

Lark closed the files and leaned back. Ending her relationship with Don wasn't an issue. Occasionally, they accompanied one another to business functions. They both agreed their careers had to come first, and when they were both so inclined, they'd have sex. Lark sighed. At least he'd been a good lay. He never pushed to stay over at her place, and she never spent the night with him. She'd miss their noncommittal arrangement.

Spike shifted on her lap as she set the seat back and closed her eyes. She'd seen photos of the estate and had a rough idea of where it was. Bless internet satellite maps. Their intrusive photographs gave her perspective on what to expect. The swimming pool on the far side of the house would be her saving grace for sanity. She swam for exercise and tension release. Often, when working through a problem, she would swim until the angst was gone and her mind clear. She'd studied maps of Long Island and business plans of each section and subsidiary of the company. So much information was inside her head that her mind just started to spin. That was when she tried to nap.

Spike woke her with a low growl as the steward approached. "Settle down, Spike."

"Ms. Braylin, we're a half hour from touchdown on Long Island."

"Thank you." She hugged Spike and stood, putting him on her seat. "Stay." Then she walked the aisle, stepping over the other two dogs on each pass until she used the restroom to brush her hair and freshen up. She never used a lot of makeup, usually just a tinted moisturizer with sunblock and a bit of mascara. Her lips were always covered with a clear gloss. She didn't believe in fancy clothing just to impress strangers.

She wore jeans and cowboy boots all the time, even at her job. She wore man-tailored shirts under a blazer. That was her usual mode of dress. On the rare occasion she had to dress to impress a client, she hated the fluffing and dusting, as she put it, changing herself to fit the image of strangers' assumptions. It didn't happen often, and her boss had quickly realized she was an asset to his firm, clothing be damned.

Well, her cousin was about to find out the same thing. As they descended, all three dogs woke, and she settled them as best she could. After all, their mood was directly related to hers, and she was antsy. Once they were on the ground, she'd feel better. She was told a car would be there to meet her. She informed the lawyer who made the arrangements to make sure they had a van or truck for the personal items she'd brought. She'd already ordered the dogs' food from an online company and had it shipped directly to the estate. At least the dogs would be taken care of.

When they landed, she thanked the steward and the pilots and took the leashes of all three dogs. She walked them directly to a corner of the field while the drivers loaded her belongings into the van. After stretching her legs and letting the dogs sniff around a bit, she headed to the black stretch limo waiting beside the cargo van with *Braylin Industries* printed on the door. The driver stood beside the open back doors, the dogs' crates waiting inside for them.

Lark smiled her thank-you and headed back to the plane, glancing into the hold to make sure she'd left nothing behind. Then she purposefully walked to the limo and let the dogs in the back. She gave the driver an overly sweet smile and tucked in beside them. “Take us home, please.”

The dogs’ empty travel crates were still in the van following behind. They’d apparently thought the dogs would be crated. Well, they were wrong. If any living thing was to be crated, it would be her new stepcousin. And the Braylin employees who’d set the plans in motion to screw her for five years.

The suits who currently controlled the company probably considered her, at thirty, an old maid or unmarriageable and most likely figured she’d just go with the flow of their directions. Lark let a full smile spread on her lips. She was about to become a major inconvenience in all directions.

Chapter Three

The photos and aerial maps didn't do the estate justice. She noted the company logo on the imposing wrought-iron gates that swung inward at their approach. The hexagon with a large *B* in gold was centered on a black background. She hadn't seen the house yet, but the gates were intimidating. She reminded herself they were just gates and took several deep breaths to settle her mind. The last thing she wanted was for them to see her anxious. Spike seemed to note her change of mood and moved closer on her lap. The other two were just napping, one on the seat across from her and the other at her feet. The driveway curved to the left and then went straight to the front door.

Another drive wound around the back of the house. She caught a glimpse of the tennis court and the pool in the back. She could explore later. For now, she wanted to get out of the car—nice as it was—and walk the dogs. Actually, she needed the walk too. Stiff from the travel, she also wanted a few moments alone before the confrontations started.

She waited until the driver stopped the car and came around to open her door. She handed him the two leashes of the larger dogs and kept Spike in her arms. Taking the leashes back, she nodded her thanks and walked away from the front door. The driver just stood there as she placed Spike on the ground. Glancing back, she gave him a second nod and kept walking. She went down the slight hill and followed the fence line with the dogs, Spike now speeding his short legs to keep pace. While she would have liked to view the garden a bit longer, she knew she'd have time later.

For now, familiarizing the dogs with the land was more important. She made a complete loop of the property, everything within the fence line. The trip took longer than she'd imagined. This would be a beautiful place to let them run once they were acclimated to the boundaries. She went to the back door. With a light knock, she let herself into the empty hallway that led to a mudroom of sorts. To the right was the kitchen and to the left what she would call a butler's pantry. When she saw three stainless-steel bowls of water waiting for the dogs, she smiled. Two were already in their raised stands for the larger dogs. The third was on the floor.

She'd emailed Edward, the butler, that she was shipping the dogs' beds, dishes, and food ahead. Apparently, the delivery had arrived. The three dogs all paused to drink. Baby, her St. Bernard, always put her paw in the dish before eating or drinking. Princess, the Great Dane, just barreled into the dishes. Spike, her small mutt of many breeds, lapped at his bowl. On a counter to the side lay the other three bowls, waiting for their food. Beside the counter were two twenty-five-pound bags of dry food she'd had delivered.

Since nobody was around, she nudged the dogs from their drinks and wandered ahead. Pushing through a swinging door, she found herself entering the grand dining room. A second doorway led to the main entry. She chose to go in that direction with a tight hold on the leashes.

"Hello?" Her voice echoed through the two-story entry. No answer. She wandered farther into the space and found the circular staircase hugging the wall to her left. She wanted to run her hands along the wood, but there would be time for that later. After all, this was now her new home. She didn't see any of her luggage or boxes in the hallway.

She heard voices and moved to the right of the front door. She stood in the arched doorway and watched the two men with their backs to her. All three dogs had automatically sat around her. Each man held a drink in his hand. She had no idea what the liquid was. The shorter man seemed older from behind, his posture slumping slightly, and his suit rumpled.

From the photos, she knew her cousin Greg was standing beside him, taller, well put together. She had no doubt her worst fear had just come true. He was the man she'd been intimate with years before. She had to wonder again if he knew who she was back then. Maybe not at the concert, but by the time they'd met at the music school, he must have had an idea. Had he asked anyone about her? Did he know her name? Was he sent there to figure out what kind of woman she was? Or was he sent to garner blackmail fodder for future use?

At the time she'd assumed his motives were similar. A quick lay with no emotions or lasting ties. Now she was unsure her appraisal had been accurate. Hell, at the time she hadn't known of his existence in the Braylin family. Answers would come but probably not quickly. Soon she'd know the truth, or at least their version of the truth. She had her version. All she could hope was that between the two, she'd find the real truth.

The men were interesting specimens of the male

being, hitting both ends of the spectrum. One young and well built; the other balding and older.

"Where the fuck is she?" the younger man asked, and she knew for sure it was Greg. His distinctive voice and blond hair took away any doubt.

"I don't know. I saw the limo arrive, and the driver brought in her bags." The man's voice sounded gravelly and old.

"Probably in the bathroom primping for us," Greg decided.

"Long trip, and everybody needs to pee occasionally," the older man said with a cynical laugh.

His tone instantly grated on her nerves. She refused to do any such thing. The dogs had had their walk. She'd pee later. She wondered if they'd seen photos of her and which ones. She only posted professional photos on her work site. Or had they done their own checking and sent someone to surreptitiously take photos and follow her movements? That idea would make her crazy, so she put it aside until she could confirm it was done. Although she now knew her grandfather had done exactly the same thing. She wondered if the extent of Greg's animosity was simply because she existed, let alone now ruled his homes, businesses, and most importantly his finances.

Greg pulled a deep breath. "Just be polite. After all, she is a stranger. And she doesn't need to know all the details."

"What details would that be?" Lark strode into the room and, after a quick survey, walked the dogs to the fireplace. It was set but not lit. She motioned for Baby to sit. She did with a thud. Then she motioned for Princess to do the same. When both were settled, she unhooked their leashes. "Stay, girls, stay." She knew every detail of her being was under scrutiny.

She walked to a large sofa and sat in the center. Spike automatically followed beside her and, with a jump, came to rest half on her lap, half on the sofa. “Good dog,” she said and unhooked his leash. She wrapped each leash around her hand and placed the leather circles on the coffee table before her. On impulse, she wanted to prop her booted feet up on the table just to annoy them, but she didn’t.

“Gentlemen, you already know I’m Lark, Maureen’s blood daughter and Greg’s nonrelated cousin. I say it that way because that was how your corporate lawyer worded our familial relationship. Greg, you’re the younger man.” She studied him for any acknowledgment of their previous meeting. And remembered asking him if he was discreet.

She turned to the rumpled older man. “You, sir, I’ve never met.” She held back a smile, thinking she liked that nickname for him, the Rumpled Old Man.

“What the hell is that?” Greg pointed to the dogs. His voice cracked. “Animals do not belong in this house. That’s what the kennel and back hall are for.”

Spike growled at Greg’s rising voice. “It’s okay,” she assured him, ruffling his ears. “The Dane is Princess. The St. Bernard is Baby. This is Spike, my protector.”

“Do they have to be in here?” he mumbled. “Is that one beside you actually a dog? It could win that contest for the ugliest dog alive I see each year.”

“Yes, they go where I go. From my first impression of you, they have better manners. And for general information, Spike is a mixed breed.” She ruffled the dog’s ears again to calm him.

When Greg cleared his throat, she decided he was

probably trying to pull back his rude attitude. He paced the length of the room on the hallway side. Since the dogs had taken the inner walkway before the fireplace, he wouldn't approach that side. She held back a smile, knowing she was getting on his nerves. That would be fun for a bit, and she'd take any advantage she could get.

Rumpled Man walked toward her with his hand extended. "Dodd, Will Dodd."

Spike growled, and Lark hushed him. "Spike, heel." The dog quieted but didn't take his eyes off Dodd. "Lark Braylin, as you're well aware."

Greg questioned her from behind the sofa. "Do they bite? There could be serious repercussions if these dogs go after guests."

She gave a half turn to witness him standing with his arms crossed in front of his chest. "Only when I tell them to. I wouldn't worry about guests for a while. It seems we have a lot to catch up on."

"Excuse me," he said loudly. Both dogs at the fireplace stood immediately, watching him.

"Down, girls, down." Both sat but didn't lie down. Instead, they decided to stare at Greg. She held back her laugh but let her lips curl into a slight smile. "Let's get this straight right now. Nobody will hurt or tease or taunt any of these animals, ever. They are very well trained and respond to certain key words. I'll introduce you to them when they've settled down. Right now, keep your distance."

"That's rich. I have to walk on eggshells around your dogs?"

"Greg, relax. They've all been cooped up on the plane for hours, and these are new surroundings for them." Dodd gave Greg an extended eye roll.

"If they'd come when they were invited, we'd all be settled by now." Greg put his glass on a side table with a heavy hand. All three dogs stood and were instantly on alert at the loud noise.

"Down, girls," she said, and they settled. "I wasn't invited. I was summoned. I also had a very busy business and private life on the West Coast. So for general information, I won't be at anyone's beck and call, ever."

"Can I get you a drink?" Dodd asked.

Lark figured he was attempting to assume the peacekeeper role. "Sparkling water, please, and lime if it's handy." She nodded to Dodd but returned her glare to Greg.

There was a tense quiet while Dodd poured the drink and placed it on a napkin before her on the coffee table.

"Thank you."

The silence in the room was almost deafening until a male voice intruded from the doorway. "Excuse me."

All three dogs stood. Lark simply said, "Girls, stay," and stood. "Edward?"

He was a bit older and grayer than she'd expected. She reminded herself he'd been very young when he came to work for the family. Her mother, Maureen, had had fond memories of him.

"Yes, ma'am."

She tucked Spike under her arm and walked to him with her hand extended. "I'm Lark, but you knew that already. Thank you for setting out the dogs' water bowls."

"My pleasure. I thought that was a central spot they could easily find. We can move them to your liking when you've had time to look around."

"Good."

"I've put your luggage in your room and the rest of the cartons in your sitting room. Upstairs and to the left, your room is the door at the end of that wing. When you're ready to unpack, just let me know." He paused and added, "I put three of the cushions in your room. Where would you like the others?"

"Here before the fireplace will be fine. They'll be out of the way there, but the dogs can still see the room and front hall."

He glanced at the two men. "I'll take care of it during supper."

"Thank you, Edward. From the glares I'm getting from Greg, I should probably stay packed a few weeks." She winked at Edward, knowing the other men in the room couldn't see her. "This is Spike." She fluffed his ears, and Edward put his hand forward, palm up, to let Spike sniff him. "All the dogs are trained to answer to 'girls' when I call. He's a bit territorial, but he'll get used to you."

"Of course, ma'am. New surroundings."

"Girls," she said, and both the larger dogs stared at her. Lark walked back and put Spike on the sofa, hoping to annoy Greg. She motioned for the other two to join her. They did, Baby lumbering across the room and Princess seemingly on alert. Both came to sit beside her. "This is Baby," she said and brought the dog closer to Edward. She leaned over and whispered to the dog. Baby sniffed Edward and lay down. Then she repeated the process with Princess. "She's a bit skittish, but she's the newest to the family. She'll settle down."

"Of course, ma'am. Can I get you anything? We serve our evening meal at seven."

"I'm fine. Thank you for getting my things

upstairs."

"Just ring if you need anything. I'll introduce you to the rest of the day staff tomorrow. Clara is our live-in cook."

"My mother had kind memories of you and Clara from her younger days."

The older man blushed at her comment. "She was a lovely child. I'm truly sorry for your loss."

"Thank you."

Greg cleared his throat as if he were trying to get her attention.

After Edward quietly left the room, Lark turned to the dogs and pointed. "Back to the fireplace." Both dogs made their way back to the fireplace and circled several times before they lay down. Baby let out a loud grunt. Spike watched from his perch on the sofa.

"I'm sure you'll want to clean up and change before supper," Greg said, taking the leading role.

"I'm fine. I don't change for supper. You'll both have plenty of time to discuss your first impressions of me and my brood afterward. For now, talk to me about Braylin Industries and the problems you're having."

Dodd spun around to stare at her.

Greg's mouth dropped open a bit. "What do you mean?"

She decided it was time to get their attention or at least annoy them. "Grandfather passed away five years ago. Why was my mother not notified of his passing or that of her brother's? Something drastic had to happen for you to send for me. What's going on? Or should I guess?" She wouldn't tell them she already knew from her research.

"We should probably let you get settled before

supper. We can talk after." Greg headed for the door.

"Why not now? We're all here, and the facts won't change after a meal."

"We thought it was time to bring you home." Dodd used a low, calm tone.

"This was never my home. So what is the reason? For five years you've known I was a part of the will, and you never contacted me then. You specifically kept my inheritance from me. Which means there is a drastic reason for your attitude and reluctance to be truthful. You've known about me all my life." She turned to look at Greg. "You've known about your aunt all your life and didn't bother to contact us in any way. How far off the rails did you run this company? What's the debt level now, and what was it five years ago?"

"We don't need to be discussing debt levels with you." Greg left the room.

"That's interesting since I wouldn't be here if there wasn't a problem. How bad is it, Mr. Dodd?"

"Lark, I'm uncomfortable discussing this, even though you are family. I'm just the CFO. Why not settle in, and we'll give you more information later."

"Does that mean you don't know the numbers, or are you trying to hide the true extent?"

"Let's leave numbers aside. I'd prefer to wait until we're all together."

"We were together until Greg reverted to juvenile behavior and stormed out. He knew I was summoned. Did he think I wouldn't ask questions or expect information?" The clock on the mantel chimed six, and she pulled a deep breath. "Fine. I'm going to feed and walk the dogs. I'll see you at supper." She grabbed the dogs' leashes, and all three stood and followed her toward the kitchen. She didn't look back to see if Dodd watched.

She stood at the back door, surveying the yard as the dogs ate. Then she leashed them and headed out. "Damn," she said once she was alone. In a verbal running commentary to the dogs, she headed with them to the fence line. "Greg has a stick up his butt. CFO Dodd is a lowlife. They've both been in charge, so they're equally responsible for the financial issues. Do they know I have their personal information? I'm sure they have ours." She paused while the dogs sniffed the fence line. "They obviously consider me the poor relation, but I hold the key to their future. If they think they'll mold me into the socialite relation to show off to creditors, they are going to be seriously disappointed."

Princess alerted to a noise on the other side of the fence. Supper ought to be an interesting meal. Had they considered she'd do some research and now had a complete file on each member of the company? Already she had no use for Dodd. His reports blatantly omitted key figures. Did Greg know—or care? "Play your cards carefully, Lark. They don't know exactly what I know. Let them dig themselves deeper before showing my hand."

She headed to the house and used the rear entrance where the dogs' water waited. Then she ducked into a small powder room and washed up. She'd be damned if she'd change into a dress or whatever they assumed. She didn't change for any man. As she was heading for the living room, Edward came into the back hallway.

"I put three hooks on the back of this cabinet." He opened a lower cabinet that held the bags of dog food. "I thought it would be easier to keep everything in one place. Of course, we'll change it whenever you'd like."

"Thank you, Edward. For now, that seems the most rational place."

"Ma'am…"

"Yes?"

"Welcome home, Miss Lark. I knew your mother. She loved growing up here."

"Thank you, Edward. She loved this house and spoke of it often, along with you and Clara from her childhood. She said you were both always kind to her. I also know she had an affinity for Clara's butter cookies."

Lark could only nod as her eyes filled. But she'd be damned if she let the tears fall before walking into the lion's den. Sniffing them back, she gave him a half smile. He produced a clean, pressed white handkerchief and handed it to her.

She dried her eyes and with a smile put the cloth in her pocket. "For later."

"They're more bark than bite, but watch your back. You and Mr. Greg are strangers, but you need each other. The rest will come to light. Just give them some time."

"Do we have that much time to waste, Edward?"

He didn't give her a verbal answer, just a nod. He pushed open the door to the entry and whispered, "Deep breath, and don't let them see you upset."

"Girls, come." She stood straight and waited for the three pets to follow her. When she walked into the living room, the dogs' cushions were set before the fireplace. Greg was dressed in slacks and man-tailored shirt. He didn't look any different than he had before, except now he wore a white shirt instead of the light blue he'd had on earlier. He didn't acknowledge her. Mr. Dodd looked the same—rumpled, cranky, and nervous sans overcoat.

Lark scooped up Spike and headed to the fireplace. “Down, girls.” She waited until they both settled. She studied Dodd while she moved to the sofa. He was beyond middle age, had thinning hair and a belly that stretched the seams of his pants and the buttons on his shirt. She held back a laugh and decided to keep a distance in case one of those buttons gave way and flew through the air as he moved.

In the evening light, his steely-blue eyes gave her a head-to-toe look meant to be demeaning. He apparently thought she should change her clothes for supper. That would be the least of his worries once she got her footing. Lark gave him the same once-over look. He blinked first, and she suppressed her knowing smile. He switched his glass from his right to left hand and wiped his palm on his pant leg. Spike watched him, and she gave the dog a quick reassuring hug.

“Mr. Dodd, Will, apparently you and Greg have been waiting until now to drop your bomb. Are you finally ready to talk to me? Maybe you’ll tell me the truth of why I was summoned.” She turned and put Spike on the sofa and headed to the corner bar, then helped herself to sparkling water. On the bar were bottles of white and red wine. Both were open beside several crystal decanters of different colored liquors. When she turned back, the two men were staring at each other.

“Is it that bad?” she asked the room in general.

“It’s complicated,” Dodd finally said.

“Well, since I’m a CPA, let’s start with the basics.” When she said she was a CPA, Dodd’s face lost all color. “Maybe you should sit down, Mr. Dodd, before you fall down.”

He shook himself from the dead stare.

“Who missed that on your research?” she asked. “Surely, you didn’t send for the black sheep of the family and not investigate me thoroughly. Or am I just considered the bad-seed relative who is now a necessity?”

“Your file said you were some kind of artist, like your mother,” Dodd admitted.

“Yes, as a hobby. But I’m a trained, licensed, certified accountant. I can multitask and enjoy both. But I’m not going to enjoy this news, so somebody just spit it out, and let’s get on with it.”

“I don’t think I like your attitude,” Greg said in a huff. “You have no right to come in here expecting private family information.”

“I wouldn’t be here if you didn’t need me. So let’s stop wasting time and billable hours for Mr. Dodd’s time card.” She glanced at each of them. “Fine. Let’s start with not notifying me about Grandfather’s death. Five years is a long period to withhold my inheritance.”

“We weren’t necessarily withholding information. Early on, details were glossed over. We weren’t aware of the extent of your…inheritance,” Greg offered.

“So why bother to give it to me at all? Do you know the details, Mr. Dodd?”

His face reddened, and his fingers fisted around the crystal goblet he held.

She glanced at him and burst out laughing. “You two are wound so tight a flea would send you running.”

“Should I hold supper?” Edward whispered from the doorway.

“We might as well eat,” she told him. “The men aren’t quite sure how to deal with me yet. I suppose I’m a bit bold and outspoken for them.” She turned to the dogs. “Girls, stay.” She picked up Spike and carried him into the dining room doorway. When she put him down, she said, “Spike, stay,” and walked into the dining room. From the reflection in the windows, she saw the two men enter and stare at her chosen seat. They were giving Spike a wide berth. But the dog never moved.

Chapter Four

Later that night, after a nonverbal meal, Lark headed upstairs. Her room looked like a gaudy French provincial suite she'd seen in magazine photographs. It was fussy and uncomfortable. Not a place she wanted to spend time in. She found solace in the second-floor library with turret windows, worn leather furniture, and ceiling-to-floor bookshelves filled with classic novels. It was the only place she felt human. She was frustrated with the treatment from her cousin—silent and brooding, meant to be demeaning.

She would have to decide if it was because of the business issues or if he knew of her before the music school and was sent to define her personality. All she could hope was the board wasn't that desperate to plant him in her midst to report back and use their private moment as blackmail material when they felt it useful. Not for the first time did she resolve to prevent sex from becoming an issue. If used, she'd say it was just sex and she wasn't embarrassed or ashamed. After all, Greg had been a willing participant. Maybe she'd do interviews and get it out in public before the company could use it against her.

Mr. Dodd was evasive and a wiz at giving nonanswers to her questions. He had, quite effectively, shut her down at every turn. Once she realized that was his plan, she stopped trying to be polite. Eventually, she'd find the information she wanted and needed.

Lark had one ace in the deck that nobody realized she held. As the new controlling partner, if they pissed her off beyond reason, she had the power to shut down the corporation and just sell it off. Or she could sign away her interest and watch them fail on their own. Neither was her first choice. She had been brought up to be a fighter, to see things through to the end. But she had options, and leaving the East Coast was first on her list. If she eventually chose that option, damn the corporation. She hadn't burned all her bridges out west. She could go anywhere and restart her career as a CPA.

****

Greg lost count of the laps Lark swam. All he knew was she made him tired just watching. He'd caught sight of her earlier from his bedroom. She wore a black one-piece swimsuit that clung to every curve and plane of her lean figure. Even in her button-down shirt yesterday, he could tell she had large breasts and a slim waist. But she was well proportioned all over. Her hips spread just enough to ease into toned thighs and strong legs. Her brunette hair flowed on the surface of the water behind her. He would have to be careful not to get lost in her chocolate-brown eyes. When she'd come to the end and turn, she'd do a backstroke. When she turned at the other end, she'd do a breaststroke. She was a very interesting package. Even if the superior tone of her voice grated on every nerve he possessed.

Beyond her clothing, he hadn't found any other annoying habits to pick at so far. But those damn walking carpets she'd brought with her were a nuisance. Right now, they were all stretched out around the pool, sunning themselves.

He tried to rationalize that since he didn't clean the house, he shouldn't care. He just wasn't used to pets of any kind. Lark came to the edge, turned, and backstroked to the other end. His bedroom door was locked. He dropped into the club chair beside the window and opened his pants. His cock had been hard and throbbing since he woke this morning. He'd handled himself in the shower last night and again this morning. Now he was pulling it out again. He'd have to be careful. He could easily become obsessed with her image.

He didn't need to fantasize about her in the abstract. She was live just below him. That brought the image of her on her knees before him, sucking him down her throat. When she turned, he'd picture slipping inside her from behind, using both her holes at his whim. He wondered what her general background was—uptight or bohemian like her mother. While he'd never met his aunt, he knew the gossip that went past him when the adults thought he wasn't listening.

His grandfather had been livid about his only daughter being pregnant and not married. Worse yet, she had been proud of her condition. That was too much for his straitlaced grandfather. Grandmother seemed indifferent and followed Adley's lead. He wrote her off as one might an unsuitable relative meant to be kept at a distance. He sent her away, never to be heard from again, only whispered about.

As Greg got older, the gossip was still heard but not with a lot of real information. Once Maureen left the house, she'd never contacted them again. He didn't think anyone from this side of the family had tried either. What he knew for sure at the time was to stay out of the issue. Self-preservation prevailed from the day he entered this house as Rod's stepson. He learned early to listen and seem uninterested. Slipping into the role and being ignored had been easy.

But now, with every flip and reach of her muscled arms, he throbbed. In reality, they had no blood between them, so they weren't related. They just carried the same last name by his adoption. Even so, screwing his new stepcousin was not the best alternative to their current situation. Hell, he didn't even think he liked her, let alone take her as a lover. No, that wasn't accurate. He wouldn't take her as a lover, maybe a screw buddy or booty call on occasion. He would never let love enter into any of his relationships. However, he'd consider laying her for the preservation of the business.

He finally accepted he'd done her before. Seeing her yesterday had brought back undeniable images from his youth and two moments in time he never thought would come back to haunt him. While he hadn't known who she was back then, he had a passing thought she might know him from the gossip sheets that always seemed to find him in a vulnerable moment. He didn't care if she'd set him up at the school. He'd never heard from her or about that night again. His life was in enough trouble with the corporate problems. He wouldn't be the one to bring up that night unless she did, and all he could hope for was she didn't do it in public.

He also became frustrated when Will Dodd continued to refer to her as the black-sheep cousin or illegitimate urchin who would ruin all their lives. One side of him was sick of the whole situation, and the other side had the nagging suspicion that he was missing a lot more behind the scenes or that was being held back from his knowledge. Suspicions led to realizations that would lead to changes in his life he wasn't prepared to accept. He only had himself to blame.

He'd accepted the free ride these last years, leaving the daily business of the corporation to the board members. Just staying the figurehead and not taking on the pressures of running the business was simpler. He was smart enough to know that was wrong, but after a while a large part of him was truly afraid what he'd find if he looked for the truth. The fear had kept him silent. Now that was coming to an end, as was his way of life he enjoyed so much. Everyone had to grow up sometime. This was his graduation of sorts, even if he was years past the time most people became independent.

Lark pulled herself up on the pool coping and finger combed her hair back. She stood, dripping wet, looking almost statuesque. In that moment, the way the light hit as she reached for the towel, she resembled a chiseled bronze with the perfect curve to her lithe body. Watching her dry off, he almost came but abandoned the process.

Greg wasn't sure if he was relieved or disgusted with himself. This whole situation was grating on him. He wasn't happy that he had to share the business with the board members, but he'd come to reason he couldn't run the company alone at that point. He'd had no choice. Time and experience taught him to find their strengths and weaknesses, and he used them accordingly for each situation to get the ideal resolution. Sometimes Dodd annoyed clients, while other times Greg couldn't connect. They worked together for the common good. But to have to share it all, have to give Lark a say from now on, went beyond every fiber of his being.

A shiver ran through him. She now ruled his life, and he hated her for it. He hated his grandfather for it.

He hated himself for not checking the will at the time. He'd allowed the lawyers to oversee all the paperwork, and the office continued to pay the bills. He had never been so wrong in his life. He couldn't go back and change any of it. He should have known better because Adley had spent years educating him on the business and its inner workings. Too bad he just hadn't been interested at that time.

Letting someone else deal with the details was easier. This was where his lack of interest had led them. Had he known about Lark's position in the hierarchy, he might have made different decisions along the way. Once he knew everything, he would have to reconsider the last five years.

None of it mattered, he reminded himself as he walked toward the hallway. "Smile and refrain from sniping. Sugar over salt, etc." The little sayings he'd heard all his life spun before him. "Ah hell, I had a good run," he said to the face in the mirror at the top of the stairs.

****

Downstairs, Greg stood beside Will Dodd at the dining room window. Both held coffee cups and stared at the empty pool.

"She sure does like to swim," Dodd said.

"Yeah" was all Greg muttered. He didn't like the tone of Will's statement or the way he leered at Lark. He would have to check these newfound protective feelings and not let anyone know they crossed his mind. He didn't want to give the board any ammunition to use against him or her.

"Got you too," Dodd said with a half laugh. "Do you think she does it on purpose?"

"I don't have a clue." He hated the idea that Will Dodd was sleazy beyond what he could have imagined. He'd never considered Dodd's sexual side. The normally demure, hard-edged lawyer was letting a new, lecherous side of his personality show through. Greg wasn't sure why now, except maybe there was nothing to lose. Leaving Lark alone with Dodd was not a good idea. Then again, Lark just might put him in his place.

He would pay to see anyone take Dodd down a few notches. In the years since Old Adley died, Dodd had gotten cocky and greedy. The reality was he was just being himself, forgoing the façade for public consumption. Greg was not his friend or buddy. He kept him close because in the last months before Lark was notified, he'd learned the entire board had been altering situations behind his back.

He would pay major money to see Lark lay the old man out flat. Hell, he just hoped she'd hold her own against him. He visualized her from the music school and remembered her statement about dealing with a bully and taking self-defense classes. Right now, he had too much on his plate to keep running interference between Lark and Dodd. She'd gotten this far. She would have to take care of herself.

He realized Dodd was talking to him and waiting for an answer.

"I said, did you think she was a true swimmer? I'm surprised she got her hair wet." Dodd shifted his package in his pants, not even attempting to cover the move.

Instantly, Greg was annoyed and sickened. But for now, he had to play the game. "Not sure. After last night when she asked over supper if the pool water was chlorine or salt, I figured she'd swim. But I never considered her…form."

He didn't mention that last night he'd used her image to fantasize in bed. He'd tried to sleep, but the throbbing hard-on wouldn't allow the rest. Finally, he'd given up and gone for it while anticipating what she would look like naked. He knew her breasts were firm and full, and she clutched his penis like a tight vise. But he'd never actually seen her naked.

"I've been considering her form since I saw her walk in the room yesterday. I'll tell you what—I'll take one for the team and be the one to do her."

Greg managed a scathing look.

"What? She's hot. I'm old but not dead. I could show her how a real man treats a lady. Maybe if we're nice to her, she'll be nice to us and leave our lifestyle alone."

"And you'll make the ultimate sacrifice," Greg uttered with disdain.

"Why not? You want her?"

Greg turned so quickly the coffee in his cup sloshed over the side.

"There it is. You do want her. Not permanently, of course, just to play with for a while. Maybe she'll let us take turns." Dodd laughed at his own joke.

"Do I get a say in who lays me for the greater company good, or am I to be passed back and forth until I succumb to your wishes and let you ruin Braylin Industries beyond redemption?"

Greg and Dodd turned to see Lark standing in the doorway, covered in a toweling robe, with her wet hair hanging down her back. Greg got a cold chill and a hot flash of desire at the same time. His throbbing cock wouldn't let his brain think straight. She might be fun for a while, but he'd been taught to protect against pregnancy at all costs and not form attachments. Considering their family history, he didn't believe in romantic love.

While he loved women in all shapes and sizes, he didn't want to keep any. He was a man who enjoyed women with the same understandings that their relationships were for fun and sex, not long-term permanence. He always let them go. Lark had him thinking outside his perimeter. She might be different. He instantly lost his erection at the idea of a relationship.

"It was just a joke, Lark," Dodd said.

Wanting to strangle Dodd for not thinking before he spoke, Greg added, "Just trying to lighten the tension."

"Your tensions, not mine," Lark said. "You've both gone out of your way to make me uncomfortable in this house. I'm not here even twenty-four hours, and you two are resorting to using sex and submission to deal with me. I suggest you take another tack. Try truth in numbers."

"We're strangers in awkward circumstances. Will and I were just joking to hide our tensions."

"There would be less tension if we stopped wasting time and talked openly about the business issues. I'll be down in a few minutes. I'll expect a real conversation then."

"This is difficult for us," Dodd admitted. "We're not used to sharing corporate information with anyone outside the firm."

"Well, get used to it. I can get information from you, or I can go to the offices and just call a board meeting. You decide." She turned and walked out. The dogs followed her up the steps.

"Fuck me," Dodd said. "Greg, we need a new plan."

"Yeah, well, maybe that's the problem. We had a plan, and so does she." Greg put his coffee down on the table and headed out of the room. Dodd stayed behind.

He never considered that Will Dodd coveted the house and his position. He realized now the older man was always on the outside looking in. Greg was still hoping to hell he didn't have to leave this house. This was his home, the only place he'd truly felt comfortable growing up. It was his solace on vacations and summers from college. No matter how much fun he had at summer camp and vacations, he was always happy to be home. This was where he lived, body and soul, and he had to figure out how to keep it.

****

Lark was in the dining room when the men reentered. They skirted Spike lying in the doorway. She could only wonder what their conversation was after she'd left. With the way they'd treated her since she arrived, she didn't care. She'd already served herself coffee and a full breakfast. Her tablet was open, and she was reading the news and checking the European numbers while waiting for the market to open. She doubted they would have considered she had her own ideas of investing, ideas she'd learned from her mother who had learned from her father. She invested conservatively unless it was an impulse purchase, which was always small until it proved itself. She knew the exact amount Braylin stocks closed at yesterday and wanted the opening numbers.

She wondered if either man bothered to do such a simple step. Time would tell. She closed the screen and sipped her coffee, watching them plate their food and finally take seats.

Greg scooped up scrambled eggs on his fork but hesitated halfway to his mouth and put the fork down. “Go ahead, scream and yell. Let’s get it over with.”

“I don’t scream and yell unless it’s my choice to prove a point. I prefer to lean in and speak very softly so the person has no choice but to give me their full attention.”

Dodd burst out laughing. “Damn, girl, are you sure you never met Old Adley?”

“I got better. I was raised by his daughter. She was his original student.”

“What do you want, Lark? Where do we start?” Greg pushed his plate away and brought his coffee forward.

“For today, I’d like to drop the animosity, get some true information, and take a tour of the offices.”

“I’m not sure that would be such a good idea. Will thinks having you around the office might make some employees antsy.” He glanced at her.

She knew it was a good call to keep her appearance the same. Jeans, boots, and a blazer, with minimal makeup and her hair pulled back in a braid.

“Antsy? That’s what Mr. Dodd thinks I’ll make the employees?” She sat back and smiled at the corporate lawyer. “My plan is to make the employees a bit antsy. I plan on making the board downright frightened.” She reined in her smile. “If Mr. Dodd thinks my presence will be disruptive, he has no idea.” She turned to stare at Dodd. “Does the entire board feel the same?”

Neither man answered.

“Well?”

“They generally keep to themselves, and Greg and I

keep to our jobs."

"Which are?" she asked.

Greg stood and glared at her. "I won't be questioned or scrutinized like this." He left the dining room, avoiding Spike.

From her perspective, his tantrum was a major overreaction to her question. "Are you going to storm out too, Mr. Dodd?"

"The house isn't that big," he muttered.

"Yet you seem to be here all the time. Do you live here, or are you just staying close to oversee that Greg keeps the company line?"

He didn't bother to cover his rude attitude. "Your presence has changed all our schedules."

Lark laughed openly and watched a blush creep up his throat to his cheeks. "Whose fault is that?" She didn't expect an answer. "Do you two carpool to the office?"

Dodd looked away.

"I'll take that as a no. Is there a vehicle here I can use until I'm a bit more settled?"

"There's a garage full of them." He had lost his cordial edge. His anger shone through in his tone. "Take your pick, but…I suggest you not touch the sports cars. All hell will break lose on that one."

"Not when you realize I can truly drive them and appreciate them as the fine machines they are."

Dodd gave her a questioning look. "I'd still save that for another day, okay? We're all on edge. Those vehicles are a line not to cross…yet. Timing is everything. I truly don't believe this is the time to assert yourself with Greg's sports cars."

"I'll think on it, but it's good to know how to get under his skin when I want to."

Dodd groaned. Apparently, he was instantly sorry he'd given away Greg's secret love of the vehicles.

She nodded but didn't say any more, opening her tablet as a distraction.

She was not surprised when Dodd stood to leave. It surprised her when he paused behind her chair and dropped his hand on her shoulder. She refrained from shaking it loose, but his touch revolted her.

"Am I going to have to watch every word I say around you?" His fingers squeezed her shoulder as if to punctuate his words.

"I'm not sure. For now, I prefer the truth. There seem to be enough secrets and lies to contend with."

"I imagined this reunion going differently, very differently."

"How? Why? Try looking at it from my perspective. How would you react if the tables were reversed?" She wanted to turn and watch his expression but didn't. "And to clarify, this isn't a reunion. This is a business arrangement I had no say in…yet."

"Whether you believe it or not, Greg wasn't aware of the will issues until recently."

"Do you, as CFO of Braylin Industries, really want me to believe you never told Greg about Adley's will?" This time she glanced over her shoulder. "Are you telling me you didn't know about the will? Because if you are saying that, then I have to question your ability as a lawyer and CFO."

He stared down at her and didn't look away. "Let's just say things were running smoothly. Why break the streak? Major changes just after Adley's death would have influenced the stock prices, etc."

"So you're saying it was easier to leave Greg in the

dark than to make waves with the truth?"

"Something like that." He squeezed her shoulder a second time.

The way he stared down at her made her beyond uncomfortable, but she refused to acknowledge him. She understood why he was making his point this way, hoping to become dominant. She'd have her moment to let him know how she felt about him soon. Now she was sorry she'd eaten breakfast.

Lark didn't dare move. Her stomach churned at his touch. This time she did use her fingers to lift his hand from her shoulder and let it drop. "I prefer not to be manhandled, Mr. Dodd. Do you understand me? Don't presume to touch me again."

He pursed his lips as if he were debating how to handle her. "Just don't judge us too quickly."

"Would you care to elaborate?" She wanted the information but didn't want to push him away by being too rude. However, she would not allow him any personal touches or fondling, even if he meant it as a fatherly gesture. She decided he wanted her to believe what he was telling her was the truth. She didn't believe it for a second, but she'd bide her time.

"Not now." He again reached to her shoulder and gave it one last squeeze. "Tread lightly, Lark. Not all things are as they seem."

"Dodd, I just told you not to touch me, and I meant it." She removed his hand for a second time. "You are a stranger. And to clarify, I intend to do my own research, starting with the company, the employees, and the board members who are hiding from me."

Will groaned. "Just be careful."

She suddenly felt cold to the bone and refused to lift

her fork, afraid her hand would shake. The loss of his touch settled her stomach. But she knew to keep her distance and not be alone with him under any circumstances. It wasn't anything she could pinpoint at that second, only that knowing feeling she got when things weren't right or as they were presented. Mr. Dodd and the board would be her downfall if she let them. What had they already planned for her, and how would they use her name?

So where did that leave her? It left her wondering how Greg might touch her if she let him. If they did have any kind of physical contact, would he be doing it of his own accord or because it could be used against her in the future? Would he make love to her to distract her from the main questions? While she didn't want to think that way, she had to consider it was possibly a fallback plan. Sex was as powerful as money, and in her new position, she knew they would use all their underhanded ways to reach their ultimate goals. She was simply a tool to be exploited and tossed when not needed. She would have to be careful what she signed.

Even though every bite bit back at her, she attempted to finish her breakfast while reading the news on her tablet. Food was the last thing she wanted right now, but she needed the appearance of calm. When she'd eaten most of it, she stood and pushed her chair in. She reached for her plate and the tablet and headed to the kitchen.

Edward turned quickly to retrieve the plate from her. "I would have gotten that, Ms. Braylin. Would you like more coffee?"

"What I'd like are several things. First, my name is Lark. We'll leave the 'Ms. Braylin' at the door unless formality prohibits. Second"—she walked directly to the woman at the sink—"I'd like to introduce myself to the lady who made a delicious supper last night."

She held out her hand, and the woman took hers from the dishwater and quickly dried it on her apron. She was well put together in a day dress with an apron covering her lower half. Her graying hair was styled, and she wore a bit of makeup, but understated. She seemed like an average older woman with a genuine smile.

"Clara, ma'am."

"It's nice to meet you, Clara, and it's just Lark when we're out of prying eyes and ears. If you keep making such amazing meals, I'll have to swim twice as much to keep fit."

"Oh hush," Clara whispered, blushing before her.

"Edward, I need a vehicle. Mr. Dodd said there were cars in the garage—" She lowered her voice. "—but not to dare touch the sports cars."

"That might be wise for a bit, Ms. Lark. I'll walk you out and show you where the keys are."

As they headed out, all three dogs caught up with them and followed along.

Chapter Five

Lark knew what the inventory was, or should be, but she'd missed a few. When Edward opened the side door to the garage, the lights instantly went on. She didn't try to hold back the gasp that escaped. "Holy shit, how many do they actually use?" At a quick glance, she saw way too many vehicles for any family. Three sedans, three town cars, and the limousine, of course, which she had assumed was hired to impress her. "Is the limo driver a permanent employee?"

"Yes, ma'am, the vehicles are his responsibility."

She spied a red sports car in the far corner and several other vintage sports cars, then two contemporary sports cars and two SUVs. "How many people drive these?" She wandered between the rows. They were three deep in each bay.

"Mr. Greg usually uses the two sports cars or the sedans during the week. Clara and I use one of the SUVs for errands."

"Who uses the old clunker in the corner?"

"Usually the groundskeeper. It's very old with a lot of miles on it."

"Is it reliable?"

"It seems to be."

"Would you ask the driver or mechanic—whatever his title is—to give it a once-over? I'd prefer to drive that for a while, especially if I want to take the dogs somewhere with me."

"I'll have him check it out today. Would you like to shop and purchase your own or have him make suggestions?"

"I think I'll use the clunker for a while and then decide. I've always been a safety-first driver. I'll look for an SUV when I have time."

"I can have the dealer bring one over for you to check out," Edward suggested.

"Thanks, but I think a gently used SUV is better for me, especially with transporting the dogs. Will my taking the old truck be an imposition on the groundsman?"

Before Edward could answer, Greg came out and hit a button on the wall. Then he walked directly to a white convertible. Without a word to either of them, he got in and started it. He revved the engine, waiting for the bay door to open, then drove off in as much of a huff as he'd left the dining room.

"I guess I won't be taking that one," she joked, and Edward looked away. "Edward, what vehicle won't be missed today?"

"Take one of the sedans for a few days, Ms. Lark. We'll double-check the 'clunker,' and you can find your own when you're settled."

"Thanks…"

"The three sedans all have navigational systems in them," Edward continued.

"Fine. Any one of them will do."

He came back with keys and smiled. "The dark blue sedan was just serviced."

"Thank you. I'm planning on leaving the dogs in the run between the garage and the house. It's gated on both ends. Do you see any issues with that?"

"No, ma'am. It was gated that way when the mister was alive. He kept German shepherds. Beautiful animals."

"Okay, the breezeway it is. I'll be back tonight for supper."

"Good luck, ma'am."

"Thank you, Edward. I'm beginning to think I'm going to need it more than I anticipated or could have imagined."

She headed back inside, grabbed a blazer and her leather backpack, and made sure the dogs were secure in the enclosure. When she was heading back for their water, Clara came out with three empty bowls. Behind her Edward carried a stand so the larger dogs could be on their feet and drink. He also carried a gallon of water to fill the bowls.

"Thank you, both. Have a good day." She turned and relocked the enclosure. "Dogs," she said, and they all looked up at her. "Be good…stay."

Lark was never so glad to be out of anywhere. She forgot to ask about opening the gate, but by the time it was in her sight line, it was opening automatically for her. Just before leaving the driveway, she checked the navigation system, which had been preset. She put her phone in the holder and hit her playlist. If her research was correct, it should take about twenty minutes to get to the office. The office was just off the Long Island Expressway.

****

Lark walked in the building with ease, no questions, no security check. The man at the reception desk nodded. He must have been told to expect her. She kept walking, figuring she'd introduce herself later. She wandered around, but nobody acknowledged her. Just what she wanted.

She found the small kitchen area with vending machines and bought a chocolate candy bar. She sat to take in what she'd seen so far on her walk. Tablet open beside her, she jotted notes. When her break was over, she continued her solo tour. When she went to the "executive" floors, she was sickened.

"The waste," she said to herself.

Before she could think further, Dodd was beside her. She noted how he tried to block her view of every open door and passing employee until they reached what looked like an empty boardroom, far from the rest of the offices. He used his hand on her back to usher her into the large room.

"You'll be more comfortable in here," he told her.

"Comfortable for what exactly?" Already she didn't like his manner and pulled away from his close position beside her. Their supper had been tense. Breakfast had been worse. If he had been sitting closer, she felt he might have patted her on the head like a child to change the topic. She'd given him a polite smile and started drafting plans in her mind to check on him further.

She understood her presence was not to his advantage. Rather, she was his nemesis because she existed and now they needed her. She wondered what might happen when things settled and they didn't need her. Watching her back was going to become a full-time job in itself. She reminded herself she had no friends here, only monetary value. Until she had a full understanding of the business, she'd keep her mouth shut and her ideas to herself.

"For whatever you're here to do." He pointed her to

a seat at the side of the long table while he took the one at the head. She didn't like him taking that seat at the head, but she sat where he pointed to keep the conversation going.

"I came to walk the offices, to familiarize myself with the layout, employees, and procedures. I can't do that from in here."

"Oh my, didn't Greg talk to you this morning? We decided it would be best if you kept a low profile for a bit."

"You know we didn't talk about this over breakfast. You were there." She pulled a breath to control her tone. "Who is 'we,' Mr. Dodd?"

"The board, of course. It wouldn't do to have you wandering the halls like a lost urchin."

" 'A lost urchin'? That's a new name for me. I bet you're real glad I didn't bring the dogs."

"Dogs? Oh no. That wouldn't be allowed." He shook his head and gave her a horrified look.

Lark knew the dogs had annoyed him over their supper. That was why she loved her dogs so much. Their inner sense was stronger than hers. "Even by the heir?" She couldn't resist rubbing a bit of salt on his wounds. She checked out corners for microphones and cameras. She assumed they had security of some kind. She needed to know who was watching and who had access to the equipment.

He cleared his throat and glanced around the room as if someone might have slipped in unnoticed. "We can't have you going around announcing you're the new owner. Stock prices…"

"I didn't say I was the new owner. You just did. But I find that interesting. Show me your office, Mr. Dodd, and the other board members' too. That way it will be a guided tour instead of an illegitimate urchin roaming the halls alone." She stood and waited for him to rise. "Are we going?"

"I find I don't quite know what to make of you, Ms. Braylin. You're beyond brazen and not dressed for the workplace. Mr. Braylin would never have approved."

"Then let's not tell Adley." She tried to joke with Will Dodd, but he obviously didn't get her sense of humor. "Besides, it's not his fault you and the board or Greg didn't contact me. Years ago, this might have been a much smoother transition. Now you're worrying about gossip. The board has skewed stock prices with their own insecurity and greed. Silence was not golden in this case." She drew a deep, cleansing breath. "I will not dress to be used as chattel for the cause."

She didn't like the way Dodd looked at her from the head of the table. She gave him the same degrading look back, and he blinked first, just like last night. That was when she knew she had him, or at least her information was correct. The research she'd done before she came east proved discrepancies in major areas, and with her arrival, all hell was going to break loose. She stood and headed for the door.

Eventually, he followed her into the hallway. He cleared his throat and motioned with his arm, directing her into another empty office. "I don't understand women like you. Your mother did you a great disservice raising you like your opinions mattered more than the company."

Lark froze in midstep. "Don't ever mention my mother again, Mr. Dodd." Her look had him shying away from her physically. "The only disservice to this company was keeping it from me." She stared at him, and he finally gave her a curt nod. "Don't try to understand me. It will only frustrate you. And you better be careful not to call me Ms. Braylin, or someone might overhear us."

She laughed aloud as she strolled down the hall with Will Dodd nipping at her heels like an untrained puppy. To her, they were all untrained pups left to run amuck. Well, she was here now, and one of her specialties was training dogs. The board wouldn't take kindly to her kind of training, but she wouldn't be deterred.

****

By the end of the day, she was mind boggled. The few board members in their offices were courteous but aloof, unable to hide their intolerance and indifference. Two of them didn't even have computers on their desks. She had no idea how the company had stayed afloat to this point. The waste of space alone stunned her.

The drive home in traffic had given her time to consider all she'd seen and heard. She sat on the back patio with a pot of tea and plate of butter cookies Clara brought her.

"My favorites," she told Clara.

"They were your mother's too. I had a feeling she introduced you to them."

"You had a good feeling. Were the dogs any trouble today?'

"No, not at all. But that Dane is a bit skittish."

"I know. She's my newest rescue. I was just getting her settled, and now we're here. She'll calm down. She just needs time."

"Just like her mama," Clara had said but was gone before Lark could comment.

She went over her notes on the tablet, put them in order, and closed her eyes. She enjoyed the quiet around her.

Back in the house again, she asked Edward where she could find a printer. He showed her to the office.

Moments later, Greg walked in, glaring at her.

"You just had to poke your nose in here too, I see. There's nothing private with you in this house."

"Part my house now too." She straightened her posture. She refused to be intimidated by his attitude.

"You're making that more than apparent strutting the halls and studying the house with that fake smile. None of it is appreciated, and we all deserve our privacy, which you trample on." He stared at her.

She didn't blink at his tone. "I would have preferred to have been introduced instead of dealing with little boys who don't want to share their toys. But it seems they're my toys now too, so don't underestimate me, Greg." She drew a deep breath and changed the topic because she could tell he was furious, fisting his hands at his sides. "I asked Edward if there was a printer in the house. So get your nuts out of your throat. I haven't breached the privacy of the desk. Heaven forbid!"

The machine kept pushing out pages of black print. "What's all that?" he asked.

"Just some notes I made while I was at the office today."

"All that? What could have kept you so busy?"

"I would have been more productive if Will Dodd hadn't attached himself to my side. He never did tell this 'little urchin' where your office was or his."

He walked to her and stood just inches away.

"I'm not intimidated by you, Greg."

"That would be a mistake." He stayed there, glaring down at her.

"No, it seems everyone involved with Adley's will made mistakes."

He stood so close she caught his scent with every inhale. He smelled of soap, not designer cologne. With each of his exhaled breaths, she caught the light scent of mint. Right now, her body was reacting before her brain could shut down the feelings. Her nipples budded, and a long-forgotten warmth traced through her body, down her belly, and landed in her core, her lower lips pulsing. She wanted to press her thighs together to stop the ache, but he might realize the movement. So she stood tall and stoic even though it took every bit of her being to stay there without reaching to touch him.

They never lost eye contact, so she knew the second it happened, watched the change come over him…his precise realization of their past. It was a nonverbal acknowledgment of their joint past. Lark had been right about the photos. He had been her music man. But she decided to hold that information for a better time. He was still staring. Slowly, he lifted his left hand to her cheek, brushing away a stray tendril of hair.

He looked at his hand on her cheek, and his eyes went wide. He dropped his hand to his side. Acceptance changed to anger and resentment in a flash.

"You smell like your wet dogs."

He turned and all but marched toward the door, leaving her confused.

"Our offices are private. Stay out of them unless invited." He stormed out.

She laughed loudly, louder than necessary, but she wanted him to hear her.

"Tomorrow I'm bringing the dogs with me," she said in a moment of pure relief. She got no response from her taunt, but she felt better. Damn, keeping her body in check would be easier if he didn't look so good. Sex was not in her best interest with any man right now. Letting her attraction for Greg be known would disadvantage her beyond redemption. She'd never find even ground if she admitted her feelings.

Supper was a tense meal. She was in the living room when Greg came in before the meal. He poured a drink but didn't offer her one or make any effort at small talk. She was relieved when Edward announced supper was ready. Even though it was another mute meal, she was hungry. When Greg wouldn't engage in any conversation with her, she pulled out her tablet and continued reading a novel she'd started before this whole debacle began. He couldn't see her screen, so she let him wonder what she was studying.

He didn't ask, but she got a good meal and another chapter read. After that, she wandered the yard with the dogs, off leash tonight. She was letting them get used to the area and the boundaries she was setting for them.

Alone in her room upstairs, she turned on the television and scanned until she found reruns of her favorite 1970s sitcom. She loved that the woman had spunk. Maybe that was why so many men didn't understand Lark's approach. She and her mother called it drive and ambition. Maybe men just saw an overachiever. No matter what, she wouldn't change to make any man comfortable.

Tomorrow she would go back to the offices again and not let Dodd sidetrack her. In reality, she could have slipped away, but she had been curious about his attitude.

He had managed to show her just what he wanted her to see and tell her nothing important. She'd tried to introduce herself to the staff, but he had whisked her away before she could do anything more than offer a smile. Now she had to find out exactly what he was hiding from her and maybe from Greg.

****

Greg canceled his date and then was sorry he had. He didn't miss the woman, just missed being out of the house. He'd been forced to come home full time after his grandfather's death. He had started to excel in his own right. He'd loved living in Manhattan and having access to the whole experience. He had to wonder what might have been if he'd had a few years longer on his own. But this house was always his sanctuary. The last weeks he'd lost that feeling. Sanctuary was in trouble. If they had a flag with a family crest, he'd hang it upside down to show they were all in distress.

He wandered into the den to watch the news but left quickly for the solitude of the office. He hoped Lark would leave him alone. It was a comfortable room since he'd replaced some of Adley's antiques with modern pieces. He put a match to the waiting kindling in the fireplace, and the flames came to life. He poured himself a scotch and settled in the armchair. At least she hadn't laid dog cushions before the hearth.

The fact that he was drawn to Lark was a major blow to his ego. He needed to dislike her for too many reasons. Relaxing and getting to know her as a person would be easy, but when he thought about that, he lost perspective. Here was this stranger who walked into his home and was about to change the course of his life to her liking—her vindictive liking.

Her swimming laps in their pool every morning when he got up didn't help. He hated that he watched her each day. He hated that she was across the table from him at breakfast and supper. What annoyed him more was the fact that she seemed to be bonding with Edward and Clara. They were his family, not hers. In the week she'd been there, he never saw any emotions. His emotions, on the other hand, were beyond raw. Now he just waited for the other shoe to drop. Or more precisely, for her to decide his future.

He managed to keep away from her at his corporate office. Even there, in her broken-down cowboy boots and worn jeans, she turned heads. The gossip mill that ran continually still hadn't broken her resolve. She never put a foot wrong and always had the polite smile and the right words for the situation. She was just too good to be true. Never losing one's cool wasn't human.

He laughed at the irony, watching her swim. It had become part of his morning routine. Yes, he jerked off in the shower every morning before she arrived, but now he found himself waiting for her to slip into the pool, watching every stroke and kick she produced in the water. Then he'd take his shower for relief. By the time they were seated across from each other at the table, he was horny again.

She was always polite, which grated on his nerves. He dismissed any conversations she tried to start. He would tune her out. But it was getting tiresome to dislike her to the level it had grown. Just once, he wished they could laugh over something, anything.

This was not the time to travel down history road. Did she ever think about that night? Did she even remember? If confronted, would she admit their previous fling or deny it ever happened? No answer mattered. He wouldn't ask or remind her. He still had a bit of pride left, although since she arrived, she seemed dead set on taking that away from him too.

His attitude and actions had started the situation. Now he didn't know how to diplomatically turn it around. He also had to keep in mind that Will Dodd was even more annoyed with her presence. Dodd still hadn't acknowledged his part in the five-year fiasco that created the situation. Greg knew he held a portion of the responsibility too. But at the time, Dodd had glossed over the will the few times Greg had inquired. Never had he heard her name in connection with the document. After a while, he just moved on and tried to restart his life. But all hell was going to break lose soon.

****

Greg hibernated in his Braylin office. No matter how he and Will Dodd tried, Lark was everywhere he turned at the office. She was always flitting around in the background. In the short time she'd been there, she'd even managed to meet several of the board members or their assistants. She seemed to skulk around until she found them and cornered them with an overly sweet smile and sugared voice. He didn't like that she had befriended the lower-tier employees and assistants. In the last weeks, he'd seen her pause to talk with the cleaning staff. He knew them by sight. She'd learned their names. From snippets of conversations he overheard, she knew about their jobs and tidbits about their families or hobbies. While the house was his sanctuary, the company office had been a secondary home. Now she infiltrated that space too. It bothered him how many people smiled when she was near.

Nobody was that good this soon. She would eventually disappoint them too, and then he'd have to deal with an employee mutiny. He had to catch her at her own game, had to get the upper hand back and soon. All he could see was the total dissolution of his life and career crumbling with her presence. He'd taken to wandering the halls at odd times just to see what was going on. He'd smile and nod to employees, but most seemed frightened or confused by his presence. He felt like a voyeur. He'd taken to roaming the halls and rooms of the house in the evenings too. As if he could connect with the spaces he took for granted in the past.

Hell, since she arrived, he hadn't taken a vacation day. Not even a day off for his own needs. He'd stopped dating. That annoyed him too. While it might not be rational, he felt he couldn't take any downtime. He hadn't gone to the Caribbean for snorkeling nor to Europe to ski. His life had come to a dead stop when she was brought into the family.

What he feared most was what information she knew or might know. Somedays he wanted to snatch that damn tablet and see what her files actually said.

After the home office incident, he watched from his company office window one afternoon as she took two printers. He'd figured they were from the office supply room. She had set one up in the upstairs library at home, and he'd assumed the other was in her rooms. Edward had confirmed his suspicion when he couldn't find where she put them. At least, he hadn't caught her in the home office again.

On the flip side, he did lose his temper that first day he found her in the home office. Being that close hadn't been smart. She'd sent him into sensory overload. It was hard to be angry with his erection doing all his thinking. He had to keep his distance from her, physically and emotionally. Walking into that room wasn't the same anymore. He pictured her at the desk and the way she looked at him. He wanted to believe it was longing, but most likely it was disgust. He still couldn't believe he fell back on the wet-dog line.

He didn't like that she spent so much time in the second-floor library. That was his grandfather's favorite room, and now she was taking it over too. Maybe kicking her out of the downstairs office had been a huge mistake, but it was a knee-jerk reaction to finding her there.

For the amount of animosity Lark caused him daily, she was just too good to be true. Fear choked him at times as he waited for her to announce changes to his lifestyle.

In the time she'd been in the house, they hadn't invited anyone over for a party, a meal, or even drinks. Only Will Dodd joined them for meals. Greg was losing patience with him too. He was crude and rude, always watching them, as if he were waiting for something to use against them. He never tried to ease a situation; rather, he antagonized it. Greg decided to stop inviting him to meals and realized he'd never invited Will. He was just always there, watching and waiting for a slip.

Greg was on the verge of firing his trusted assistant because the man was polite to her. When she'd seen the photo of his cat on the desk, they'd launched into a conversation about pets and their care. Damn that woman. She kept photos of her rescue dogs on her phone. If he heard the word *rescue* one more time, he'd throw up. Many people adopted pets from the shelters. Why couldn't she just be quiet about them? *Rescue*? He was the one who needed to be rescued.

It struck Greg that with the passing of time, he was losing his hatred of the dogs. When he was alone, he found himself petting the damn dogs. Talking to them as if he'd get an answer. Hell, even the little nasty one that was too protective of her was worming his way into his heart. The dog was so ugly he found himself talking to him too. He didn't do pets. They left hair on his clothing and were just one more thing to take care of.

He would give Lark credit for one thing. She seemed to be on top of their care all the time. Many a day he'd seen her out in the yard sitting on the ground with them, petting or brushing them, and talking as if they could understand her. Then again, since he had gone silent with her, who else would she talk to?

Last weekend he'd tried to get into her email and failed. She didn't keep a high social media profile. In reality, the only thing she put out for public consumption was her pets. She never mentioned the company or that she was even on the East Coast. Greg had gone so far as to put a password cracker on her laptop. He'd known he screwed up when she found it and removed it without comment.

She made a point of burying her nose in her tablet. Every morning over breakfast, he wanted to snatch it from her hands and stomp on it until it was just bits and pieces or slam it against the wall. He didn't do either, but he wanted to. Why couldn't she just holler or show some emotion? Then they could have a real fight. He couldn't fight back against her silence. He'd leave the house without a word spoken between them. That she hadn't mentioned the password issue made him start checking his media accounts. He found no changes or breaches, which meant she probably already had access.

Living under the same roof was just awful. How could he be smitten with a woman who was about to wreak havoc on his life? It didn't help that when he was alone, she was all he could think about. He fantasized about how he'd sweet-talk her into submission. That idea made him laugh.

Greg didn't think any man or person would push her into submission. While she might give up control for a bit, she was too much like him to turn over full control. While she might give the appearance of relenting, she always had an alternative plan. Just like Old Adley and Rod and, apparently, Maureen too. Lark had been raised to consider all angles before acting.

Chapter Six

Outside, Lark walked the fence line, letting the dogs wander freely. In the weeks she'd been there, the dogs had learned the boundaries. What would winter be like here? She got an instant chill. East Coast winters were never an experience she wanted to try. Hell, the few times she'd been skiing, she'd been glad to get back to San Francisco. Yes, they had cold and damp and rainy days, but she didn't relish the snow on a daily basis. She paused to stare at the sky. Out here she breathed differently than inside.

Spike growled, alerting her to a presence. Greg headed toward her. She'd see what he had to say before confronting him.

"That dog is so ugly she'd win the ugliest dog contest they have every year."

"You used that line already. And Spike is a he, although I figure you call him a her to be annoying." She drew several deep breaths while she considered how to deal with him. "Don't judge a dog by his looks. Actually, it's what attracted me to him." Lark smiled, remembering seeing him at the shelter, but she didn't share the memory. This wasn't a friendly conversation over a drink to get to know each other. "It's just like judging a person on their looks."

"I'll agree I haven't always been on point in that direction."

"Why, Greg, we're actually having a conversation. What's your ulterior motive?" She had to wonder because until now he'd done nothing but snarl and bark at her or freeze her out. Now he was showing up all friendly. Like Spike, she was instantly alert.

"Is there any more to your revenge plan we need to know about?"

She gave him credit for keeping her gaze. "There is no revenge plan. If you, Dodd, or any member of the board would talk to me, let alone listen to options for the future, things would go smoother."

He straightened his posture, looking affronted. "We know you have plans. Just tell me."

"I've tried to. In the last days, I've left folders of information for you at breakfast. You never once opened one, just tossed them back at me." She paused and looked directly at him for a moment. "Why do you want to listen now? Did Dodd send you to find out what I have in mind?"

"I can't handle this stress." It was a blunt statement.

"You poor boy. You're under stress? Try being inside my stress level. I was pulled from my home and business and traveled across the country to be ignored and dismissed. To have Dodd insinuate I'm the poor relation looking for an open door to your bank account." She paused and drew several deep breaths.

Greg looked away as her breasts rose each time she inhaled.

"The man calls me an urchin! I think it is time you all remembered you came to me in a totally untimely manner. Now you shut me down at every turn when I try to get information. Information I'm entitled to." She studied his features. Did she see remorse or what she wanted to believe was remorse?

“These haven’t been my proudest moments.”

“Like my first day here? When you literally walked away mad because I recognized you have no oversight at the company? Hell, if you didn’t need the money, I’d still not know about my inheritance.”

“I didn’t know all the details.” He paused and added, “Granted, I didn’t push for information.”

“It was easier to ride the gravy train than actually work for a living?”

“I’m sorry. I was wrong. Can we move past this situation?”

“Thank you for the apology. But why now? What’s changed?”

“I can’t handle the tension between us.” He hedged and finally said, “I don’t trust Will Dodd anymore.”

“What’s changed?”

“You did, damn it! Ever since I found out about you and the will situation, I’m seeing a different side of him. One I should have caught earlier. If the tables were reversed, I’d want revenge, and I have to assume you do too.”

“This isn’t revenge, Greg. It’s just common sense.” She continued her slow trek around the yard, whistling when Princess started to wander away.

“Old Adley raised shepherds. He had a knack for training them. It was like he had a sixth sense when it came to those dogs. I was actually sorry when he didn’t replace them as he aged.” He paced his steps to hers. “I don’t hate your dogs.”

“I know, but it’s easier to bark at them than me. I bark back, and you’re not sure how deep I’ll bite.” She finally laughed. “I’ve seen you with Baby. I find she’s a good listener too." He halted, and she laughed again. "Relax. Your secret is safe with me."

"Are all my secrets safe?"

This time Lark paused. Long seconds passed as they stared at each other. "I didn't know you'd remembered."

"I didn't for a while, and for a while I refused to accept the truth. My mind was so full of company bullshit I just figured you looked familiar because of the family resemblance. Adley had a photo of you and your mother on his desk in his bedroom." He let out a breath. "His private space. It wasn't a room we were invited into. I was only in there once after he took ill." He stretched and looked up at the night sky.

"You remembered the photo from seeing it once five years ago?"

"After this mess began. I went in there one day looking for…inspiration or answers. I saw it again then. You seemed familiar yet not. I didn't push further. At the time, it wasn't important," he admitted.

"And the photos that were gathered when you were doing your background check?" Lark reached down to pet Baby's ears.

"I didn't see it then either. I only checked your driver's license photo. It wasn't until I heard you talking with Clara and Edward in the kitchen one night. That's when I couldn't deny we'd…met in the past. It was your laugh that triggered the memory. After that, I couldn't forget or ignore the issue."

"At least we don't have the onus of being related by blood. Besides, those two meetings were a fluke, a one off, and we both knew it at the time. The concert was neutral ground. The music beating through us, the hordes of people so close all you had to do was sway with them.

It was like perpetual motion without effort." She laughed at the memory.

"It was a chance meeting, and I didn't even know your name." His lips curled into a smile, but he pulled it back when she glanced at him.

"I didn't know yours either. But I knew how you kissed me in the midst of that crowd and how you held me against you with your cock throbbing against my butt."

"I suppose going behind the stage wasn't the smartest place to think we'd be alone." He laughed.

She laughed too, finally letting go of the tension she'd been holding since he approached. "Probably not, but there wasn't privacy anywhere." She called to Spike to follow. "I still remember the look on your face when I pulled the condom from my pocket." She stopped dead. "I will tell you, whether you believe me or not, that was the first time I ever did anything like that. I wasn't bold with men back then. I usually intimidate them. But that night with the music…"

"Yeah, it was a strange night for me too. Being brutally honest, I saw you at a distance and figured when I got close, you'd look different. You did. Better." He shook his head.

"I'll give you this, Greg. You made me come just sucking my nipples. When you unzipped my jeans and slipped your fingers against me, well, let's just say I got a twofer that night. And I remember your erection pulsing in my hand and thinking about how you'd stretch my body. I wondered if you'd use both my openings."

"Too bad we were interrupted. We almost managed to connect that night."

"I remember leaning on a bank of amps while we

fondled. The beat pulsing through us…" She stopped talking when she realized she was being too open and honest with him.

"It's more that the whole situation was forbidden in so many ways." Greg gave her a wide smile.

"That was part of the appeal. You were a good kisser. I always wondered if you were a good licker too." Lark watched Greg's neck and cheeks blush in the exterior light. "I never did get a chance to suck you off. Just to fondle you."

"We did manage to get farther at the charity event." He smiled and shifted his weight.

But he didn't shift his erection, as she assumed. Somehow, she was disappointed yet not, considering their inappropriate behavior each time they'd met in the past.

For the first time since she arrived, she felt a genuine smile cross her lips. "Agreed. I have fond memories of that practice room. By then I was more forward with my wants and learned what I liked and wanted and to go for it when reasonable. I wasn't looking for emotions, just pleasure."

"I was so angry with you when you finally arrived, I couldn't see past the issue." He looked down and shuffled his feet.

He paused, and Lark was about to interject.

"I know," he cut her off. "That was my doing. But damn, girl, you walked into the room, and I took one look at you dressed to be unimpressive, and my brain stopped working. It was like a lightning bolt of memories invaded my being. I'll admit it was hard to concentrate on anything at that moment." He hedged and looked away. "When did you realize?"

"You looked familiar from the photos in my research package, but in person…the scowling put me off a bit."

"I suppose we can't pick up where we left off. All the time lost and this business crap."

"We surely can't do anything about it now." She gave him a head-to-toe look and smiled. "Too bad." She drew a deep breath.

"Could you imagine if the tabloids found out we'd been together back then?"

She stiffened when he said tabloids. She would know it was him if she showed up on the front page of some slimy magazine or website. "Especially if they found out I knew you at different times. Or if they make up facts like I'm still doing you now."

"I agree, and it wouldn't be the same. It's too bad we're in this situation."

"We might have enjoyed each other when we're in the mood." Would her idea offend or interest him?

"I'm not trying to prove my prowess anymore." He hesitated. "But that night at the college concert, I would have taken anything you let me. I was in lust literally across a lawn."

"When I first got your summons to come east and started to do my own research, I saw your photo. I wondered and decided it couldn't be. What would be the odds of meeting a stranger in Los Angeles and have it turn out to be someone I'd meet again on the East Coast?"

"Once I realized, I decided I had to keep my distance or you might remember those nights and use it against me. I still wonder if your ploys aren't because of that time." Greg turned to watch her.

"I'm not that cynical. And believe it or not, my mother loved this family, especially her very gruff and unemotional father. Even though he disowned her because of me, she didn't hold it against him. At least by the time I was old enough to understand. She always said one day she'd show up and just give Adley a hug and see what his reaction was."

"Why didn't she come back?"

"While I'm not one hundred percent sure, I think it had something to do with the way her mom's family treated her and Rod, and especially her mom and dad." She pulled back a sigh. "It didn't help that when Adley finally reached out, it was always as an order instead of a request."

"They were a strange group," Greg agreed but didn't offer information.

"I think she was waiting for Adley to contact her with a real invitation, not a missive sent with intimidation. By the time she accepted his pride wouldn't let him, she'd taken ill. Traveling then wasn't possible."

"Why not contact him anyway? Why didn't you call the old man?"

"She asked me not to. She didn't want him to see her sick. She wanted him to remember her as she was when they parted. Healthy, smiling, and with me, the product of their argument, prospering."

"I knew Rod had a sister and that she had a baby. I was young but knew not to ask questions about touchy subjects. Then came boarding school and college and summers abroad."

"I don't blame anyone for the past…well, at least before the last five years."

"So what do we do now?"

"I decided to keep our musical adventures as a memory. You can't go back. It's never the same. So as long as we agree, that's just private memories." She called Baby back when she realized she'd begun to wander too far. "Besides, if it was used against me, I'd deny the situation."

Greg gave her a full smile. "Interested in a quick lay on the lawn?"

She managed to hold a blank stare for several moments before laughing at his concerned look.

"Or maybe around behind the garages," he goaded.

"Why not in the back of one of your fancy cars, or have you been there, done that already?" She didn't hold the laugh back from her tone.

"At least I had you before this strange mess."

"I wouldn't word it quite that way."

"So, what happens now? What if our pasts come to light? You know the board will use it against us."

"I don't know. The first thing that comes to my mind is deny, deny, deny."

"We can't let anyone, especially Dodd, know we had this conversation."

"Or that we're forming a carefully worded truce?"

"I'm trying, Lark. This whole situation is partly my fault. I can't go back and change any of it, but going forward, I know I've been used by the board all these years."

"We need to keep up the animosity in public. In private, it just takes too much energy."

"Agreed," he said and smiled. "How can I help you settle in at work? What do you need?"

"For now, I think we have to keep up the distance and attitude, or Dodd will become suspicious. But I want him kept away from me. I don't trust him on any level, especially a personal one. He's tried to casually touch me several times. I've told him not to, but he did it a second time. He didn't like my warning, and I think I might have made the situation worse. Now it will become a goal for him to manhandle me."

"He tried to put a move on you?" he asked.

"He tried to make it a 'fatherly gesture,' but I got his underlying connotation. His leering look didn't help."

"Can you take care of yourself with him? I'm not sure how to get you a bodyguard without him knowing just how much he disgusts you. What do you think? Are you afraid of him?"

"Frankly, yes. But I don't want to let him know that. It's better to keep him guessing than blatantly embarrassing him. However, if he continues to try and touch or corner me, I will explain it to him in physical moves."

He laughed. "I'd pay to see that. But you're right. For now, we keep him guessing. If he thinks we've found common ground, he'll stop talking to me, and we'll lose information that might be helpful."

"Agreed. For now, we keep up the pretense. But, Greg, you have to tell me the truth. How bad is the situation?" She stared at him.

"Truthfully, until the last months when I was told they were bringing you in, I had no clue. Now I'm finding I was a fool to let Dodd and the board members just run things. It was simpler than asking questions I wouldn't like the answers to. I admit I had a grand time, and now it's over. It's about time I grew up and took responsibility for the mess we're in right now and for the future."

“It will all come out at some point, but for now, I don’t have another argument in me. I just want to let my mind go blank.”

“I agree with you there. Tomorrow’s going to be a long day.”

“Yes, it will be. Although in different directions, I’d guess.” She called out, “Girls, come,” and waited until all three animals were beside her. “I’m going up. I’ll see you at the office tomorrow afternoon. I have to be here for my truck delivery in the morning.”

“What do you want me to tell anyone if they ask?”

“Nothing. I wouldn’t have given you my schedule. That would mean we talked. It’s not their business, and they’ll all know by the afternoon when I show up in a different vehicle.” She turned and headed back to the house. “My mom described this house to me over and over. But I never realized I’d become attached to it so easily and quickly too.”

They walked side by side back to the house. As she was about to round the garage, Greg touched her arm and pulled her to him. His kiss started out light, just a hint of his lips against hers. When she didn’t stop him, he kissed her again. This time with more pressure. She should stop this now, but she let her hands run up along his chest, his hair filtering through her fingers. He pulled her closer until their bodies were lined up, and she felt his hard-on pulsing against her. Even fully clothed, she felt his erection. They battled with tongues for control of the kiss. When she dropped her hand between their bodies and grasped his erection, he pulled back.

“This isn’t a good idea.” He turned away, staring up at the sky.

“I know. But I figured if we got past it, well, maybe

it would take the stress away." As soon as she said the words, she laughed. "That didn't work out. Now we're both horny and can't do anything about it."

"Probably not the best idea I've had all day or all year," he admitted. "Good night, Lark. Good luck with your new vehicle." He started toward the back door but paused. "This can't happen, can it?"

"No, it can't. It's not a good idea," she told him. "I'll be in later. I'm going to let the dogs run a bit longer. Good night."

He walked away, and she didn't realize she was holding her breath until she heard the back door close. Damn, keeping her distance from him was going to be a problem.

****

In the week that passed since Greg and Lark shared their kiss behind the garage, they had been cautious around each other. He was careful not to show any interest in her, especially when they had any kind of audience. He was on edge, always pulling back a smile toward her or the occasional lift of his hand to touch her. Dodd had taken to showing up at breakfast and evening meals with no invitations or warning. Greg was on his last nerve with the old guy, but he knew better than to confront him at this time. Until he knew the depth of trouble, he'd keep quiet.

Yet another file was lying beside his supper plate. As in the past with all of them, he made a show of tossing it across the table toward Lark in full view of Will Dodd. He made the move to impress the old guy he now held in disdain.

Lark never said a word. The only thing she did do was grab the file before Will could. Several times over the last weeks, he'd reached for the discarded file and she'd pulled it away before he could see the contents.

"I've told you before. If I wanted you to see what's in the file, I'd have given you your own copy," she said.

"It won't do to have you keeping secrets from me. Everything in the company runs past my desk."

As with all the past files, she gave him the same curt line. "Then when the time comes, these files will too." She made a production of walking to the living room and tossing them in the fire each night.

Greg noted how the vein over Dodd's left eye would pulse when she refused him access to the pages. He silently gave her credit for not including the old man and simply pissing him off.

This went on for four nights. Then there were no more files at the dinner table.

She did, however, push them under Greg's door for the next two nights. When he found them, he refused to open them, refused to break the tape seal on them to read the contents. What he did do was walk down the hallway and push them under her door.

After that, she stopped trying to give him information. Now that she had stopped, he was more curious about what he missed but wasn't man enough to ask her directly. He knew it was childish and not to his benefit. He still couldn't bring himself to open the files and actually read what the issues were and worse yet, what her solutions might be.

Greg was beyond defining his emotions. Saturday, he had plans to go out for the evening but canceled when he saw Dodd's car pulling into the driveway. As usual, their supper was sullen. He hated the lecherous looks Dodd flashed at Lark. Later that night, he went to the living room table and picked up a heavy glass vase. He weighed it in his hand. No, he wouldn't toss it through the window. He did, however, spike it into the empty fireplace. It shattered and filtered down over the logs waiting to be lit. "Damn, this family," he said to the walls.

He wandered the room and tried to make sense of the whole situation. When he was alone, he'd admitted that he wouldn't like her ideas even if they were valid for the business plan. He wouldn't know because he still hadn't read any of her notes or files. Now it seemed childish even to him. Not that he'd tell her. The minute he saw her, his cock swelled, and he couldn't think straight. All he could picture was feeding it down her throat. He pictured Lark, wet from her swim, on her knees before him, swallowing him to the hilt. It wasn't the best plan, but considering the tense days they'd all had, he knew emotions were on overload. A man could dream. At this time in his life, that seemed to be all he had left.

He had to alter the house dynamic before he reacted and did something he couldn't change. He hadn't been out with any of his regular women. He didn't do relationships. He was more intent on preventing pregnancy at any cost. He would not be tied to any woman or child because of an hour of lust.

After all, that was how he came to be. His parents fucked around and weren't careful. Yes, they'd married, and it fell apart before it began. He'd known his father, and even as a child, he felt only relief when the man walked away. Yes, his mother got a check each month, but the fighting had stopped. Greg had rationalized long ago that when she started seeing Rod, he wasn't happy.

But at least Rod didn’t hit either of them.

None of this was getting him anywhere. History couldn’t be rewritten. Only the future could be influenced or protected. At least that was how he felt. He walked to his bedroom and considered slamming the door. He didn’t because he wasn’t a child anymore. He dropped onto his bed.

“Damn it,” he said and finally laughed. “I’m fucked in all directions, and I’m not enjoying it.”

Chapter Seven

The next Monday morning, Greg stood at the dining room window. He stared out, watching a white SUV being released from the back of a flatbed. When the vehicle hadn't been delivered the day after their late-night walk, he figured she changed her mind. He hadn't asked, and she didn't offer a reason.

Watching the scene, he didn't like the easy interactions between the stranger and Lark. Then he had a brilliant epiphany. What if he introduced her to someone, a man he considered the least harmful, maybe a nerd with no sexual experience? Lark might like having a man she could train to her preferences.

Since she arrived, he'd spent many an hour considering what her type of mate might be. He knew a few guys who wouldn't jump her on the first date. If given the proper incentive, they might fish for information he could use as ammunition to get his future plans implemented. Maybe he could find one who might defend him. He might not trust any guy willing to work like that. But that might be better than letting her come home with some stud with model looks and a hard body.

He studied her with the delivery man and didn't like the instant connection they seemed to have developed. It was a hard pill to swallow when he realized he and Lark had started a similar connection that fateful night so long ago at their random meeting at the music school. He had to wonder what might have been if they'd left together that night or seen each other again. Then again, their identities would have come out, and that would have destroyed any fun or relationship they might have been building. He let out a disgruntled breath.

"I'm in deep trouble here," he said to the empty room.

Beyond the business, he still liked her. He was still attracted to her. He would just have to wait and see what happened. *Old Adley is rolling in his grave*, Greg thought as Edward came in and placed a covered serving dish on the sideboard. Rod too, probably. So he was fucked and not enjoying it. This was not fun in any direction. Damn, what if she was right about some of the company stuff? He should have read through the mass of files she'd been tossing at him. He'd hoped the information was all bullshit, but Lark was smarter than he'd assumed.

That was his problem. He assumed too much about her and assumed Dodd was honest and his information correct. Dodd fucked him too—only so politely he didn't take notice. Which pissed him off to no end. First, to be used by him. Second, to know she saw it before he did and would probably never let him forget Dodd and the rest of the board had used him.

****

Lark was very careful where she kept her paper files and her laptop. They were always with her or locked away in the small safe she'd ordered online and had delivered to her bedroom a few weeks before. Greg might know about it because the shipping box boldly told the world what was inside. Once she'd unpacked the safe, she tossed an old cotton throw over it and moved a table lamp on top. Even her tablet was always in sight.

After finding the attempted password cracker, she didn't trust her cousin with her files.

Part of her wanted to believe Greg was coming to understand the situation. Yet there was still too much of the unknown to assume he would now be on her side. She couldn't trust his motives. His turnaround was too quick.

She was annoyed beyond reason when she found that bug on her computer. She was thankful her friend Steve had set up the notifications of any new programs. But she bit back the initial anger and urge to taunt him with her find and removed it. She never mentioned the bug after it was removed. She waited for Greg to confront her, but then how could he without acknowledging he'd put it there? She was also careful to never leave any of her things unattended or where anyone else could get to them.

She went online to a "spy store" and purchased a new gadget of her own—namely, a bug-and-camera finder. It would notify her if a camera was looking back at the gadget. She used it in her bedroom and took it to the office to check for bugs in the room Dodd had stashed her in. When she was alone in the house, she also checked the main rooms but didn't find any bugs. For a while she thought she was overreacting.

She'd spent four weeks wandering the halls of the company and exploring the home. In the attic one afternoon, she came across a bedroom suite she considered modern, with clean lines and a natural oak finish. It was from the 1950s. She fell in love instantly with it in comparison to the white-and-gold French provincial stuff that overcrowded her room. With Edward's and a groundsman's help, they'd managed to swap out the furniture. Now she felt welcomed in the room. She'd also swapped out the gaudy furniture in her sitting area for older, worn, mismatched tables and overstuffed chairs that had been abandoned up there long ago.

So many treasures were up there—furniture covered with tarps and old trunks with rusty locks. It was the cleanest attic she'd ever seen. She promised herself on the next rainy weekend, she'd explore further. For now, just having simple furniture in her room settled her.

She'd kept the combination gold-and-white linens and curtains that were there, but eventually, she'd choose her own, if she decided to stay long term. There was no reason to tell Greg her backup plan was to walk away. She made a good salary on her own. If Braylin Industries went under, she'd still excel. Keeping her distance from the name and company all these years had insulated her from their problems. The only nagging issue was the many employees who would suffer.

Greg showed no interest in her daily life beyond worrying about their paychecks and perks. She felt no loyalty toward him. Since their talk and kiss in the yard, making assumptions about his motives was becoming harder. But there were too many roadblocks to start a relationship, even if it was just for sex. She still didn't trust him. She didn't trust anyone easily or quickly but Edward, Clara, and her dogs. Some days she couldn't believe she'd been here two months now.

With the new safe and furniture arrangement, she'd told no one where she kept her research. She had more files than she could carry, but they all held information she wanted to have with her. When the end of the quarter neared, she sent out a carefully worded email memo to the board. Short and sweet, it simply said, "Your presence is requested on Monday at ten a.m. in the conference room. Attendance is mandatory." Every member of the board got one, including Greg. She followed up with printed copies too.

Not a single person said a word to her about them. She checked each one on her list and knew the emails had been received and opened. Seeing who showed up and with what kind of attitude would be interesting. She went one step further.

On Thursday night before the meeting, she pushed another memo under Greg's bedroom door. That was worded just as carefully. *Family meeting Saturday, ten a.m. in the house office. Attendance is mandatory.*

Friday, she was alone in the dining room at breakfast. On her way out, she stopped to tell Clara she was leaving.

"Greg mentioned he would be out for the evening. Is there something special you'd like for supper?" Clara asked.

"Anything will be fine. However, can we forgo the dining room formality and just eat in the kitchen? Or is that overstepping my place, insinuating myself into your mealtime?"

"Of course not. You go ahead and have a good day. We'll see you tonight."

"Thank you, Clara."

In her new…used SUV, she settled behind the wheel and looked forward to having warm bodies to eat with. She hated the dining room in this house. While beautiful, it was uptight in all ways. She wondered what response she'd get from her memos and decided she wouldn't know until she got to the office. She doubted the board would approach her and Greg. She had no idea what his daily office routine was, nor did he seem willing to inform her.

At the Saturday meeting, she would have a quiet discussion with him before next Monday's board meeting. If he didn't show up tomorrow, she'd have her answers, and that would dictate her attitude for Monday. She didn't think he knew about her correspondence with Harvey Masters. Her mother had trusted Harvey, and Lark did too. When the summons first arrived and demanded her immediate appearance, she had gone directly to him. She paid him separately to keep him out of the fray and to keep him as her personal counsel. He'd been helpful with getting records for her and explaining the issues she was unfamiliar with. In the weeks it took for her to finally head east, he'd given her a crash course in Braylin Industries and their business tactics.

That day she left work early, with Mr. Dodd watching her leave from his office window. Out of spite, she turned to wave at him. He took a step back from the window, and she smiled. She didn't tell him where she was going. She didn't tell anyone. They'd stuck her in a huge office at the far end of the computer area with no staff and minimal furniture. Blinking lights and whooshing sounds of the machines were all she saw or heard all day. She didn't care. What she saw was wasted space. With the roof about to blow off the house tomorrow and the offices on Monday, she just wanted to get away.

At home, she gathered the dogs in her SUV and headed to the vet. Each got a wellness check, and she made sure their vaccinations were on file and their chips updated in case they got lost. They were up to date, but she wanted to meet the vet and let him see the dogs were cared for to head off any problems. After all, every time she caught sight of Greg, he was grumbling at the dogs, even if they were just sleeping before the fire. Spike grated on him the most, and she didn't care.

This was a preventive appointment. Just because they kissed in the yard or because she caught him talking to Baby when he thought they were alone, she wouldn't let her guard down. Yes, he'd admitted he didn't hate her dogs, but that didn't mean in a crisis he wouldn't use them against her. There was still too much history she wasn't privy to.

That night, she ate beef stew in the kitchen with Clara and Edward. Lark hadn't laughed since her arrival. They were kind with stories of her mother when she lived there, and they glossed over any issues that might be uncomfortable. She made a point of being careful not to put them on the spot.

When they were lingering over coffee, Greg came in the back door. The dogs were used to him and didn't stir, except for Spike, who gave his normal growl. She reached down and settled the dog.

"Now you're taking Edward and Clara away from their duties," Greg said with a growl that mimicked Spike's.

"Their duties, as you put it, include meal breaks. I just joined them. It's less work than setting the dining room for one person. I find their company holds less animosity too." She rose and took her mug to the dishwasher. "Thank you both for a lovely meal. The stew was wonderful, Clara."

Lark waited for him to say something about the meeting for tomorrow, and when he didn't, she snapped her fingers and directed all three dogs out the back door for their evening walk. What was usually a quiet time of reflection took on a new onus. She knew he watched her, at least until she was away from the house.

Tomorrow would be interesting.

From going over the household accounts, she'd learned that they usually had company at least once a week. A full-out party. Whether it was just a few people or hordes, no expense was spared. The alcohol bills blew her mind.

It was hard to miss that they hadn't invited anyone over except Mr. Dodd. They apparently were still trying to hide the poor relation from the public. That was about to change. She smiled at her thought. "Hell hath no fury like a woman scorned or mistreated." She felt both. After the last weeks, she was ready. She'd waited for the month to end, as requested. If Mr. Dodd thought he'd hold her back longer, he was dead wrong. Come Monday, there were going to be a lot of cranky men at Braylin Industries.

****

After walking the dogs on Saturday morning, Lark had breakfast alone. She didn't bother to change. She just gathered her files and headed to the "sacred office." While one side of her wanted to take the seat behind the desk, she used the seating area to set the mood.

Edward came in with a coffee tray and put it on the sideboard. He left quietly with a nod. Half an hour later she was about to get her second cup of coffee. Her attitude was swiftly decaying. Edward came in with fresh coffee at exactly eleven o'clock.

"Edward, is Greg in the house?"

"I believe so. Shall I check his room?"

"No, thank you. He knows where he's supposed to be."

He left quietly with the pot containing the cooled coffee.

Lark rose, refilled her cup, and returned to her seat on the sofa, the files still spread out on the coffee table. The information before her was ingrained in her brain.

Greg sauntered in at eleven forty-five. If he was trying to provoke a negative response, she wouldn't give him the satisfaction.

"I'm here. What do you want?" He dropped into the chair across from the sofa.

"I wanted to try and be cordial and professional. Not so much now. Is your time more important than mine?"

"Yes." It was a rude answer.

So much for their moonlight truce. His change of attitude wasn't surprising. She hadn't fallen into bed with him. That had to be a shot to his ego. He reverted to a company man.

"Fine. We'll skip the pleasantries." She slid down onto the floor and used the sofa to rest against. Then she took a file and tossed it to Greg. He caught it and tossed it onto the side table, not opening it. She glared at him, and he blinked first, letting out a deep sigh. Finally, he reached for the file and opened it to the first page. He sat straight and took a second look.

"You can't be serious," he snapped.

"But I am." She didn't let him ruffle her.

"Fuck no, I will not—"

"Fuck yes, you will. I've spent months going over these records. I've been hidden from view, ignored, and generally made to feel like I'm an interloper. Which, according to Adley's will, I'm not. In reality, you brought this on by hiding my inheritance and letting the board go unchecked for five years. This is the result."

"I don't have time for this crap," he spat.

"Fine. But you can't come back to me when the changes are implemented and say you were clueless and I didn't attempt to include you."

"What are you thinking? This is not how the company works. You have no idea about how this business runs."

"You sounded just like Will Dodd." Lark sipped her coffee. He seemed so annoyed she had to hold back a smile. She got him. Yes, he messed with her time, but he would know better than to present a divided front before the board Monday.

"You can't take away our expense accounts…" Greg said. He sounded annoyed now.

"If you read it carefully, it said expense accounts would be restructured and double-checked from now on. That's the start," she said, staring at him. She wouldn't let his green eyes get to her. Even though her body was heated at the thought of a repeat performance from the music school, she couldn't let that happen.

"You can't do that. They're all business expenses. You're just trying to rile me."

"Look, we can do this in private, or we can do it in front of the board on Monday. It's your call, but you can't say I didn't try to keep family issues private."

Finally, Greg scanned the rest of the pages and tossed them back on the floor. "No."

"No?"

"No, you may not make these changes. I won't have it."

"Yes, you will. By keeping me away for the last five

years, you gave me all the power. Besides, Adley gave me the power first. It's all very simple. We make these changes, or we go under. It's your call."

"You have no idea how this company works. You have no right to consider any of this. If you were smart, you'd shut your mouth, sit in the corner, and learn before thinking you can change Braylin Industries."

"I can see you'd rather discuss it on Monday in front of the board." She gathered her files and pushed up to sit on the sofa. "Are they aware you were going to remortgage the estate for…petty cash? And what would have happened when you blew through that cash and there was no equity left to pull?"

"That's not your business." When his voice rose, Spike sat up beside her on alert.

She whispered to the dog, who sat down but kept staring at him.

"And keep these dogs away from me, or I'll have them taken away!"

She laughed aloud. From his glaring at her, he didn't appreciate her laugh. When he said the word *dogs*, all three had stirred.

"No, you won't. Unless you want to find a new place to live and work."

Greg fisted his hands, apparently floored by her statement.

"Don't begin to consider touching my pets." She pulled a breath to control her temper, realizing he was trying to bait her into another argument. "That's your problem, sir. I use the term loosely. I don't run from bullies. I put them down." She stared at him when his jaw dropped slightly. "You've all underestimated me and my power for years. Now the devil has come for payment."

"You expect me and the board to live on our salaries. Are you are kidding me?"

"Most of the world lives within their means or close to it. It's a novel concept for you, but it's your new reality."

He stood and walked to the door. He didn't take his copy of the files with him. "I'll fight you, Lark. Trust me—you don't want to fuck with me or my finances."

"Considering that's what you've done with me for the last five years, I'd think you'd be more careful with your admissions of fraud."

His face turned bright red. "Fuck you."

"Fraud in any way is never the best approach. It's the one we have left after all the backroom crap you people have worked. See you Monday at the meeting with the board."

She gathered her files and snapped her fingers, waiting for the dogs to rise and then follow her out of the room. Greg remained in the same place. She was so thankful she hadn't fallen into bed with him just for the hell of it. She locked her files away and took the dogs downstairs for their walk to blow off her anger.

She stopped to peek into the kitchen. "Is Greg going to be home for supper?"

"No, ma'am," Clara said. "He came through, said he'd be out for the evening, and left."

"Fine. Let's just relax tonight, then. I'd prefer to have supper on a tray in the den and the television for company. If he comes in and sees us enjoying a meal, I'm afraid he'll cop an attitude with you and Edward."

"He really is a nice man most of the time," Clara said.

"It's the rest of the time that's the problem." She drew a breath. She knew better than to discuss business with either employee. It wouldn't bode well for them. She'd be accused of trying to subvert their loyalties. She headed out with the three dogs. As they neared the garden, the sports coupe squealed out of the garage.

"At least I got his attention," she said to the dogs. She put in her earbuds and hit her playlist on the phone, hoping the music would settle her.

Her biggest saving grace was that Will Dodd stopped appearing at every meal. She wasn't sure why the change, but she enjoyed the food so much more when she didn't have to deal with his leering looks and condescending tones. He'd given her a wider berth at the office, but she knew her every move was being watched.

Chapter Eight

Monday morning, Lark skipped breakfast and was at the office before seven. After putting place cards before each seat in the conference room, she took the head seat and waited. She'd put Greg on her right. His assistant came in and placed a tray of coffee on a sideboard.

"Thank you." She wondered who normally brought coffee to the board meetings. Somehow, she didn't think Greg's assistant was assigned this duty. Whoever else that might have been, they, meaning the board, were trying to keep her away from other employees. For now, that was a detail she'd put aside for later discovery.

"You're welcome, Ms. Braylin. Good luck today." He turned and left quickly.

She decided it wouldn't be good for his future if the board thought he was on her side.

Just when she thought the board would stand her up, the members slowly filed in, each with a glare. When they saw her sitting at the head of the table, they started mumbling among themselves. Apparently, a little makeup went a long way with this group. She didn't interrupt. Instead, she just waited. Half an hour late, Greg sauntered in with Mr. Dodd beside him. Their faces dropped too when they saw the seat she had commandeered.

"That's Adley's place," Greg said.

"Adley left it to me in his will. Please have a seat. You've already kept us all waiting." More grumbles came from around the table. She stood, and there was a universal gasp in the room.

Today she wore a form-fitting linen dress designed to fit her bust and hips. The black-and-white vertical stripes made her look even slimmer. Her heels were killing her, but she wouldn't admit it to a soul. She'd tucked back the top and sides of her hair from her face instead of her usual braid. It cascaded down her back in waves. She'd applied full makeup, the kind she only used for formal occasions. Even to her own gaze in the mirror this morning, she'd looked good. As she was leaving, Clara had caught sight of her.

"Oh, miss. You look beautiful. Almost the spitting image of Maureen yet different."

"Thank you, Clara. I'll be home for supper. I can't speak for Greg." She'd left and driven herself to the office in her new secondhand SUV.

She looked good, she knew her subject, and she was about to start a war with the board members. The issue wasn't about what she wore. Their plan was to blame her when stock prices plummeted.

If her entrance into the company wasn't handled carefully for the public, people would speculate about her presence. That wasn't her goal. She understood they would use any means necessary to vote her out as soon as they had her signatures. They needed her momentarily, but when their purposes were served, she'd be disposable. She took offense at that concept.

When everyone had found their place card and taken their seats, she stood and pulled a piece of paper from the top of the pile.

"I'm glad we were finally able to get the entire board in one room today. Let's not waste any more of *my* time." She drew a deep breath. "I'm officially notifying everyone in this room that all board meetings will be recorded for future reference." She didn't elaborate in what form. They didn't ask questions as to why they were being taped. They simply erupted in anger and began to threaten her. They claimed she had no right to change the dynamics they'd been entrenched in for so many years.

Lark held herself tall and didn't flinch. Instead, she stared at them until they quieted. "I do have the right. Everyone in this room and beyond handed it to me." Then she read from the paper before her.

"In terms from the dictionary and various other legal resources, fraud is defined as deceit, trickery, and cheating. An intentional deception to cause a person to give up property or a lawful right along with something said or done to deceive and trick." She paused for a breath. "From a separate source, fraudulent is defined as the intentional perversion of truth for the purpose of inducing another to part with something valuable or to surrender legal rights due to false representations. This includes misleading allegations or *concealment.* I'm sure you're getting my point."

Lark paused and looked at each face at the table. Most wouldn't return her gaze. "Moving on, fraudulent alienation boils down to the act of an administrator who wasted assets of an estate by giving them away or selling at a gross undervalue with intent to defraud." She let that settle when she heard the groans from the men in the room. Not surprising, Mr. Dodd was silent and wouldn't look at her.

“I could continue with definitions of fraudulent alienation, concealment, misrepresentation, but with all the degrees in this room, I’m sure you’ve gotten my point.”

“This is slander,” one of the men yelled from the other end of the table.

“Actually…” She turned another page and continued. “Slander is speaking base and defamatory words to prejudice another’s reputation, standards, business, or means of livelihood. Oral defamation is speaking false and malicious words concerning another resulting in injury to their reputation.”

“You’re not a lawyer. Anyone can read a dictionary,” someone commented.

“Yes, and so did my lawyer before I ever got on a plane to come here. My counsel assured me these terms are accurate.” She held up a hand. “Before you ask, I paid him privately, not from company funds.”

There were a lot of mumbled comments and outraged attitudes about letting an outsider into their company. But she knew she had them. Not a single man at that table refuted her definitions.

“I had hoped to work this out before we got to this point, but none of you seemed interested in discussing anything with me, especially concerning Braylin Industries. I’ve been in this building for months, and whenever any of you caught sight of me, you ran in different directions. Am I wrong?”

She waited out more mumblings. She made a point of slowly walking to the coffee tray and pouring herself a cup. When she was back, seated at the head of the table, she took a pile of reports and handed a stack to the men sitting on either side of her. “If you would pass them down, please."

Lark sat back and sipped her coffee as their reactions almost blasted the roof from the building. "Settle down, gentlemen, so we can have a civil discussion."

Another round of objections began.

"You can't take the plane away. We don't fly commercial," someone said.

"You can't mean to monitor our expense accounts…" another yelled.

The list went on just as she expected. She let them talk it out. Greg hadn't said a word, hadn't opened the report. Will Dodd was the first one who took a point and talked to her.

"I don't think condensing the offices is a viable option. When clients come into Braylin, they expect a certain level of opulence. If you change the perception of the company, we'll lose business."

"Do you take clients to the fourth floor?"

"Well, no, that's mostly—"

"It's wasted space. We have storage capabilities in the basement that will fit everything currently on the fourth floor. I've measured it, Mr. Dodd. Considering we own the building, we can lease that floor for…" She reached for her files and rattled off a dollar amount.

Dodd didn't challenge her. Another man hollered, "You can't presume to take away our company vehicles. That's ridiculous."

"How many vehicles can you drive at once?"

"What?" he asked.

"According to the records, the company leases three luxury vehicles just to you personally. Even if you let your spouse use one, that still leaves another vehicle sitting in a garage."

He had no comeback to that one.

"I think the board members have forgotten one thing." She waited until they calmed down and gave her their attention. "The board represents the shareholders." Lark waited another beat for effect. "I'm sure they'll be quite interested to learn how you have spent their dividends since Adley's death. None of you would have dared try anything like this when he was alive."

The board members continued to argue. She glanced from Greg to Will Dodd. Neither met her look.

An hour later, she put her hand up to stop the rude comments and accusations. "We could be doing this in court. I chose to try this approach first. Trust me—you don't want to bring the legal system into our corporate workings. You'll lose by *five* years."

The room went silent. "That's what I thought," she said under her breath. She caught Greg holding back a slight smile forming on his lips. "I'm not looking to dismantle this company. In fact, I'm looking for ways to salvage it and make it prosper. I could have just sued the corporation when I first found out about Adley's will. I chose a higher road. But I've been assured by several uninvolved sources that it's still my right to go in that direction. Don't push me, gentlemen. You all knew Adley. You know he didn't do things lightly or recklessly. I'm choosing to try and find a rational and reasonable direction to keep the company afloat."

There was another dead silence. "Since Adley's handwritten letter was delivered to me already unsealed, I have to assume most of you in this room knew the contents. So, you all know Adley had dirt on all of you. I don't need his research. All my research was from public records." They started whispering, and she cut them short. "You just have to know where to look."

Silence, dead silence, accompanied steely glares. She knew they wouldn't begin to take her seriously. "I'll expect each of you to bring a list of at least three changes that can be made to your departments to minimize spending and maximize the current staff." After another round of grievances, she gathered her files and stood. "We'll meet again on Friday morning at ten. I suggest you are on time and you've done your own research. You'll find I'm not reckless with my numbers or ideas."

She slowly walked to the door, refusing to give in to the blister on her toe from being squished into the show shoes, as she referred to them. At the doorway, she paused with her hand on the knob. "It might be time for some of you to reconsider your retirement packages. And I don't have to remind you of the nondisclosure agreements in each of your contracts." She opened the door and paused one last time. "Friday, ten a.m."

"I don't work on Fridays," someone hollered behind her.

She didn't turn around. "You do now." Then she took great pleasure in gently closing the door behind her. She didn't need to stay to listen. She'd put her own bug in the office before they arrived and had been recording the entire meeting. Later, when she was alone, she'd replay the recordings.

After all, the law required her to notify anyone being recorded in any way. She did make a point of telling them at the start of the meeting. They didn't verbally challenge her, so she continued. Her protection was that she did tell them upfront.

****

A part of Lark didn't want to go back to the Braylin

estate that night. After she reviewed the taped conversations of the meeting's aftermath, her anger was on a short leash. The change in her appearance from West Coast casual to East Coast professional attire had surprised everyone in the office, including her cousin. That didn't mean she'd dress to impress every day, but she'd changed the impressions of many minds that day. They had better start taking her seriously, or she could and would make trouble for all of them. Since she was alone in her huge office with nothing but her laptop, desk, chair, and empty sideboard, she didn't hold back her smile and eventually her laughter.

Apparently, none of the board appreciated her suggestion that they work on Friday. They did, however, discuss her opening to the meeting and the definitions of fraud she'd read aloud. She was still surprised that there was no real backlash to recording the meeting. After listening to the tapes several times, she had pages of notes on a lined yellow pad. Her information was all ammunition to be filtered in at their Friday meeting.

She found one part of the recording the most interesting. As they were filing out, Mr. Dodd had stopped them.

"If we don't show up for her meetings, what can she do? I suggest we just ignore her for now. Let her stew a bit and give me some time to figure out what she thinks she has on us," he'd said.

She had information from the men's muttered comments. Ultimately, she understood no board meeting would happen on Friday, at least not with the board members. But she'd show up, just in case they tried to double-cross her. In the meantime, she had decisions to make. Huge decisions. If her own future was the only issue to consider, there was no doubt as to her next step. But beyond her cousin, she had employees to consider. She would have to give this all some serious thought. Her attempts at corralling the board for the company's benefit wasn't going to happen as she'd hoped.

Lark usually thought through major decisions with clarity. Right now, all she saw was red, along with the initial impulse to sue all the involved parties and ultimately shut down the company. She wouldn't let that happen, mainly because her mother would be disappointed. She would give them one more attempt to solidify the situation, even if it was eating at her stomach.

Arriving back at the estate, she was surprised to see the sports car in the huge garage. That meant Greg had come home. In the past weeks, avoidance was easier if he didn't come home before eleven p.m. That was fine with her. She hadn't meant to send him fleeing from their home, but it was his choice to stay away.

The dogs greeted her at the back door as she kicked off her shoes. She dropped to the floor to give them some attention, not caring her dress would wrinkle or be covered in fur. She just wanted contact and felt guilty for not spending more time with them lately.

When she walked into the dining room barefoot, he was waiting for her. His direct eye contact was how he acknowledged her presence. She took her seat, and they had a very polite meal with *please* and *thank you* when the salt was passed or a platter handed across the table. Afterward she went to her room and changed into her everyday uniform of comfortable clothing to take the dogs for their evening walk. In reality, she was taking herself for a walk. Returning, she was surprised to find Greg in the living room.

"Can we talk?" he started. "Are you interested in a drink?"

"Just sparkling water, please, with lime." She snuggled back on the sofa, Spike there before she settled. The other dogs took to their cushions. It was hard not to look at Greg and want to see him as human and not one of her money-grubbing relatives.

Again, she reminded herself he wasn't her relative, just the adopted son of Rod Braylin. She had nothing against adoption. She did hold their five-year plan against them. Now if she could just get her hormones in line.

Greg stood tall. His piercing green gaze followed her every breath. He watched her chest rise and fall. He only turned away to fill a glass of water and place it on the table before her. She noted how he followed the dogs' movements more than hers.

"Thank you." Lark decided he was waiting for her attention.

"You surely made the board squirm this morning," he finally said, taking the club chair across from her.

"I didn't say anything that wasn't true."

"We know. The thing is, Lark, your approach was a bit…brusque."

"Brusque! That's an interesting choice of words."

"What would you call it?" He actually gave her a small smile.

"What approach would you have preferred? It's not like I didn't try to talk to all of you. I spent weeks in that office only to be shut out and ignored in all my attempts to discuss the situation."

"That probably wasn't in our own best interest," he said. "I've begun to realize the error of my ways. So if we could put aside the last years and weeks temporarily, I'd like to discuss the plans you've drafted."

"Fine. I'll be right back." She returned with her files and tablet. She spread her files on the low table before her and took her seat beside Spike.

"I feel blindsided," he said. "How could you do this to us?"

"You feel blindsided! Did you ever consider how I felt?" She took a deep breath before she continued. "Again, I tried to talk to you numerous times. All I got were rude attitudes, no-shows or late arrivals, and you walking out. I tried private meetings here, tried to give you the files, only to have them tossed back at me. I tried to talk to the board, but Mr. Dodd continually ran interference. He is going to be a problem, if you're not already aware of that." She watched him roll his eyes. "But you're already aware of his dealings. When did you realize he was a problem? Before or after the board relented and called me home? Is that why you keep him so close?"

"To a point." Greg put his drink on the round table beside him. "Dodd is a separate issue that I agree has to be dealt with. Could we put him aside for a bit?"

She nodded and waited, resisting folding her arms across her chest. She took Spike onto her lap instead. "Your charter, where do you want to start?"

"Your reports and your numbers. Where did all that information come from?"

"From the company files. Don't you check the weekly, monthly, or quarterly statements?"

"I'm ashamed to admit I left a lot of that to the board members. Are you sure your information is correct? How can you be so sure so quickly?"

"I'm a CPA. It's what I do. It's just how my mind works." She held back a smile. At least this was some communication. She didn't want to shut him down before more answers. "I also have a degree in theoretical mathematics." She petted Spike's ears. "How could your background checks miss that?"

"There are members of the board who don't take kindly to change. *Resistant* is the first term that comes to mind." He watched her. "Your comment about their retirement packages was not appreciated. In fact, I'm sure most of the employees could hear their loud comments through the walls."

"I did, too, as I left." She toed off her boots and crossed her legs up under her on the sofa. "It wasn't out of line. When was the last time you had a conversation with some of the younger employees about how their departments were run?" She hesitated and added, "That's what board meetings are for."

"It's the way it was always done," he said, obviously annoyed. He appeared dismissive of her whole being and the reason she was there in the first place.

"When Adley was alive? If you hadn't noticed, we're not in his time anymore. Even he had the sense to consolidate all the subdivisions to the headquarters here instead of leaving them around the country. Less travel, more communication. It was a good decision."

"Why do you hate the board members so much?" He rose to refill his drink.

"I don't know them well enough to hate them. I do feel the injustice they've done to me personally, and by you letting them skate on without overseeing them, they all feel so superior. They won't dare let anyone in their departments change anything that's done. Hell, three of them refuse to have a computer in their offices. I'm not asking them to become technicians, just to know how to pull up a report or the stock prices." She paused for a deep breath. "Do you realize all those televisions in their offices never run any news or stock prices? These old men go in there and watch television…like daytime entertainment shows."

"How would you know?"

"Because I've stopped by unannounced on each of them. I've tried to introduce myself, and each time they have televisions running, and none of them have anything to do with the outside business world. Hell, one of them has three stations of fifties sitcoms running." She put up her hand to ward off his comments. "I watch the old reruns too. But I'd like to think they would at least make the appearance of having world news or the market numbers running, even if they're muted."

"Some of your observations are on point. It might help us all if you weren't so verbal about them."

"That's a tall order after their treatment." She dropped her feet to the floor. "Have you ever truly done a day's work? Because I can't figure out what you do there."

"Are you saying I'm not pulling my weight? Because you have no idea what I contribute to the company." His voice rose, and Spike sat forward. "I'm the face of the company. I do all the public appearances and appease the clients. Are you planning on retiring me too?"

"Let's just say there are big changes on the horizon for all of us."

Greg let out a disgruntled laugh. "You're considering firing me, and you think that's just a change?

What gives you the right?"

"You did. You and every person that withheld the will." She paused for a calming breath. "Have you bothered to consider this was a huge change for me too? I did have a life before you realized you couldn't mortgage the estate. I'm surprised someone just didn't sign my name!" She watched his face go red. "Oh my God! You did try, but someone was smart enough to ask for proof, weren't they?"

"Can we just admit things were done improperly for a while? We're trying to change that now." He paced the length of the room. "Is this where I'm supposed to grovel with apologies?"

"I'd prefer apologies from the board and yours without attitude, but I can wait."

"Then tell me this, cousin, what are your plans for the company? We do have a say in the decisions. I'd prefer not to be caught short at Friday's meeting."

"Relax. I'd be surprised if there is a Friday meeting. I will show up, but I assume I'll be the only one there."

"Why?" He seemed confused, shaking his head from side to side.

"Wait until Friday and see who shows up."

"You think the board will boycott your meeting?"

"Absolutely. Just to prove their point that they don't respect me. But that's another conversation. You were in the room when Dodd made the suggestion."

Greg's head snapped up. "How did you know?"

"I stated very clearly at the beginning that the meeting was being recorded. For now, let's just deal with the facts at hand."

"Do you have any idea how many employees will lose their jobs if you implement your threats?"

"I'm not looking to fire employees. I just want to lease wasted floor space that could be used for income."

"You going to take away our cars too?" Greg started pacing the room. He wandered along the hall door instead of in front of the fireplace, where the dogs lay.

"Two per management employee. Any others, and you buy them."

"That's why you're driving a used SUV, then, to prove a point." He shook his head, grumbling about his automobiles.

"You saw the vehicle. I've purchased a gently used SUV. Sorry to disappoint you, but it's only three years old and not a fleck of rust in sight. And before you ask, I used my own funds, not the company's."

"Why used? Don't you believe in buying anything new?" Finally, he shook his head and laughed. "You're trying to prove a point about efficiency."

"What embarrasses you about a used vehicle?" Then it struck her. "I was raised differently. We think through large purchases. A new vehicle didn't make sense for my lifestyle."

"That goes for your wardrobe too?"

Lark turned to him. "You are embarrassed. Just because I wear what's comfortable and practical?"

"Seeing you today brought the point home. You could be so much more than you are on a daily basis, but it seems like you don't care about your appearance." He gave her a shoulder shrug.

"Sorry. I don't think you appreciate the time and effort it takes to put on a façade for the public. When absolutely necessary, fine. But daily, this is me. Get used to it."

"Leaving your wardrobe aside for now, have you

considered what you'd do if the board decides to quit or retire? I hope you have a backup plan." He dropped into a chair across from her.

"If you would have read my files, you'll note there are options for each board member's replacements. I've scouted two per member, three for a few. All promoted from within their division."

"You better watch your back, Lark. Those men do not like their lives or lifestyles being messed with, especially from a stranger."

"Why didn't you bother to consider changes?" She didn't let him answer. "Because it was easier to go with the flow? Because you didn't want to consider having to change your own job, to actually work at something each day beyond golf, client lunches, and suppers?"

"Would you believe I'm actually trying to be honest here, just for a moment. You're not making any friends at the company. That could be dangerous on many levels."

"Is that a threat from you or the board members? Or both?"

"Not from me. It's just general information that's floating around."

"I heard that rumor the second week I was there. You see, I talk to the employees. I listen to their issues and their proposed solutions."

"What do you expect me to do, Lark?"

"I'd like to be given the benefit of the doubt instead of patted on the head and sent on my way to an empty office. And if Dodd calls me an urchin one more time, I'm going to lay him out. How's that for being politically correct?"

"I'd love to see that," Greg said. "I'd love to see old

Dodd flying commercial, even if it is first class."

"Business class. Their contracts read air-travel expenses. They don't specify first class." She liked sparring with Greg when they weren't sniping at each other.

"If you're taking away the company plane, they're going to assume first class."

"Aren't they lawyers and accountants? Didn't they draft their contracts? Somebody screwed up big-time because there are a lot of perks that are taken for granted." She cleared her throat. "That includes the amount they travel. While I've left this out, I will say it would be much cheaper to bring the clients here rather than to go to them. After all, we have this huge, opulent office that clients rarely see." Again, she paused. "And there's the fact that they use the corporate plane for 'business' travel that doesn't seem to exist, or at least I couldn't find any records of those clients."

"One minefield at a time." He walked back to the bar but didn't pour a drink. He came and sat across from her.

She let out a sigh. "I'll tell you what. Why don't you continue being the company's golden boy as figurehead and try to soothe ruffled egos? I'll take the heat for the decisions. After all, I am the poor relation they hid from. It would make sense for me to be the disgruntled employee."

Edward came into the doorway. "Can I get you anything?" he asked in general.

"Yes, please. Fresh coffee would be appreciated. We're going to be here for a bit longer."

He nodded and left.

Greg groaned and sat forward. "That means you've

got more on your list. What else are we losing?"

"Me for five minutes. I'm going to take a bathroom break and get my laptop." She jogged up the stairs, wondering what his thoughts might be while she was gone. She was back the same time Edward carried the coffee tray into the room. "Thank you." She paused to put the computer on the sofa and poured herself a cup. Then she sat back down and opened her laptop.

"Go ahead," Greg said.

"Fine. Leaving this estate aside, can you tell me why the company is paying for five other family compounds? According to company records, there are three beach properties and two ski chalets. Yet you ski in Europe. You went twice last year. My suggestion would be to keep one of each. We can sell the others or lease them for the income. Do you realize we employ at least ten other people to keep homes that are rarely used?

"If we keep them, it's only reasonable to let the rental income pay the salaries and taxes. Are you familiar with websites that lease vacation properties? The people who would lease them would expect some staff. At least it's a positive proposition instead of a costly one. I haven't seen any of them, just photos. You decide which ones to keep."

"You are fucking crazy, lady. You're not taking away my homes." His tone had the two larger dogs standing up and staring at him.

"I thought this was your home and the others were vacation properties. Can you honestly tell me when you used each of them last?" She gave the dogs a hand signal, and they came to lie before the sofa where she sat, Spike glued to her side.

"I hate your fucking dogs." He stormed from the

room.

"I assume the conversation is over." She sighed and let her head drop back against the sofa.

Greg came to the doorway and let out a huffing breath.

"Just think on it, Greg. Maybe you will see it's a positive step. Considering you haven't used either of the ski properties in two years, and you only used the Caribbean property once last year. It's an option. If you can think of something else to make them self-sufficient, I'm willing to listen."

"It's been two years since I've been skiing in the US? I didn't realize." He walked over and poured himself coffee.

"Just think about it. I'm not trying to strip you or the company of all the assets, just lighten the load of ones that aren't useful." She pushed forward and stood. "I'm going to walk the dogs and get some fresh air."

"Wait, Lark." He set the coffee down. "Are you putting us on austerity here too? It seems like you're trying to penalize us all for slighting you."

"Believe it or not, Greg, I'm just trying to keep us current. The mathematician inside me can't stand to see the waste, especially when we could be doing other things that are profitable." She headed out, and the dogs followed her.

The rest of the week went by as usual. Everyone at the office ignored her, and Greg was a no-show for breakfast and supper. That was fine with her. She preferred to enjoy her supper on a tray before the television and the evening news.

Chapter Nine

The following Friday, Lark sat in the boardroom, alone in her normal, comfortable uniform. At least her feet didn't hurt. None of the members had set foot in the building. Eventually, Greg showed up.

"Go ahead, say it," she uttered.

"You really didn't think they'd show up because you demanded it, did you?"

"It was a test of respect. They failed." She sat tall in her seat at the head of the table. "It's okay. The next scheduled board meeting will be here soon. They'll show up for that meeting."

She decided it was interesting that Greg did show up and on time. He probably just wanted to rub in the slight, but he came. Progress was progress, even if at a snail's pace.

"What makes you so sure?" He headed to the sideboard and poured coffee for himself. He raised the pot to Lark.

She shook her head. "I went back through the records. They always show up for the end-of-the-quarter meetings. They want to be able to estimate their bonuses. It's the only Friday any of them ever work."

"So we're just supposed to wait three weeks for you to shut us down?"

She shook her head again. "I'm truly not trying to shut the company down."

"I wish I could believe that," he snarled.

"For a minute, I thought you finally accepted that my agenda isn't revenge. I want to make my mother proud. I want to make Old Adley proud, even if both are in the abstract. I'm trying to become invested in this company and make a future for myself too." She paused and drew a breath, realizing she was referring to him as Old Adley too. "Have you considered that if I wanted revenge for the way I've been treated, I could have stayed on the West Coast, gone the route of news-show interviews, and just sued you all to hell?" She let out an exasperated breath. "I can't stay here and be afraid to deal with every issue I see. I won't pussyfoot around a group of old fossils that are too set in their ways to accept I'm offering possibilities that they haven't considered."

"We're all off-kilter, Lark. None of us expected you to come in and assume all the power. We figured you'd be a little more…reflective before threatening to fire the board members and dismantle the company."

"You know, Greg, all those files and meetings at the house when I tried to talk this through were a waste of time. But just to clarify, maybe if you looked at the research without an attitude of entitlement, you'd realize this whole situation could be easily fixed."

She gathered her tablet and headed for the door. She paused with her hand on the knob. "Maybe you should just sit down and think about what you expect from the future."

"I have, at least since our kiss in the yard. I can't reconcile this side of you with the woman I met at the music school."

"That woman is long buried since this estate thing came up."

"I'm admitting things were not done properly. I'd like to meet up with that woman again one day."

"I'd like to meet the man from the school too. But sex would be too easy. And afterward…well, you don't respect me now. I'd never get any respect or companionship after." She let out a breath. "Sometimes I think I should just lay you for the fun. But that would be short-lived relief, not good for long-term anything."

"This all would have been simpler if we'd never met before."

Lark stared at him. "Can I get a truthful answer? Those meetings—were you sent to me? Did you know who I was? Did the board suggest you do some recon about the urchin heir?"

"No. Whether you believe me or not, I had no clue who you were. I was just attracted. You were different than most women I meet. The draw was you didn't want anything but sex from me."

"That's true. You're hot, handsome, and you made me horny. I figured you'd be a safe stranger never to be seen or heard from again." She shrugged.

"That didn't quite work out."

"No, it didn't. But I can still remember how your erection stretched me until I came."

"You have such beautiful breasts. I became enamored with your nipples. You're so responsive to my touch."

"It was a fleeting moment in time," she told him.

"Any chance we could reconnect, even just in private? Nobody would have to know."

She laughed at him. "No, I don't trust you not to use the circumstance against me if I piss you off, which, you are well aware of, I seem to do daily."

"We could make a truce not to do that. At least we'd both get some stress relief."

"If only we could," she mused. "Those days are gone. Maybe you should try swimming."

"You drive me crazy when you swim. You're so graceful, so beautiful."

"Thank you." The heat of embarrassment flooded her cheeks. She was relieved when his phone rang and he left to answer the call. While one side of her would have liked to know what the call was about, the other side wasn't sure she could process more stress at the moment.

She turned and left, thankful she hadn't bothered to turn on the recordings before the meeting was due to start. She walked with her head up to her austere office at the far end of the building and shut the door. Only then did she allow the anger to overtake her.

She had three weeks to get this straight in her mind before the end of the quarter. She stared out the window, and the realization resurfaced again. Everything in the past was gone in all ways. She had choices to make that would affect many people. None of them were going to like her decisions.

****

The next day Lark woke to a full-out rainstorm. She was glad it was Saturday and she didn't have to be anywhere early. Since the dogs hadn't stirred, she pulled the blanket over her head and went back to sleep.

When she woke the second time, Baby was sitting beside her on the bed, panting and whining.

"Baby, get down." The dog didn't stir. She knew the dog needed to go out, but before she could get her feet to the carpet, a clash of thunder struck in the distance. Even she startled while Baby managed to hide her head under the blanket. If the dog wasn't so huge, it might have been funny. By the time she stretched and woke up a bit more, the dog had nuzzled her whole body on the bed under the blanket.

By then all three dogs were awake. Lark pulled on her comfortable worn jeans and old sneakers. Baby needed to be coaxed off the bed, but eventually she managed to get them all downstairs. Out the back door, she made the executive decision to forgo the leashes and the long walk. She stayed close to the house, waiting for each to wander for a while. With a quick trip back to the door, she grabbed an umbrella. She knew they wouldn't do anything without a proper walk.

Even though it was a short walk, it was still a walk. She made sure each one peed before allowing herself to head back. With a clap of thunder in the distance and a streak of lightning too close for comfort, she decided the walk was over. Baby was at the back door before she was. Spike didn't seem to notice he was wet; neither did Princess.

Inside, she paused in the hallway to towel off the dogs before letting them loose. She accepted a mug of coffee from Clara and savored the first sips.

Spike paused to eat, Princess drank from the bowl, and Baby sat by her leg, whining. "This is a new side of you," she teased, reaching to scratch the animal's ears.

Edward appeared at the doorway. "More coffee?"

"Yes, please." She walked into the kitchen and accepted a refill of the mug of steamy brew. "Thanks. I slept through the news. Is it going to rain all day?"

"That's the forecast," Edward acknowledged.

"So much for a swim." She lifted the mug in a mock toast. "Thanks for the coffee."

"Breakfast?" he asked.

"No, thanks. Is Greg here today?"

"No, he left early, although he didn't tell me his plans."

She nodded and walked away. A few steps back into the hallway, she turned around. "Edward, where are the old family photo albums? My mother used to tell me about all the photos taken when she was young."

"They're all stored up in the attic." He hesitated and walked toward her with the coffeepot, pausing to top her off again. "Rainy days are good for attic exploring. I believe they're in an old black trunk. Would you like me to find them and bring them down?"

"No, thanks. I'll look around." She snapped her fingers, and the dogs followed, all making it to her bedroom door before she did. They were starting to feel at home, and to them, this was their safe place.

After a hot shower, she let her hair air-dry and pulled on her oldest sweats, the ones she almost didn't pack. But for a day in the attic, they seemed appropriate.

****

Lark wasn't sure how long she was up there. With no sunlight and only a few bare bulbs, she couldn't tell the time. It didn't matter. She had purposely turned off her phone before going upstairs. She was enjoying the trip through her family history, or her extended family history. She didn't grow up knowing them, but they were blood. The only relatives she might have ever known. Now they were all gone. She was the lone Braylin blood here.

Beyond furniture, she found cases of old clothing. She found one trunk with what she assumed were Nancy's clothing from the styles. At the bottom was her wedding gown. She resisted unfolding it from the layers of tissue to see the details, figuring she'd find photos of it. A few cartons contained baby clothes and what looked like christening gowns, although she couldn't decide if they were worn by Rod and Maureen or their parents.

There was a pole lamp with a leaded-glass shade that had a slight crack in one of the panels. She wondered what it would cost to have it returned to the manufacturer and repaired. If possible, it would be a beautiful addition to the library. A few cartons contained ornate silver tea and coffee services. There were also two complete sets of china, one with a garish design in bold colors. Those dishes were ugly, and she understood why they were packed away. The second set had a spartan design in silver, although it carried the stamp of a famous company. Apparently, someone didn't care for that service either.

Eventually, she came across two trunks she hadn't explored. That was her gold mine. She lifted the cover of the first and saw framed photos from many generations. The second held the precious albums she'd sought.

Her emotions ran high as she flipped through the books. What had she expected to find? Surely, posed portraits with staunch-looking parents. What she found was unexplainable.

After a cursory look, she went back to the oldest album and scanned the photos of her grandmother's family. They were stiff collared and posed. In each one, their expressions were the same—stern and pinched. But taking time to look through the rest, she was startled with each page she turned.

The wedding photos of her grandparents were staged. Maureen had told her that Adley and Nancy had eloped. Apparently, these photos were produced for social purposes. But a few candids had been tucked near the back of the album. Those showed them smiling and touching. There wasn't a single staged photo of anyone smiling.

The next section showed their early life together. Lark understood Adley was trying to prove himself to Nancy's family. Her impression was when Nancy was away from them, she did smile. In some they laughed, and in others they looked at each other with love and affection.

Then came Rod and Maureen as infants and small children. Smiles and affection abounded. Only the few with Nancy's parents were back to the formal, staunch photograph.

Then came the change. That was when her mother, Maureen, was around five or six. Insecurity on Nancy's expression took precedence, while Adley still smiled. Photos of pool parties and the children's birthdays along with ones from Christmas mornings were filled with smiles.

Photos from the next few years allowed her to watch her mother and uncle grow. She saw the distinct difference in her grandparents. Nancy seemed on edge, and Adley seemed annoyed. The rest of the albums mainly contained pictures of the children, including the required school photos from each year.

Lark closed the cover and sat back, contemplating the changes her mother had diplomatically relayed. Her mother had been unwilling to denigrate her parents' memory even under the tense circumstances. Her mother had chosen to remember the family in happier times. None of it mattered. One thing Lark knew for sure—she couldn't change the past, only influence the future. She carefully packed the albums away and shut the trunk.

She headed back downstairs but changed her mind. Instead, she returned to the first trunk and retrieved two of the framed photos she'd seen earlier. One was from her mother's high school graduation. She wore the required pearl necklace and black sweater.

The second was a photo from her mother's younger years. Adley sat in a chair beside a Christmas tree. Nancy sat on the arm of the chair, her arm draped casually around his shoulders. Rod sat on the floor with a truck in his hands, and Maureen sat on her father's lap with a rag doll. To the side of the chair was the leaded lamp she'd admired in the attic. She would have loved to know what was said before the photo was snapped, because their smiles were wide and seemed genuine.

She took the two framed photos and headed back to her bedroom. After a quick polish with a washcloth, she put them both on the mantel over the fireplace in the seating area, and then she promptly fell asleep in the large armchair. She woke with a start when Baby started whining. Glancing at the clock, she saw she'd slept for two hours.

Downstairs, she let the dogs into the run, knowing with the steady rain they wouldn't stay out long. She grabbed a bottle of water from the refrigerator, and while she waited for the dogs to return, Edward came in.

"Can I get you anything, miss?"

"No, thank you. Just letting the dogs run."

He nodded and turned, but she called him back. "When I was in the attic this morning, I saw an old pole lamp with a leaded-glass shade. Are you aware of a problem with it beyond the crack in one of the panes?"

"Not to my knowledge. It used to sit in your grandfather's office. When he passed, Greg had some of the older things moved out and replaced with more modern items."

"Could you have it brought down and the electrical checked? If it works, I'd like to put it in the second-floor library. It's too beautiful to sit in the attic."

"I'll have it brought down and checked."

"Thank you."

The dogs were all back. Spike was barking, and Baby and Princess were huddled against the door. She retrieved the old towels placed in a cabinet near the door for just this purpose. After she gave each dog a quick dry, they followed her upstairs to the second-floor library, which was becoming her favorite place in the house. She set a match to the logs and dropped into the reading chair. The dogs settled before the fireplace.

With her laptop open, she made notes for next week. Two hours later, Edward knocked on the door and entered with the lamp. It had been cleaned and sparkled more than she would have imagined.

"The wiring seems intact. I believe it was a style issue rather than an electrical issue."

She stood as he walked into the room. "Thank you. It's beautiful," she said as he plugged it into the outlet near the door to show her the shade design.

"Where would you like it?"

"Over here by my reading chair." She met him and bent to plug it in. It bathed the whole room in a kaleidoscope of colors. "It's stunning. Thank you."

"You're welcome. Supper will be at seven."

She nodded and stood before the lamp, appreciating its colors.

****

While she'd thought to see the room before, she'd never breached the privacy of Adley's bedroom. Today she did, just because she could. The scent of tobacco was the first sensory memory she made while standing in the doorway. Then she saw it, the glass piece she was familiar with. It was a piece her mother had made years before. Lark didn't think but walked straight to the mantel and took it. She decided to leave exploring the rest of the room for another day. Her emotions were already stretched. Seeing the glass piece in Adley's private space pushed her to walk away.

Back in the library, settled in her favorite club chair, she watched the reflecting light from the lamp and the fireplace. Her mind continued to wander. Since her time in the attic, her thoughts hadn't cleared. Rather, they'd become more befuddled. All she knew for sure was what her mother had told her about her family and her upbringing. She had no reason to question her mother's version, especially considering they had abandoned her or rather, sent her away with one choice they'd considered a mistake.

No. She wasn't a mistake, as her mother always reinforced. She was the gift the Braylin family wouldn't accept. What struck her most was the other side she'd never known. Maureen had told her Adley was an orphan, but she never clarified the rest of his history. Maybe Maureen didn't know the actual details. She had regaled Lark with stories of her childhood filled with laughs and hugs. But she'd never elaborated on what had changed. What had been the one moment in time that set the family on a different course? Maureen had said her mother had become fragile.

Maybe her grandfather never offered answers to that question. Lark had never thought to ask the question. From conversations with her mother, she'd always assumed Nancy was delicate from the start and child-rearing had left her weak. But now that she'd seen the photographs, she saw another side to the Braylin family.

The ones of Rod and Maureen's youth struck her most. There had been laughter and smiles. There had been fun and love. Especially from Nancy. In those early photos, she wore the smile of a proud woman and mother. So what had changed and when?

Lark abandoned her line of thinking and settled in to enjoy the fire and the shadows of the lamp. The library door flung inward.

"So now you're stealing family heirlooms," Greg taunted.

She was in no mood to appease him. After their conversation about sex, she found it hard to be near him without thinking in those directions. She had to keep her distance before she actually reached to touch him and made the situation worse. "No, I simply took one from the attic to be used again. I was told it was in Old Adley's office for years until he died and you wanted a 'modern space.' As you can see, it's still in the family home." She pointed to the lamp behind her chair.

He didn't have an answer to that statement. Instead, he shifted his weight from one hip to the other.

"And for general information, it's all partly mine too. So just fuck off. I've got enough on my mind right now. I'm not in the mood to fence with you, Greg."

He laughed. "Well, a real emotion." He moved into the room and bent before the fireplace to add a few logs from the reserve pile.

"I thought you were out for the day?"

"Now I have to clear my plans with you?" he asked.

"Why start now? Look, I'm not in the mood to be pandered to or berated for bothering to read the corporate reports."

"What happened to you?" He rose and took the club chair beside her.

"Nothing. I'm just done placating people and taking their bad moods."

"Wow, something did happen. Did Mr. Dodd call you today?" He stood and moved to the door, reaching to partially close it before he sat beside her again.

"No, was he supposed to?"

"Not that I'm aware of. It just seems he's the only one who pushes your buttons into anger." He paused to look at her.

His scrutiny heated her body, but she refused to give him any inkling that she still had feelings about him, even if they were just sexual.

"Well, I do that too," he said, not holding back a smile. "What happened, Lark?"

"Besides finding the lamp in the attic, I found something…else." She hesitated and pointed to a large glass bowl on the mantel.

"I've never seen that before," Greg said.

"I found it in Adley's room." She waited for him to explode, but he didn't.

Instead, he stood and walked to the mantel. Taking the dish from its stand, he studied it in the light. "It's beautiful. I'm not sure I've ever seen this before. You said it was in Adley's room?"

She again waited for him to throw a fit, but he didn't, surprising her. "After the attic, I wanted to understand the family. I just stood in the doorway, looking around the room. The first thing that hit me was the smell of cherry tobacco. Then I saw that on the mantel in his sitting area." She shifted in her seat and held back a comment about him being careful with the dish. "I took it from Adley's room so I could see it whenever I needed a reminder."

"A reminder of what?"

The piece glinted in the light. The swirl of the dark-blue color within the opalescent glass reflected against the walls. She had an instant memory of when the piece was made. She was young, doing homework in her mother's studio. Her homework was forgotten as she watched how the color was layered and refired. In this moment, she could almost feel the immense heat that enveloped the area as the piece was formed. Although the end result amazed her, she never had the dexterity to make anything as beautiful. She was taught the procedures, but it didn't click within her brain. Numbers were different. She just had to look at them, and she understood the way they worked.

"Lark, what did you mean?"

"It was a piece my mother made when I was a child. I remember when she was working on it. Then it went to the gallery and was sold. I never thought to see it again, yet there it was in Adley's private bedroom. The man is a total enigma to me."

"To most of us." Greg carefully put the piece back on the mantel. "Your mother made it. Wow. I've never seen it before. Then again, Adley's master bedroom was his private space. I don't remember anyone ever going past the threshold after Nancy died. I wonder if it was in there when she was still alive."

"I'd bet if it was, she didn't know their daughter was the artist." She let out a sigh that took too much effort to hold back.

"I'm going to tell you something I probably shouldn't. But shortly after you arrived, I did some research on the internet. I saw photos of some of your mother's pieces. The ones in the museums. They were beautiful."

"Thank you. Her works are beautiful."

"Did she ever marry? I've never heard you mention a father or stepfather."

"No, she never married. She dated a little when I was younger, and when I was older, she had a few long-term boyfriends. But she never felt the need to marry any of them."

"Did that bother you?"

"No. She was careful what men she introduced me to when I was little, and we had a wide circle of friends and families we socialized with. They were mainly connected with the arts. If she wanted an escort to a specific event, there were always male friends to call on. They considered it more networking than dating."

"Do you know why she didn't marry?"

"It never mattered to her, mostly because her work mattered more. Once you start working on a piece of glass, you have to follow through. Not all men appreciated being told they were being canceled for her work." She laughed at a memory she didn't share.

"That didn't bother you, not having a male figure around?" he asked.

"I had plenty of male figures around. Mom just never felt the need to marry any of them." She looked at him and decided to continue. "She had a longtime lover.

He spent the summers up in San Francisco and the winters in New Mexico. He was a painter. That is where I learned to love and ride horses."

"And where your first pair of cowboy boots came from?" Greg teased.

"Sorry to disappoint you. I took riding lessons when I was finishing grammar school. Mom wanted me to be comfortable around large animals. That's when I got my first pair of boots. The time in New Mexico was pure fun."

"I suppose asking about your biological father is off-limits," he said, more as a statement than a question.

"He was a topic we never discussed. I only found out his first name after she passed away. I figured she could have found him if she wanted to, but she never did. So, I won't either."

They were quiet for a while before Greg finally spoke. "This is amazing. I can't believe I never noticed it in Adley's room. Then again, it wasn't a public room to snoop in."

She let out a deep breath. "I didn't look around Adley's room. It felt wrong. But I couldn't leave that in there."

"Maybe one day we'll go into the room together. We can explore it and see if we can find some hint of the man I missed. We missed."

"He was always a concept, never a reality in my life. But to find this…it's all very confusing. I choose to believe that even though he sent her away, he loved her in his own way, even if wasn't a way I could understand."

"I lived with him from the time I was five, and I never understood him. Even after Nancy died, I could never get a handle on him. But I will say that at times I'd see the mask slip. See him actually laughing at something or taking joy in being with his dogs. He raised German shepherds. They were amazing animals. They were his pride and joy."

"I knew he raised them. That was why the kennel and run were put in. Edward told me that when I first arrived. You mentioned Adley had a sixth sense training them when we were outside that one night."

"You look as if you're ready to burst into tears. Talk to me."

"I'm confused, and if I ask, I'm afraid it will leave me vulnerable." She stared at him, hoping to see an expression she could trust.

"At this point, does it matter?" Greg said, walking to the window seat but not actually sitting, just looking out the window. She wondered if he saw the same patterns the rain made against the glass as she did.

"Fine. I can only hope you don't use this against me, and I'd prefer nobody else know about my curiosity, even Edward and Clara."

"If you're not willing to talk to either of them, you are worried. Go ahead, Lark. Ask your question."

For the first time she began to hope they were putting aside the animosity and finally forging some type of friendship. She decided to trust him with her questions. The worst that could happen was he would betray her and she'd use it as a lesson. Since all the involved parties were dead, they couldn't speak for themselves. Nor could they reach down and retaliate for her curiosity.

Chapter Ten

She straightened in her seat and tried not to see the handsome man in the room with her. Between the light from the fire and the glass lamp, he looked different—softer, not so stern and rough. He was extremely handsome, and again, she silently accepted he still made her hot and horny. That she wouldn't reveal, but she pressed her thighs together to stop from squirming at the thought.

"You grew up here. Did you ever overhear conversations about Nancy, my…our grandmother?"

"She always seemed sickly," Greg said easily. "As best as I can remember, she was always treated as frail. I was little, but she seemed to spend the days in her room and only came down for supper. That was a very formal meal in this house. Strict manners and hushed conversation. After that, she'd disappear back to her room. I remember dreading supper. Why are you asking?"

"I was looking through the old photo albums, the ones from Rod and Maureen's childhood. Both Nancy and Adley seemed so in love with each other and with their children. They laughed and hugged, and the photos seem like a different family. At least for a while." She let out a sigh.

"I remember Rod cautioning us when Nancy's family came for a visit. When her parents died, her dotty old cousins felt it was their responsibility to continually remind her that she was a disappointment to the family. They were loud, rude, and generally disagreeable. Those were the strictest days in the house. Rod and my mother trotted me out to be viewed and then sent me back to my room. I used to wonder why they were embarrassed about me." He returned to the chair beside her and sat, turning to look at her. "I'd sneak out of my room to the top of the stairs and listen to the adults downstairs. They were never kind people. In fact, as I got a little older, I became thankful I didn't have to be on view."

He settled and crossed one leg over his other knee. "No noise, no backtalk, no talking at all. If I was asked a direct question, I had to answer with *ma'am* or *sir*. I always had to dress up and be seen and not heard until I got a reprieve. I remember Nancy being remote after the visits. But Rod and Mom reverted to their personalities, albeit relieved."

"Any idea why?"

"Supposition. I'm not sure, and I was just a kid. But it seemed to me that no matter what Adley and Nancy did, it was always wrong with her family. The dotty old cousins never had a kind word to say to my mom or Rod. And I have memories of them talking loudly about what a disappointment Nancy was to their family. It was like she could never live up to their vision."

"How?"

"I'm not sure. It was just an impression. When I first came to the house, Nancy was different, kinder. But after each visit with her side of the family, she withdrew." He fidgeted, folding back the cuffs on his shirt, obviously uncomfortable. "My mom once told me to just go with the flow while they visited, that bad behavior would reflect poorly on Nancy and Adley, beyond her and Rod. To be honest, I never knew my mom to be anxious around anyone, even Old Adley. But when Nancy's family came, even she was on edge. The whole house and staff seemed to be on alert."

"I find that extremely sad," Lark said. "I have to wonder how different all their lives would have turned out if they didn't influence Nancy. Or if Nancy had the guts to tell them to shove it. It makes me wonder what might have been different with my mother's life if Adley and Nancy hadn't allowed themselves to be influenced by the extended family."

"I can't prove it." Greg hesitated before continuing. "I once overheard Nancy's cousins berating her for her contemporary ways of raising her children and even their clothing. It was like they were embarrassed by her. That even though Old Adley made more money than God, it was never enough for them. As a kid, I learned there was no way to win with them. Did you ever meet those kinds of people? No matter what you did or said, it wasn't good enough? That's how it was on those visits."

"Unfortunately, yes." She relaxed back in the chair, studying the patterns of light from the newly found lamp. For a few moments, she couldn't look at Greg, afraid she'd say or do something to show her hand and leave her vulnerable.

"After those visits, Nancy receded to her room for days. They hammered her with their disappointments. And remember she was a grandmother by then. She could have told them to fuck off. Apparently, their hold over her was too embedded."

Lark stiffened. The comment was another reinforcement of what she and her mother had lost in not being a part of the family, good and bad. In this instance, it gave her a deeper insight into Maureen's reasons for not coming back to the family.

"Wait, I didn't mean you or your mother. Their disappointment was about Rod not fathering his own children. That it was Nancy's fault I wasn't their biological family. Like she had control of his sperm count. I truly never heard anything about Maureen. In reality, her name was rarely mentioned. And never when Nancy's family visited. Never."

"It's all so confusing to me. When Rod and Maureen were children, they seemed so happy and vibrant. The photos tell a story. I've seen enough pictures of Adley and Nancy to think they tried to raise happy kids. They seemed so in love in the photos, and they line up with some of the stories Mom told me over the years."

"That might have been part of the problem," Greg admitted. "My young impressions led me to believe they were jealous of Nancy and hated she was enjoying her life and family. If she seemed happy, her family would be ruder than the last time."

"Even when you were little?"

"I was a kid that Rod tried to keep out of the line of fire. I do remember a few arguments where he would try to defend his mom and dad, but that only made matters worse. Nancy's aunt called him disingenuous once. I remember that because I had to come upstairs and look up the word." He paused before continuing.

"I remember one argument where Nancy's family threatened to cut off her inheritance. Old Adley got nasty and told them they hadn't ever helped them financially, and neither he nor Nancy ever asked for financial help. He pissed the aunt off big-time by reminding her of the monthly check he was now sending them. All he ever wanted was his wife to be happy, and they just couldn't accept she found that with him." He shrugged.

"None of it makes sense. My mind is spinning, and I'll never get answers. So, I have to let those questions go with history unresolved." Lark straightened in her chair. "I turned my phone off on purpose today. Why did you think Mr. Dodd was going to contact me today?"

"It was just the look on your face, like the bottom had dropped out."

"I guess we'll never know the answers for sure, and it wouldn't make a difference. I was just looking to understand this family dynamic."

"Greed," he told her. "Simple greed. In my opinion, Nancy's family was waiting for Adley to fail. When he didn't and he didn't need their money, it made them angrier. That took away all their control over both of them, and eventually he was subsidizing them." He stretched out in the chair. "Besides the photos, what brought this up?"

She let out a deep breath. "I suppose seeing the 'happy family photos' of Adley and Nancy with their children opened up another door into hell for me. You see, I grew up knowing that Adley Braylin didn't want my mother or her illegitimate child anywhere near him or his family."

"I don't know. I suppose any of them could have made the same overture. Rod included."

"The one tossed out doesn't make the call unless they need help. My mother never needed their help when she was still in their good graces. Even if the bottom fell out, she never would have asked either of them for anything."

Edward knocked lightly on the half-open door to the library. "Supper will be ready in half an hour."

"Thank you," Lark said, but he lingered in the doorway. "Edward?"

"It may not be my place to say this, but I can tell you that Mr. B did consider bringing your mother back. It was Nancy's mother, your great-grandmother, who forbad it. When Nancy's parents passed, her aunt and uncle kept hammering home issues of disrespect and family honor."

"What about Adley?"

"He wouldn't go against his wife's wishes even though she had passed away. When she married him for love instead of the husband her family arranged, it left them both in an awkward position. He knew he'd broken that family bond. Nancy tried to repair it for years—literally until she passed away—but he never lost the guilt or the family strain of the situation."

"Who were these people?" Lark asked out of frustration.

"They were from a different generation, and they didn't expect their daughter or niece to go against their wishes even for love." Edward cleared his throat.

She realized he was uncomfortable talking about the family. "Thank you, Edward. I understand it's difficult to divulge family issues, especially to the bad seed."

"Not the bad seed, Miss Lark. Just the one nobody got to know." He turned and walked away.

"I feel bad making him tell family secrets."

"If any of us were the bad seeds of the family, I was," Greg told her and laughed.

"I guess this is why my mother never broached the topic with me. Then again, I don't know that I ever asked her for an explanation. I'm beginning to think it was because I was afraid of the answer."

"Let's get some food. Maybe it will make us both feel better." He stood and walked to the doorway.

"Smartest thing you've said to me all day." She paused to look back at the lamp. "I'll be right down. I want to wash up." She waited until he left before attempting to push herself out of the chair. Her mind had been reeling for months. Now it reeled in yet another direction.

She had one more question but wouldn't ask. Were any of her grandmother's family still alive? And if they were, would they talk to her, or would she be ignored because of who she was and the circumstance of her birth? After learning what she had today, she decided they didn't deserve her time. It didn't matter. She wouldn't try to find them out of respect for her mother's memory.

****

Later that night, Lark realized it was the first time she'd enjoyed a meal with Greg since she arrived. For just that one hour, they seemed to have found a truce. Now if she could only get him out of her mind in a different direction. Sex was so ingrained in her mind these last days she couldn't escape the fantasies. She hoped it was just temporary hormonal issues. But the feeling was still valid. Unfortunately, she couldn't do anything about it. Approaching him for sex wasn't a good idea. What approach could she take that wouldn't leave her as the pursuer? What if she did and he rebuffed her advance? She didn't want to choose between the company or the man. She wanted them both.

But that brought to mind a question she hadn't

verbalized. Over coffee after their meal, she broached the subject. “While I’m not trying to start World War III, can I ask why Will Dodd stopped showing up for meals? Don’t get me wrong—I’m thrilled he’s not around. But was that his choice, or did you ask him to stay away?”

“Actually, I was wondering about that myself the other day. He’d only started hanging around when you were due to arrive. I’ll admit I was grumpy with you and him in the beginning. When I started skipping meals here, he seemed to stop showing up. Truthfully, I figured you’d said something to him.” Greg looked up at her and smiled.

“Not directly, only comments about him not touching me and keeping a proper distance from me when we were in the same space.”

“I’m thinking he stopped showing up when you began to assert yourself at the office.”

“Maybe he decided it was a waste of his time since I wouldn’t talk to him about anything when he shut me out,” she mused.

“I will say I’m grateful he’s not hanging around here all the time, but now that you’ve mentioned it, I’m beginning to wonder what ulterior motive he’s working on now.”

“Me too. I’m sure he’ll drop whatever bomb he’s building soon. After all, I’ve pissed him off, along with the entire board.”

He nodded. “For now, let’s just enjoy the reprieve. I didn’t appreciate his being the first face I saw in the morning and the last at night. Even at the office, he’s been keeping his distance. Before we called you here, he was always in my office, looking over my shoulder. Not so much these last weeks.”

"I guess we'll just have to wait until he decides it's time to throw another hitch in our lives." She smiled and sipped her coffee. "I'll admit I'm much more comfortable with my morning swim knowing he's not watching from the windows."

"Your point does bring up questions. Maybe he's afraid we've banded together against him."

"If he thought that, I'd assume he'd be here all the time." She continued to enjoy her coffee. "I feel like I'm waiting for another explosion and have no idea how to protect against it. I will say this—I've been extremely careful what I write…anywhere. There shouldn't be any samples of my handwriting or signatures in that office. If we find documents or checks signed by me, we'll know what tack he's taken."

"I…never mind." Greg turned away.

"You what? What do you know that I don't?" She leaned forward.

"I'm wondering if he had access to your signature before he contacted you."

"Great. Now I'll worry about that all night," she teased. "Oh hell, this is giving me a headache. We'll find out when the bottom drops."

"I was thinking about taking in a movie. You interested in joining me?"

It was the first invitation she felt was truly genuine. "Thanks, maybe another time. I'm exhausted from my attic snooping, and now my mind is swirling with the possibilities of what Dodd has in mind for us." She stood and stretched. "You go and have a good time. This will all work out eventually. I'm going to let the dogs run before I go up. Good night." She hesitated and added, "If we're seen together and it gets back to Dodd, all hell will break loose."

"Good point. Night, Lark."

"Girls," she simply said, and the three dogs were at her side. "Out." They all scrambled toward the kitchen door with her close behind them.

Waiting at the door while the dogs ran, she reviewed all the conversations she'd had with Dodd in the last weeks, especially those before the board meeting. After that, she knew from her recordings exactly what he thought of her and how he encouraged the rest of the members to boycott her meetings. When her headache began to worsen, she decided to let it go for a while. She had no real information. Right now, chasing the concept would just make her angry and her headache worse.

That night, with the rain still beating against the roof and windows, the dogs returned quickly. As usual, Spike was the last to meander back. Upstairs in her room she decided to take a hot bath.

While she soaked in the hot water, her mind wandered. Closing her eyes, she let the water wash over her and dropped her hands under the heated liquid. She tried to picture Greg with her as they might be now, but it all became a blur of light hair and green eyes. Of large hands all over her body.

Dried and stretched out on her bed, she tried to remember how he kissed. She still remembered the shivers that man produced with his kiss in the yard just a short time before. Even years later, she'd never forgotten how they touched and kissed. She'd never forgotten his cock either. He was long and thick. This man knew how to drive her crazy. He made sure she came before pushing her over the edge into another orgasm and taking his own release.

****

When sleep was evasive, Greg headed down to the kitchen for a snack. Maybe a sandwich would help him relax. For sure, the things wandering through his mind were not conducive to rest. Replaying how he'd kissed Lark outside in the yard wasn't helping. Hell, since that night, all he could think about was that kiss and how much more he wanted to do to her and have her do to him. Their earlier conversation had him handling himself since he'd gotten to his room and locked the door after the movie. None of it was constructive to his current situation.

Yes, he'd been looking for emotions from Lark. He was prepared for her anger. Actually, he found himself baiting her for an angry reply. All he got was a resigned distance.

But earlier in the library, he saw the vulnerable side she'd never let slip in front of him. Now his situation was worse. He had no choice but to accept she was human. He hated her for making him consider her upbringing without any family around. From his perspective, she was lucky on one hand because she escaped his grandmother's family visits and their biting temper and disdain.

But she also missed the good times. Holidays and family vacations were always fun and stress free when away from their normal routine and the prying eyes of the extended family. Maureen must have been one tough lady. She'd been a survivor and taught her daughter to behave similarly. He couldn't accuse Lark of being spoiled by money or the family name.

The night-lights were on as usual throughout the house. It wasn't until he rounded the corner into the kitchen that he saw her sitting at the table with a half-eaten slab of pecan pie and a glass of milk before her. When she saw him enter, she paused with a bite of pie on her fork halfway to her mouth. If she hadn't looked so sleepy and vulnerable, he might have been able to keep up the persona of hate he forced when she was around. Tonight he just didn't have the strength to hate.

"Sorry, I didn't realize you were in here. I didn't see the dogs."

"I put them out for a last run."

She stared at him, and her cheeks flamed red. Before he could ask what she was thinking, she finished the thought for him.

"I was horny and figured food would distract me." She brought the fork to her lips and slid the bite of pie into her mouth.

His mind worked overtime to come up with a curt answer. He had none. "I guess it depends on where you were planning on putting the food."

"I was never into mixing food and sex. Too messy, especially if it's my sheets."

Despite his erection, he walked to the fridge and took out a platter of leftover baked chicken. He put the plate on the counter and pulled off a leg. He offered her a bite, but she shook her head. She lifted her plate of pie as an offering, but he shook his head. He took another bite of the chicken and continued to stare at her.

"I tried masturbating, but it didn't work."

His mouth dropped open. He tried to school his expression but figured he only managed surprise.

"Well, at least I got your attention." She laughed and took another bite of pie.

"I could help you with that. But there would have to

be ground rules," he said in a serious tone. Having spent time with her outside of work, he was beginning to remember what drew him to her all those years back. It was just her initial attitude that had been so off-putting. With good reason, he didn't make that admission aloud.

"Again, do I have a say in this?"

"We're just having a discussion," he quickly added. "Here and now, alone in the house with no one to overhear us, we should discuss this. We now know our paths have crossed in the past." He studied her. "Are you interested?"

"If circumstances were different, probably. But come morning, I don't know what side of you I'd encounter. This personality or the one that hates me because I exist? Will you revert to being a jerk again?"

"I suppose I could try to curb that behavior. In private, yes, I could be this guy. But for now, it would be best if we kept an antagonistic façade for the public." He shrugged. "Realistically, if we were polite at the office, people would notice. Behind these private walls, nobody but the two of us would have to know what goes on. I can be discreet." Greg looked at Lark.

"Oddly, I think that has happened to us already because of the changes in the situation." She finished the last of the milk in her glass and pushed back from the table. "And since I'm the oddity in this situation, I'm not sure if I could truly trust you. You talk a good game, but is this a pretense to get the company back or to make me look bad? You have to admit we've been on tenuous ground since I got here. And that was before we acknowledged we had past acquaintance."

"Here's a bit of honesty I'm uncomfortable with," Greg offered. "Since this whole thing started, I haven't dated."

"Why? Because of money issues or because you didn't trust me alone in the house?"

"Both. The first week you were here, I was in the dining room, watching you swim, and thought about 'doing you' for the company's sake. Actually, I was thinking through the topic. I wanted to figure out if I had a romantic interest in you or not. If not, then I'd be free to pursue you without guilt."

"What was the final decision you figured out?"

He noted she was still using her indoor voice, but he wasn't sure for how long. "Hell, I've had an erection since the day you walked into this house, dogs and all."

"Sorry to be such an inconvenience." She settled back in her seat.

"Look, I'm just saying I was attracted and still am. But I haven't gone outside this house looking for relief."

"Why? Because it wasn't in your best interest until you figured out my agenda? Or was it because you didn't want to piss off the woman who signs the checks?" She stood and moved to the dishwasher with her plate and glass. "Did you ever consider that I had a life before being summoned? Did you care, or is all this just convenient because I hold the money?" She shook her head. "Ya know, upstairs in the library tonight talking to Edward, I thought we were beginning to bond. And our conversation over supper gave me hope. Now I understand that was all a façade too. Keep the girl happy until you figure out how to take control of the company back from her."

"Lark, that's not what I was saying."

"Maybe not right now, but it is the ultimate goal. Once you get what you want, I'll have served my purpose, and you can get back to your life."

"I thought we were making headway to being closer."

"I thought so too, but we all have ulterior motives. It's just that they're different. I want to save the company long term. Mainly to prove Adley wasn't wrong about my mother and me. You just want control of the money again. Will you give Will Dodd free rein to run the company again at that point?" She walked to the door and paused. "Sex would have been fun. But I don't trust you. And if there's one thing I need in sex, it's to trust my partners." She went to the back door and whistled for the dogs. Once they were in, she disappeared with them.

Well, he certainly screwed that up. He wasn't sure where he went off the rails, but he did. And just when he was trying to be honest and open. But she was right. He wouldn't trust himself either if he were in her position. Maybe she'd sleep on the idea and see it from a better perspective in the morning. Yeah, he wouldn't bet on that. He managed to dig himself deeper than he'd started out. She was right about the library tonight. She showed him a bit of vulnerability, and just hours later he managed to turn it into a dare. Not what his original thought was, but he saw where this all went wrong.

Too bad she wasn't horny enough to do right now and get past the awkward place. He should have just jerked off in his room and skipped the snack. He tossed the chicken bone in the garbage and leaned against the counter. How had this night tanked, and what would be the repercussions in the morning? Nothing good came to mind.

If someone told him they'd lay him to get past the awkward places, he'd probably cop an attitude too.

****

Lark kept her attitude until she was safely locked in her bedroom. What had started out as a joking matter quickly turned dark. Did she trust this guy? No. Did she want to? Yes. But the reality was she didn't know this man, and so far, since she was the one holding the cards and money, she wouldn't trust him or anyone associated with Braylin Industries. To these men, she was a bank, waiting to open for their convenience. And that was one thing she wasn't in her life, a convenience to any man or person.

While sex with Greg was an interesting idea, she couldn't just lay him without repercussions. What little advantage she had right now, she had to keep. Horny would come and go, but for now she'd let it go. Even though the idea continued to spiral through her mind and body, she had no choice but to push it aside. After all, she didn't know for sure what agreement he had with the board members. And she was still the uninvited outsider who now literally controlled all the Braylin employees' futures. Self-preservation made her leery of everyone she'd met so far, Edward and Clara being the exceptions.

For the foreseeable future, she would stay quiet and continue to figure out how to keep the company intact. If that meant sometime in the future she might get to bed Greg, fine. Not now. Not until she knew who her friends and enemies truly were. *Respect* was a big word in her vocabulary. He didn't respect her or her judgment. He just wanted her to side with him and hand over the checkbook.

While she could be totally off base, she considered that Rod might have overcompensated with Greg to keep them insulated from the family politics. When she'd done the background checks on Greg before coming to the East Coast, she got the impression he was a spoiled young man who never worried about money or the future, only enjoying life.

Was his behavior a knee-jerk reaction to the way he saw his parents treated by Nancy's family? Did Adley give him a looser rein to disguise Rod's mother's frailty? That didn't make sense because from the photos, she wasn't a frail woman to start with. Ultimately, Lark had to figure the berating treatment by Nancy's biological family broke her spirit.

Was Adley making sure his children never felt that same weight? They'd both traveled as teens, but both kept up with academics. Had Maureen's announcement about her pending motherhood been the last straw? Was that the moment Adley conceded he would never be accepted by Nancy's family? It seemed to Lark that was a foregone conclusion. No matter what had happened, she continued to thank her mother for keeping her out of the fray.

Maureen never seemed unhappy with her life. She was proud of her self-reliance and the career she'd build for herself and her daughter. If her mother had second or third thoughts, they were never verbalized. Yes, her mother had a temper, but it wasn't usually directed at Lark. Rather, she'd become annoyed with the banal social structure she found so restrictive. Maybe growing up striving for her grandparents' approval had taught her it wasn't worth the time to worry. Too bad Nancy couldn't find that peace.

She couldn't change the past. She could only influence the future.

Chapter Eleven

Sunday Lark woke to a cloudy sky, which was an improvement over yesterday's torrential rains. She'd gone out early and let the dogs run while she swam. All three had taken to her routine of letting them run and returning to rest poolside near her. So far, she hadn't had to chase after them. Spike began a low growl, and she stopped at the side to see why.

Then she heard it. Greg arguing loudly and getting closer. He approached using hand gestures that put her on alert. She settled the three dogs, who had all noted the commotion. As he neared, she steadied herself for the next onslaught of the power struggle. At that very moment, she was thankful she hadn't spent the night in his bed.

After all the family revelations last night, she felt vulnerable. In general, she wouldn't let society crush her. She'd fight harder to prove her worth. She wondered if he saw her in a different light now. It was too late. She took a calculated risk to open up to him. If he used her vulnerability against her, he would show his true colors.

"This is the first time you've come to the pool. From your phone conversation, which I could hear clear across the lawn, something has happened. What am I getting blamed for now, and how bad is it?" She continued to tread water by the side while reassuring the dogs.

"Social media is exploding." He waved his phone.

"Who would do this?"

"Do what?" she asked, continuing to calm the dogs.

He leaned down to show her the phone. When she reached for it, he pulled back. "Your hands are wet."

"Fuck me." She swam to the steps and climbed out, pulling on a toweling robe she left at the coping. Then she grabbed a towel from the nearby lounge and blotted her hair. "Let me see." He handed her his phone, and she stood rooted to the spot. Then she started scrolling. What she saw astonished her in too many ways to verbalize.

"Well." Greg stared at her.

"I didn't see this coming," she said in a resigned tone. "I should have anticipated someone leaking this…me to the press."

"Did you expect it?"

"*No*, did you? Have you dropped hints or just made statements that could be taken out of context or misconstrued?" She continued to scroll through the posts.

"Of course not. I haven't socialized since you showed up."

"Don't even start, Greg." She moved to the table where she'd left her phone. She gave him his phone back and started checking hers. The headlines got worse.

"Are you sure you didn't drop hints because of the circumstances? Were you feeling put out and decided to place me in a vulnerable spot? Maybe talked to an adviser back home before coming here? Maybe in a moment of anger told someone you thought you could trust?" He took deep breaths before continuing. "I don't want to think you would do this. It's not to your advantage no matter how angry or annoyed you are with me."

She scrolled while Greg debated if she was the leak. Then she caught it. “Stop arguing,” she said loudly to get his attention. “This is a fucking press release! Son of a bitch, I never thought they’d do this to the entire company.” She placed her phone back on the table and tossed off her robe. She dove back into the pool. She swam laps as hard as she could until she was breathless.

Greg read the headlines aloud. “ ‘Disinherited Braylin Heir Returns, Braylin Heir Disrupts Business, Braylin Fortune in Question.’ ” He paused and shook his head. He took a seat on the edge of one of the lounge chairs and kept reading. “ ‘Illegitimate Heir Challenges Will, Braylin Boy Twists When Forgotten Heir Surfaces.’

“Fuck, this is on…” He said the name of a known tabloid site. “ ‘Braylin Family Dirty Little Secret Surfaces.’ ” His body literally shook as he continued to scroll on the phone.

Lark was furious. “Who would have put that together?”

“This one is worse,” Greg said, reading aloud. “ ‘Gold Digger Braylin Heir,’ and it’s got photos.”

When she heard that one, she pulled herself up on the side of the pool. She grabbed her robe and dried her hands while Greg handed her the phone she left on the table. “What the fuck.” She sighed. “It’s like they went out of their way to find awful photos. That’s my driver’s license and my college yearbook.”

“What other photos will they find?” He sounded beyond mad. “What else are they going to find?”

“I don’t know. What are they going to find about you?” His jaw dropped just a bit, and she knew he finally realized the repercussions to both of them. “That got your attention," she said. "I've never taken nude photos or had them taken that I'm aware of. No videos either. Hell, I barely keep a social media presence."

Greg sat farther back on the lounge as they looked at each other. "I don't know…I never considered it. Never videos…but I erased it." A blush crept up his throat with the comment. "That was years ago, back in college."

"But you know it's all in the cloud. Nothing is ever truly erased." She sighed heavily.

He let out a stilted breath. "Fuck, fuck, fuck."

"Wait, go back and read past the headlines." She looked at the phone. "These are all basically the same, written as a press release."

"You're right." He buried his head in his hands for a moment. "This is a press release. Who stands to gain the most from something like this?"

She had to rein in her tone before actually saying the words that came to her while she'd been doing laps and Greg was reading headlines. "Your precious Mr. Dodd and the board, you asshole."

"Why?" Greg asked, sounding completely oblivious.

"To discredit the two of us. Because if the stock drops, it becomes our fault. Think it through." She put the phone down.

"The question is, what do we do about it? We start by not posting on our media sites." He asked and answered his own question.

"That goes without saying. No denials or explanations, no posts at all," Lark told him as she scanned her phone. "My Facebook page only listed basic business information from my old accounting job and posts about the dogs and the rescue center."

"Shit," he said with a quake in his voice. "Mine is blowing up." He started reading blurbs from his posts.

"They range from disturbing to threatening." She rubbed her temples.

"A few of the later ones are, 'you go, guy, good for you,' stuff like that." Greg tossed his phone on the cushion beside him. "Should we delete the pages?"

A look of what she defined as dread overtook his features, his scowl deepening. Their business situation had suddenly gone real world. Now he was finally beginning to understand this was personal to both of them. She wanted to bask in his misery but couldn't bring herself to be that person who delighted in another person's problems. She wouldn't let the people behind the press release change her core personality. She wasn't a true Braylin yet.

"No," she said, "we might need them as ammunition at some point. Just don't post anything. Have you made any calls this morning?"

"No," Greg retorted.

"Then who were you talking to on the way here?"

"To myself. I was yelling at the phone and the posts. I haven't begun to check my voice mail. I'm almost afraid to. This was the first thing I saw this morning, headlines about…us."

She was lost in her thoughts when she realized Greg was snapping his fingers to get her attention. Spike started to growl. "Spike, down. And you, don't snap at me. The dog sees it as a threat."

"Then stop spacing out," he said angrily.

"Just be quiet a minute. I saw something…" She went silent, ignoring him while she scrolled back and forth until she found it. “Go back to the original posts, the first ones from three a.m.” She kept looking and waited until he caught up. “Don’t you see it?”

“Urchin! Who else but someone inside the company offices would know Dodd called you that? I’ve heard Dodd use that all over the offices.”

“It’s his damn signature. And it’s a taunt. He thinks he won.” She struggled to put her thoughts in order. “In reality, I bet by close of business Monday, the stock will go up a bit. Let’s hope someone outside the company fucks up early in the week so this gets pushed aside.”

“I hope someone else fucks up quick, too. What day do the print tabloids come out?”

“Not a clue,” she said. But Greg had walked away, only waving his hand as he left.

“Where is he going?” she said to Spike and pulled a breath, trying to think through the situation. *Get a grip, girl. Damn tabloids!* She’d seen them folded in the kitchen desk area. Clara read them. Which meant Clara was going to be reading those headlines too.

“I think she’s the least of our worries,” she said to the dogs. She gathered her towel and phone.

Greg walked back, waving the newspaper as he rejoined her. He followed beside her, almost tripping on Baby, who pushed between them to be near Lark.

“Dates don’t matter with the internet sites already blaring,” she said. “The print headlines will be old news. But we need to be prepared.”

“Can we stop the print headlines, threaten to sue?”

“I don’t know. What I need to do is see these in print right now.” They approached the kitchen door, and the dogs went ahead. “I’m going to get dressed. I’ll use the printer in my bedroom for…” She named one of the sites.

"Can you print the others?"

"What good will that do?" His tone was beyond exasperated.

"I'm a paper person. I need to put them side by side to compare them. It's just how I work. Ten minutes." She wandered away with the phone in her hand, then stopped. "We'll need anything in print from your social media accounts that sounds like a threat."

Edward came to the kitchen doorway. "Can I help?"

"Yes, don't answer the house phone. Let it go to message. Tell Clara too and be careful of your private phones. Nobody gets past the gates, nobody including Mr. Dodd. If the press gathers, ignore them." Greg paused. "Have you seen the headlines?"

"Not yet," Edward answered. "Why don't you two get settled? I'll feed the dogs and have fresh coffee sent to the office."

"The dining room, please. I'll need space to spread out." Lark headed away but got sidetracked. She returned a moment later to thank Edward for feeding the dogs.

He gave her a quick nod, and she walked away.

Greg met up with her in the hallway. "You need to see this." He held out his phone for her to see.

"Fuck." She continued toward the stairway, mumbling. Someone had breached the privacy at the house. There was a photo of her leaving the pool, wet and dripping. The headline read "Braylin Heiress Literally Wet!" That was her limit. Even on the estate, she wasn't safe. Her privacy had been breached at her home. She studied the picture. It appeared to be taken from outside the hedge line. They had crossed her nonimaginary limit. She saw red, vengeance. Finally, clarity brought options.

"Tell Edward and Clara to be careful. Nobody else is allowed on the property until further notice, not even day staff." She'd let Greg fill them in. For now, she needed to be dressed. Clothed and not vulnerable.

"I already told them," he assured her.

"Yeah, okay." She headed up the stairs toward her room.

****

Lark turned on her printer and found the site she wanted. She hit Print on the way to the bathroom. She jumped into a quick shower and was using the washcloth a bit too vigorously to just be washing off the salt from the pool. When her orgasm was elusive, she tossed the wet cloth to the bottom of the tub and showered off.

"Talk about a strange morning," she said to herself. She pulled on comfortable jeans and a T-shirt, let her hair air-dry, and headed downstairs. She hoped things hadn't gotten worse in the few minutes she'd been gone.

While the material was printing, she couldn't stop thinking about the headlines. "Not now," she admonished herself. But a small part of her couldn't stop the smile on her lips. *Braylin Heirs Sex Partners.*

She chose to believe Greg hadn't planted the headline. Anyone at the company could have made a statement in passing. But the word *urchin* stuck with her. Her mother had taught her to listen to her intuition. Not to let it guide her life, but to acknowledge those feelings. Sometimes, information wasn't what it appeared with people and situations. For now, she'd give him the benefit of the doubt. Not to would be a great disservice to her and Greg, and she was beginning to like him.

"Lord help us all," she said.

****

Lark joined Greg in the dining room. He was surrounded by stacks of print material. She added her printouts to the pile. He looked up at her with uncertainty. Or was it fright? Had he finally accepted the company men would take him down to get to her?

"Just checking to make sure you're okay after seeing the photo?" He handed her a cup of fresh coffee.

"I need to know if I'm alone in this, or are we a united front?"

He gave her a rueful laugh. "Don't you mean sex partners?"

"Call it what you want. The headlines have gone beyond just vicious gossip. Saying we're having sex parties is over the line. So is photographing me poolside." She let out an exasperated breath.

"Too bad," he said with a smile. "If we're getting blamed for doing it, maybe we should try it."

"You've lost your mind, too. No matter how badly I want you in my bed, doing it just for revenge against a newspaper or Mr. Dodd is not the way I want you." She shook her head and went back to the printed pages.

"Reluctantly, I agree with you, but it was a good fantasy."

"Could we not give away any more ammunition right now?" She glanced around the room. "I've wondered in the past if there were listening devices, cameras, or other issues inside the house. Can I trust you? Seriously, the photo on the website could have been taken with a long lens, but who would know I swim each morning? More important, who would suggest the photo at all?"

"I didn't have anything to do with this, Lark. I admit I've been rude and annoying, but this crosses the line for all of us. This isn't my style even if I was trying to piss you off."

"Dodd knew I swam each morning."

"Fuck me, the old bastard didn't back off. He just took a new direction."

"All right, then. From our private social media, we need to separate the threatening comments from the 'attaboys,' and I need to figure out where the initial information came from."

She was bleary eyed from searching the printouts. Something was there. She just couldn't spot it. Her mind was fried. "How good are your computer skills?"

"Passable, I guess. Why?"

"There's something we're missing. I can't find it. We need to figure out where the initial press release came from."

"How?" Greg asked.

She gave him a crossed-eyed look.

"I guess that look means if you knew, you'd be doing it yourself." He pulled out a chair beside her and stared. "Just say what you're thinking, and we'll figure it out."

"How was this information sent? If phone, is it traceable? If email, is the address traceable? I need to know who put out the original press release."

An hour later, Lark pushed back from the table. "I'm exasperated, but I can't give up. I can't find what I'm looking for." She looked at Greg. "You'll have to trust me on this. I have a friend out west. I'm going to call him." She placed the call in front of him on speaker. She informed Steve Greg was in the room and made the introductions. After he'd acknowledged he'd seen the mass media headlines, she told him she needed help finding out who started the rumor. Hanging up, she shook her head. "If he can't find it, we're screwed and not in a good way."

Edward came in and asked if they were hungry. Just moments later, he appeared with a tray of sandwiches and fresh coffee.

"I'm not hungry," Greg said, taking half a sandwich.

"I eat when I'm mad, annoyed, or anxious." Lark took a half and wandered around the room, pausing to look at the different piles of printouts they'd separated.

When her phone rang half an hour later, they both jumped. She grabbed it, checked the caller ID, and put it on speaker. "You're on speaker, Steve. Did you have any luck?"

"Who did you piss off, Lark, or should I say who did the two of you piss off?"

"Tell me you found something," she all but pleaded.

"I've got information to send you, but I don't want to do it over email. Any chance you still have a working fax machine?"

"A fax machine?" Greg asked. "Does anyone still send faxes?"

"Not really, but it's a safer way under the circumstances. Do you still have a landline at that address?"

"Yeah," Greg said, "but I haven't seen a fax machine in ages."

"I have," Lark said. "Give me a couple of minutes. I'll be right back." She left him hanging around her phone, silent. She didn't know if he and Steve had a conversation while she was gone, only that she struggled down the steps from her bedroom with the bulky machine. "I'm back," she said into the phone. "Give me a second to set this up. Damn, this thing is heavy."

"You bring that with you, Lark?" The voice laughed. "I remember you never traveled light, even when we were in school."

"Actually, I had a printer issue when I first came here. I found a few old machines in limbo storage at the office and brought this home for after-hours use. It's a printer, scanner, and fax all in one." She looked around the dining room and sighed. "I've got to find a landline connection in a different room. Could you carry this?" she said to Greg as she grabbed the phone.

"Yeah, I got it. The office still has a landline." He lifted the huge machine and stomped to the office.

Lark came in with the phone in hand. "Hang on. I think we found one." She put the phone on the desk and bent down to plug it in. It took a few minutes to come to life. "Paper?" she asked. Greg opened a drawer and handed her a stack.

"Okay, my dear genius friend." She rattled off the phone number.

"All right, listen to me." Her California computer guy went on to tell them, "Print these off, then trash the machine. Literally trash it so it can't be traced."

"What do you mean traced?" Greg asked as the machine started to whirl and swirl with lights and beeps.

"Every printer has an imbedded code that prints on each page. It's invisible to the naked eye. Unless you're looking for it under magnification or special light, you'll never see it. But if someone does find these fax copies and they want to, they can find the code and trace it back to you or to whoever purchased the machine. It will lead back to the office. I don't think you want that to happen. I know I don't want that to happen." The machine continued spitting out pages. “And cut off the top and bottom boarders of each sheet. Burn them. It’s easier to read the codes in those areas.”

“You are a god, Steve,” she teased. “Thank you. I owe you one.”

“Consider this payback for getting me through finals in senior year. But, Lark, be careful. Whoever this is went out of their way to circumvent the system, unless you know who lives in Connecticut.”

“Dodd.” Lark and Greg said the name at the same time.

“Holy fuck, you are my hero,” she told Steve.

“Just check the pages and remember it never came from me. Print it and get rid of the machine.” He hesitated. “Don’t let any piece of the machine remain intact. If you’ve got a firepit, that would work best. But don’t breathe in the fumes and make sure you have an extinguisher handy. Chemicals in the plastic will flare up.”

Greg spoke up. “Even if it is deleted, won’t it still be available on your machines?”

Steve pulled an exasperated breath. “Okay, a crash course. You can delete an email or file from your hard drive. But it can still be found if someone is really looking for it. The only way to cover it is to literally rewrite over that specific space on the hard drive, and it has to be real garbage that can’t be deciphered.”

“So how do you do that?” Lark asked.

“I have the specific space on a separate hard drive I used to send the file. I will go back and rewrite over it with a program I’ve been working on. Besides, if anyone thinks they can come back at me for getting into your company files, I’ll say I was hacked. I’m working from a public line, not a private one. Anyone could reroute a public signal. It's the safest I can get right now. Just don't mention my name." He let out a breath. "And, Lark, don't let anyone you don't trust get near your phone. I'll be sending you an express package with new chips for all your phones. When you get them, reconstruct your contact lists by hand. Don't send them to the new chip. Then immediately destroy the old chips."

"What about work files?" Greg asked.

"My suggestion is to print what you need from a different machine and keep them in a safe place. I wouldn't use your phones or tablets until you have a better hand on security and you're past the boiling point with this issue."

"Any chance you want to come to the East Coast and work with us?" Greg asked. "We could use a person we trust. Lark trusts you. You've helped us here. Your help gives you the benefit of the doubt with me too."

"Thanks, but no. I just got a contract to set up a new corporate system out here. Besides, I'm a West Coast guy. The cold shrinks my balls."

"Think on it, even if you want to just get a short paid vacation," she told Steve.

"I'll think on it, but don't count on me. If you still need help down the line, I'll make a few calls and see who might help out there."

"Thank you, my dear friend. I do owe you one." Lark felt somewhat relieved.

"If you need me again, don't call from your phones or house. Find an old-fashioned pay phone. They're still in some municipal building lobbies, gas stations, maybe a library or diner. Find one. Trust me on this. Don't trust any home or company phones."

"I trust you, and so does Greg. Unfortunately, we don't have your computer savvy."

"Not a lot of people do," he answered, laughing again. "Got it?"

"Yes, I got it. Thanks again."

Steve cleared his throat, as if to stall for time. "Lark, the wet photo. You still look good, girl, even to a guy who doesn't truly appreciate the female form. But you know to be careful. Someone is watching you. Right now, I've only seen pictures that were from a distance. I don't know if that's all they've got or if they're in the house too."

"I'm wondering that too. Thanks." She disconnected and started reading the pages as they spit out from the old machine. She handed each one to Greg in turn as she finished the page.

After they had a chance to read the files, Greg lost his temper first.

"Son of a bitch." He picked up a vase from the mantle. He weighed it in his hand and put it back down. "We have proof it was Dodd. What do we do now?"

"We keep our mouths shut. We go through the motions like this didn't happen. If we're directly approached at the office tomorrow, we act like it's a joke. Like it didn't bother us. Use phrases like 'any press is good press for advertising even if it is fiction.' Then we don't engage."

"Are you serious? We can't just walk into the office like this isn't happening." He looked at her as if she were crazy.

"If anyone sees this is bothering us, it will get worse. Right now, we're a united front. If pushed for an answer, we say someone is really pissed at us, most likely jealous, etc. How we handle this will reflect on us forever." She shrugged her shoulder. "You have a better idea than punching out anyone who opens their mouth?"

"No. But it would be satisfying."

"Look, tomorrow the entertainment news will be all over this. The legitimate news will mention it because of the stock issues. Hopefully, they'll let it go quickly. Then we ride it out. We use the in-house gossip to our advantage. Ears open, mouths shut. We'll be able to figure out a lot about our employees by the way they handle the situation. Soon enough we'll know who's in our camp and who is the enemy."

"Your mind works in mysterious ways." Greg took a deep breath.

"Baffle them with bullshit." Lark gave him a half laugh.

"That's what they've been doing to us. That's what the board and Dodd have been doing for the last years. This is not how I pictured spending my Sunday off." He headed to the bar.

"What's the old saying? If you want something to screw up, tell the universe your plans," Lark joked. He didn't smile. "Too soon?" She didn't wait for an answer but went back to her printouts.

"We have another issue," she finally said. "I'm going to take the dogs for a quick walk. I'll wear a hooded sweatshirt for cover, and I want to look for vulnerabilities in the hedges."

"The hedges? Have the dogs gotten out?"

"No. I think the fencing is intact. But if there are light spots in the plantings, someone might use it to photograph through. If they were using a drone, I think I would have seen or heard it." She stood quietly for a moment. "I'd ask you to go with me, but I'm afraid it will look suspicious in case someone does have eyes on us."

"Don't take long. While you're gone, I'll figure out who to bring in to check the house for bugs." He paused and looked at Lark. "What? If they're getting photos of you swimming, how do we know the house hasn't been left with issues?"

"You mean Dodd has been in and out of here for months."

"I never bothered to consider he might be leaving anything behind. Fuck, I really hate that old man." Again, he started rubbing his temples.

"While we're heaping on bad news, you remember a kiss by the garage in the moonlight. We don't know if they have that. So even though the idea sickens me, we have to be prepared for that to show up if there's another round of headlines." She stood, and the dogs stood with her. "I'm just saying it's a possibility, and I don't want us to be blindsided again."

"Go walk the dogs. I'll try to figure out who we know that we can trust."

"Who set up the house security and alarm systems?"

Greg's voice was tight when he answered her question. "The company set it up, and they do all the monitoring."

"We need an outsider. I'm going to text Steve. He'll get us an outside referral we can trust."

"But no one that works or has any affiliation with the family or the company. We still don't know who we can trust." Greg picked up the vase he'd weighed earlier and arched it into the fireplace. After the dogs all started barking, he looked at Lark. "Sometimes it helps to break something. Other times it just makes more of a mess."

"I need air. Not someone local. It will pay us to bring in someone from out of town, maybe the West Coast, to check out the house and offices. Let me know what you think."

"Now we're importing security details." He shook his head.

"For now, we're just talking about clearing the house."

"Can't we just find something online that would let us check for basics and not have anyone in the home?" He went to the desk and started a new search for bug-detection equipment. "Man, you should see how many sites sell security shit. My God, no wonder it's so easy to stalk people."

"Greg, just wait." She left and returned shortly with the gadgets she'd brought after finding the password cracker. "These are just basic, but let's see if anything shows up before we decide to buy more equipment. And if we do use outside security, they should have their own equipment."

"Why would you have these?"

"I bought them when I found a password cracker on my laptop weeks ago." She stood with her hand on her hip, letting her lips fold into a smirk before she laughed. "Remember that now?"

"I was hoping you forgot about that," he admitted.

"This was my insurance policy to feel secure, so let's just scan the main rooms and see if we find anything. I'm going to walk the fence lines." She left before she had to navigate the rest of their conversation. Right now, she was looking at him in a new light. A light that would be difficult for them in too many ways to consider. She had to get the business set before worrying about her sex life. Considering this walk was to get her away from him for a few minutes, she had to forget sex.

While they had been working in the dining room, Greg had dropped his hand on her shoulder when he looked at what she was pointing out. It felt good, warm and soothing. Her fingers brushed against his when he handed her hot coffee. His fingers were warm from the hot cup, but she had an instant visual memory of how those fingers stretched her body to distraction so long ago.

She laughed aloud as she scanned the hedge line while the dogs wandered. If someone had told her a year ago she'd be here, right here in this situation, she'd have told them they were bat-crap crazy. She was a West Coast girl. Then again, she never considered that her mother would become ill.

"Control is elusive," she said to Baby, who lumbered along beside her. "It's all an illusion, and we get through the day assuming we have it."

Would she give up her control to Greg? She decided only temporarily and never outside the bed. Her West Coast boyfriend's cock was on the smaller side, and he didn't do much foreplay, or at least with her. They were truly convenience buddies, and that was okay at the time. The truth was she didn't have to put any emotions into the relationship. Neither was truly vested.

Lark knew this man was hung. She swallowed hard at the idea of taking him into her mouth. Her lower lips pulsed, and she wondered how he might lick her. Both their encounters had been quick and forbidden, or at least not in the most advantageous places. That was the point.

Get what she wanted and get out before emotions took hold. She hadn't wanted anything lasting with anyone during her college days. Men were for experimentation. This Braylin man had been her best-ever experiment in choosing a mate strictly by looks and initial impressions. "Let's hope I haven't lost that ability to make a clear choice."

She whistled for the dogs and headed back to the house. Right now, she wasn't sure what to expect. Distance from Greg might be her friend, along with a couple of aspirin and a nap.

Back at the house, Greg told her he hadn't found anything, no recorders or cameras. But they decided to bring in an outside team for a thorough check and to update the security system used at the house and especially for the system where it was used for the boundary views.

"Will Dodd used the in-house IT for the setup. I don't know who he owns or what he holds over the security department and staff."

They also decided to find a separate forensic accountant to go through the company books, emails, and phones, as a start. While she had done exactly that over the last weeks, the company would claim her information was tainted by greed and anger. The outside firm was on her list for the next executive meeting as a threat, but now it was a necessity.

Even though she came to the East Coast prepared with her own research, her searches were nowhere deep enough. The rest of the day went by in a blur. Keeping her distance from Greg's occasional touch was imperative. He didn't push to stay near her. Instead, he seemed to understand she needed or wanted her personal space. In the end, they went to opposite corners of the home. She skipped supper in the dining room and ate from a tray in front of the television in her room. She had no idea what was flashing on the screen before her, nor could she say the food was good. She ate it to take away her headache.

That night she lay awake, wishing Greg would knock on her door and offer her…himself. He did not. But she realized she wouldn't be played again. The board screwed with the wrong woman. They had crossed the line too many times to ignore them any longer. She would soon educate them all on their mistakes and live with the consequences.

For now, she and Greg seemed to have an unspoken agreement to keep to separate spaces. She couldn't speak for him. She was on overload in too many directions to consider.

Chapter Twelve

Early Monday, Lark sat in the office Dodd had put her in when she first arrived. It was at the far end of the building, set apart from the rest of the employees. While she was prepared for an onslaught of questions and looks, the few employees she passed had kept to normal greetings. Nothing seemed to change from the weekend onslaught of lies by media outlets. But it was still early in the day. By agreement, Greg would keep his distance as usual, and they'd meet up tonight at home to compare notes on their day. She was tempted to check the social media sites but didn't.

This morning, a credible television news program mentioned Braylin Industries, but they seemed to be hedging their bets before committing themselves. For that small reprieve, she was thankful. But the entertainment-news shows would use the fabricated lies as their lead. Salacious headlines brought viewers.

She knew where Adley's office was but hadn't made a big deal about being kept away. Mainly because she couldn't escape Mr. Dodd's prying eyes. Until yesterday, taking over the conference room was enough of a confrontation. After her time traveling down memory lane in the attic and the media storm, she just didn't care who she pissed off.

"Fuck me." She pushed back from the empty desk, grabbed her backpack, and went directly to the office beside the conference room, the one she'd been continually steered away from.

Opening the double doors, she swore she could still smell cherry pipe tobacco, similar to the scent in Adley's bedroom. She never smelled it anywhere else in the house but in this room, Adley's private office. The scent overwhelmed her. It wasn't off-putting but rather a comforting memory. Her mother had mentioned that Adley smoked a pipe with cherry tobacco. Apparently, he smoked in his office. The room felt like a time capsule waiting to be explored.

The large desk sat before a huge window overlooking the wooded area at the rear of the building. His leather desk chair seemed huge, and the fabric was worn in places. Behind his desk on a shelf was a large glass ashtray. Beside it, a pipe stand with a covered amber glass bowl in the center waited to be replenished, as if he'd walk through the door any moment. The framed family photos propped within view brought tears to her eyes. Nancy on their wedding day. In this photo, she wore a simple beige suit, and Lark realized the photograph was from their elopement, from happier times. Others were of Rod and Maureen as children. Copies of Rod and Maureen's college graduations, the formal portraits she'd seen.

Though she felt like a thief in the night, she sat in the chair and ran her fingers along the worn wooden desk. The side drawers were locked. The center drawer slid open, and she wondered if a key was in there. What she found brought more tears to her eyes. With trembling fingers, she pulled out two more photographs. She recognized one immediately. In a silver frame was a copy of a photo she'd seen in one of the albums. The one of the family in the backyard pool, all wet and laughing. The second was of her mother and her in her college graduation gown standing side by side. *Why* was all she could wonder. Just how stubborn was this great man to disown the daughter he obviously loved?

Then she heard noise in the hallway and steeled herself for a fight to take the office. No matter what Mr. Dodd thought, she would take possession of the office to annoy him. Besides, she was sick of being the bad-seed urchin they were forced to deal with. From now on, she would go back to the accomplished woman she was brought up to be. Fuck them all, including the board and her stepcousin.

While his jaw dropped slightly when she opened the door, the thirty-something male settling at the desk outside recovered and smiled at her. "Welcome, Ms. Braylin. I'm Herb." He rose and offered his hand to shake hers. "I was your grandfather's assistant."

"We met briefly." She extended her hand to shake his. She was intuitive about people sometimes. In her opinion, Herb was caught off guard and anxious.

"Yes, ma'am."

"You seem on edge, Herb. Is there a problem?" Right away she figured he wouldn't want to work with a female.

"I was told not to extend you any courtesy or information if you asked. I was to send you back to the managing partner." As he said the words, he looked directly at her.

She gave him credit for keeping her gaze. "Who gave you those orders?" Immediately, she knew it was Dodd. "Never mind. Mr. Dodd will find out I'm moving into Adley's office eventually." She glanced at her watch. "Do you have a problem working for a woman?"

"No, ma'am. I was instructed not to offer any help. But…" He drew a deep breath. "I don't feel that's right, considering I'm collecting a paycheck from the corporation. Mr. B made it possible for me to finish grad school while I was here."

"Consider it a tuition program," she said offhandedly.

"That's what Mr. Braylin told me. It wouldn't be hard work, I could use my slow time to do schoolwork, and he'd have someone he could trust at his door."

His remark startled her. It was an interesting choice of words. Had Old Adley known he was being screwed toward the end? She'd let it go for now, but she wouldn't forget about the wording.

"Okay, Herb. How about you start to work for your pay?"

"I'd hoped when you came someone would notice I can do more than answer the phone and put together the monthly reports."

"I see. You may regret those words soon." Lark gave him a shoulder shrug. "Life as you knew it at the corporation has just taken a turn. We have about half an hour before the rest of the employees start to show up. Would you help me gather my belongings from my other office?" She realized he had no intention of mentioning the media storm and relaxed.

They walked side by side to the far end of the hallway. She learned he started at the company seven years ago, was married for four years, and had a two-year-old son. She liked that he wanted to earn his pay. He was about to find out firsthand not to mess with the Braylin urchin.

They gathered the few items she'd left in the old office. She emptied the desk drawer of her hairbrush and a few stacks of articles she'd torn from papers and magazines but hadn't had a chance to read. There wasn't much more. She unlocked the desk drawers and pulled out several paper files she'd been accumulating.

"Herb, can you be discreet?"

"Yes, ma'am. That was why Mr. B chose me as his assistant. I was just starting grad school, and he gave me a chance to learn the business from the inside out." He cleared his throat and added, "He was a good man."

She could only nod. She had no personal experience to offer an opinion. She took one last look around the office and grabbed the framed photo of her mother on the corner of her desk. "That's it."

"What about the information in your computer?"

"I never used it. I never knew who had access to it, so I've used my laptop."

"Smart woman." He faked a cough.

Back in her new office, he placed the stacks on the edge of the desk. "Should I file these for you?"

"No, I'll go through them. Most can be tossed. Was there a computer in the office when Adley was alive?"

"Yes, ma'am. He used it regularly. He had televisions on the credenza tuned to the stock exchange and a world news station. He did all his communication on the computer. He was quite tech savvy for a gentleman of his age."

"What happened to that computer or rather the hard drive?"

"Mr. Dodd came in the morning after Mr. Braylin passed and just took the whole thing."

"I see," she hedged and looked at him. "Okay, Herb,

here's the new deal. Between us, I'm Ms. Braylin. *Ma'am* makes me feel a bit stuffy."

He nodded.

"And from this point on, you work for me. Can you handle that, and can you keep Mr. Dodd out of our private loop? If you prefer, we can transfer you to a different department."

He nodded. "I work for Braylin Industries, ma'am…Ms. Braylin. You are the corporation along with Mr. Greg. I'd appreciate a chance to earn my pay."

"Has Mr. Dodd asked you for any work, reports, or information in the last year?"

"No. He gives me looks that make me feel like I'm ready to be fired daily, but he's kept me on. I still check all the mail and keep the in-house reports up to date."

"Herb, did Adley back up his files, and if so, did anyone else know about it?"

His wide smile surprised her.

"Yes, ma'am. His files were backed up daily."

For the first time in ages, she felt better. "Where are those backups now, and has anyone asked you for access or copies?"

"Not a single person ever asked for them." He walked to the door and locked it. Then he walked back to the pipe stand. When he lifted the center glass container, the bottom of the wooden stand was hollowed out just enough to house a small thumb drive. He picked it up and handed it to her. "To my knowledge, nobody knew about this. If they did, it was never mentioned in my presence. Also, I kept a separate copy in my files. Nobody ever asked for it, so I hid it in my desk. I lock my desk at the end of each day."

"Thank you, Herb." She realized she'd been holding

her breath and let it out slowly.

Herb looked at the floor.

She slipped the small slice of history in her jeans pocket. “Herb?”

“This is difficult, but you are my boss.” He moved behind the desk and opened the center drawer. Then he pulled out the frame with *her* college graduation photo. The frame was heavy silver. He placed it facedown on the desk, and after slipping the two metal stays that held the back in place, he removed it and handed her an old-fashioned disc. “I believe he kept more personal information on this, but I’ve never run it.”

“Thank you, Herb. I won’t insult you about our conversations being private.”

“No need.” He stepped back. “If there are other items he hid, I didn’t know about them. But you might want to look around just in case.”

Lark smiled at him as he put the photo backing in place. Then he put the frame back in the desk drawer. She pushed the disc into a pocket on the exterior of her backpack.

“Come on, Herb. I’ll buy you a cup of coffee,” she said with a smile. They walked down the hall to the small break room, and each poured coffee for themselves.

“You will have to let me know what you expect of me and what your preferences are on personal calls, office appointments, etc.”

“We’ll figure it out together. After coffee, could you appropriate a new desktop computer for the office? There seems to be a lot of spare office machines on the fourth floor.”

“Limbo.” He covered his words with a sip of his coffee.

"Maybe you could find someone from IT to help you gather a few monitors from up there too. I'd like three if possible."

"For the far wall over the credenza?"

"Yes, I like to keep in touch with the outside world."

"I'll take care of it."

"If Mr. Braylin comes in today, please let him know I'd like a moment of his time." Lark gave him a nod and topped off her coffee before leaving him in the break area.

As she walked back to her office, several people watched her. She likened it to her breaching the ivory tower. "Fuck them all." It simply meant that Mr. Dodd would show up unannounced at some point…soon. She considered locking her door, but she'd wait until he intruded before taking that step.

She wandered around the room, running her fingers over the wooden filing cabinets and admiring the artwork that graced the walls. In that moment, she decided it was time to breach the sanctuary of the master bedroom at home too. She'd avoided opening the doors to that room, figuring she had no right until the weekend with her cursory look and finding her mother's glass art. But at this point, she just didn't care who she annoyed. She was comfortable in her suite at home. She wouldn't move into the master, but she could see how Adley and Nancy lived behind those closed doors.

She would make one concession to the family. She grabbed her cell phone and texted Greg a simple message.

—WD will blow a gasket today. Keep your distance.—

There. If he was curious, he'd come find her and ask

or realize immediately she'd moved into Adley's office. If he didn't look for her, then he could fend for himself. She had no idea what his schedule was or if he'd even be in the office this morning. Most likely the rest of the company employees already knew. Had any of them contacted Greg or Mr. Dodd after seeing her enter the office? She sat back in the seat with a wide smile.

Today was going to get interesting, very interesting. Besides the office change, she had the media crap to deal with. Some restless sleep, aspirin, and lots of caffeine had given her the grand realization. Her new perspective became clear. Every situation always had three sides. The two opposing views and the truth in the middle.

Her only issue right now was the distraction of sex with Greg. As she ran her fingers across the polished slab of wood, she pictured him taking her over the desk from behind while she balanced herself, grasping the sides. How would he do her these days? She had been with him at a different time in her life and his. No matter what, she still remembered how he kissed and touched her. She pushed aside those frustrating thoughts.

As she swung the chair to view the outside world, she had a lightning bolt of thought. Did anyone put any kind of listening or recording devices in here? Did Old Adley set anything up? She would have to be careful when she looked to not get caught. Tomorrow she'd bring in her personal bug/camera finder to ease her tensions in the room. Ultimately, she'd let the new security crew do a full sweep, but the little handheld hadn't disappointed her yet. Then she'd have to talk to Greg. They had decisions to make. If they found anything, did they leave it in place and avoid it, or did they dismantle it? Then it would be up to the person who planted it to approach her. Both had different appeals.

Tonight when they got home, they'd have to decide what level of security they felt comfortable with in the office and at home. She didn't forget a few of the media posts that were beyond creepy and others that were downright dangerous. Whoever was doing this, they'd breached her home, her safe place. She was determined to find that aura—or now illusion—of home again. Nothing less was acceptable.

****

Lark was checking personnel files on her laptop when the door was opened with such force the doorknob hit the wall. Herb and the IT guy who were setting up the monitors above the credenza across the room both startled.

"How dare you think you can use this office." Dodd dropped his briefcase and glared at her.

"Herb, you can finish that later," Lark quietly said.

Herb all but pushed the IT man out the door, then closed it behind him.

Lark closed the cover on the laptop. "Mr. Dodd, this is a place of business. You will not speak to me in that tone again, ever."

"I don't care what you say or think. I run this company. All we need you for is a figurehead and to sign checks. You will not second-guess how this company is run." He gave her a rude head-to-toe look of disgust. "You wild, ungrateful urchin, with your blue jeans and boots. You're not fit to be seen in public, let alone be associated with the company. Keep to your place, Lark Braylin, or you will be sent home. Do you understand you can't come in here after five years and think you have some hold over us?"

“I never thought that. I know it. You gave me that when you waited five years to contact me about my inheritance. The way I figure, you created this situation. Tread lightly, Mr. Dodd, and leave my office.”

“You will regret this move. Move back to where I put you this instant.”

“It would have had more effect if you stomped your foot like a child when you said that.” She gave him the same rude head-to-toe look he’d given her when he entered. “My days of being hidden are over, Dodd. As of this date, the ‘urchin’ Braylin heir has come into new times.”

“I knew you’d be trouble. I was right to keep you away.” He hissed the words more than spoke them. If he’d been closer, he would have sprayed her with his saliva.

“More so now that I know the press release was sent from your Connecticut residence.”

While he seemed shocked, he recovered quickly. “You can’t know that. It’s just a guess. This media shitstorm will send our stock through the floor, and you’ll be to blame.” He paused to draw a deep breath. “You’re unfit to inhabit this office, you illegitimate bitch. We all considered you dead like your slut of a mother.”

She stood and measured her tone. “Mr. Dodd, you will never refer to or utter my mother’s name again.”

“You watch your back. You were only a means to an end. We have other options without you. Now that you’ve brought shame to the company name, I can get rid of you.”

“Did it make you feel superior to leak those lies to the media?”

"I don't think they are lies. Why else would you come here except for the money? That boy had no clue how to deal with a bitch like you. Just like your mother…not worthy of the name."

"I told you to leave my mother out of the situation. It seems you feel I've outlived my usefulness already, and you just confirmed you're the leak to the media. So your goal was to blame me for any stock slump that might occur. Branding me the 'illegitimate urchin' was a mistake. Not the first one you've made."

"You will leave this office immediately, or I'll have you removed."

"Try it, Mr. Dodd. Try to have me physically removed from this office. Do you think I'm sitting in your chair? Have I not acted according to your presumptions? Get out, Mr. Dodd, right now."

He started sputtering and cursing at her, using Adley's and Maureen's names. Then suddenly his posture changed, as if he remembered something, some grand realization she'd eventually find out.

"You can't make any changes without board approval, and I assure you no matter what you suggest, you'll never get their votes." He stood tall.

She took his posture as a dare. "Out of my office, Dodd, before I call security." When he continued to stand and glare at her, she added, "This 'urchin bitch' has reached her limit. You have no appreciation how much time and effort it takes to become this quality of bitch." She pushed a button on the telephone console. "Herb, please call security to my office."

His eyes went wide, then sliver thin, and she stiffened. Did he have the in-house security in his pocket?

"You'll regret thinking you have a place here." He turned and left.

As he did, Herb appeared in the doorway. "Are you okay?"

"Yes, thank you. However, from now on, if that man attempts to come in this office, your first action will be to call security. Then I want you to join us in the office. Grab your tablet or something so it will look like you're taking notes."

"Of course. Do you want a security officer up here now?"

"Actually, I'd like to talk to the head of security as soon as possible."

"I'll call him immediately."

Moments later an older man knocked on the door and opened it slightly. "Ms. Braylin, I'm Tom Simmons, head of security. Is there a problem?"

"Just a few questions. Please have a seat." She motioned with her arm to the other side of her desk. She studied his pinched expression. Did he not want her in this office either? "Before I came here, did anyone ever ask you to man the reception area?"

"Not directly."

"Define 'not directly.' " She pushed back in her large seat. She got an image of a child sitting in an adult chair with her feet dangling and held back a smile.

"Just before Mr. Braylin passed, he was considering stationing a guard there. But it was decided it was a waste of manpower just for show. We monitor the cameras from the security office."

"Who made that decision?"

He gave her a blank stare.

"Never mind, Tom. From now on I want a guard

positioned at the reception area. Low profile but on view."

"It's a waste. So is that secretary sitting down there greeting people. Let them read the directory."

"When I assigned the assistant to that area two weeks ago, I requested a guard there at all times. Why hasn't there been one posted?" Every time she passed the desk and didn't see a guard as requested ate at her. But she'd been waiting for the best time to use it against Dodd.

"Took you a long time to notice. Not very observant, are you?"

"I've noticed. Make it a security guard who doesn't ogle the staff. That's all for now."

"You get that superior attitude living out west? It doesn't work here. And you're not a fit either. I've seen the headlines about you and your cousin. Must be nice to snap your fingers and have a man service you to keep his paychecks coming."

"Yes, if it were true. But it's not, although you don't care because it doesn't push your or Dodd's agenda." She shook her head and wanted him gone from her sight. "Be on alert. There may be press snooping around the next few days. None of them are to cross the threshold or any other place in this building. Keep the entrances clear, and nobody gets past the reception area without their ID badges."

"I'll run it by Mr. Dodd." He stood to leave.

"Excuse me?"

"I said I'll run it by Mr. Dodd."

She had known he was one of Dodd's men the moment he came into the office. His personnel file would be the next one she pulled up. Originally, she'd looked at all the files, but since she didn't know the players, the information had no context. Now, having met most of the employees, even just in passing, she was able to put a face with a name and a history. "Do it immediately. Then you go ahead and run it by Mr. Dodd. If Dodd has a problem with this, tell him to come find me." She waited for a beat and added, "You're excused."

It was a standoff, and Lark knew it. She had a few directions to go but wanted to choose wisely. If he were completely insubordinate, she could fire him with cause. If he threatened her, that would be better. Then she could punch his smug jaw just for the satisfaction of the action.

"I said you're excused." This time the tone of her voice had become caustic. She thought he'd call her bluff.

"I don't need this crap." He turned on his heel and walked out.

Herb was immediately at the door. "You okay, Ms. Braylin?"

"Yes. Please call back the man from IT to finish. His name was James?"

"Yes, ma'am. I'll call him right away."

She motioned for him to come closer. "Send him in to finish. Leave the door open. If Tom or Dodd comes back, buzz me. And find me a listing of private security firms…quietly. Nobody who's done any business with Braylin in the past. I want this kept low-key but effective." When he turned to leave, she added, "Can I count on you to watch my back until things settle down?"

He stood a bit taller and nodded. The next thing she heard was him phoning James to come back in and finish.

Lark kept her head down, watching the screen but

only seeing a blur. She was seething and wanted to break something. But she wouldn't. It was enough to remember she was a burr under Dodd's and Tom's saddles and most likely a few other people. That was her satisfaction for now. The feeling gave her insight into Greg slamming the vase into the fireplace.

Just after the televisions and computer were all set up, the door opened again without a knock. She steeled herself for whatever form the confrontation would take.

"What the hell?" Greg closed the door behind him. "Dodd has been screaming into my voice mail for the last hour."

She hated that her initial impression that Greg was quite a handsome specimen of the male being hadn't changed—tall, fit, with enough personality to back up his attitude. It didn't help that she knew how he kissed and how he touched her. *God, what a man*, she thought, before reining in her thoughts.

"How bad is the feedback so far?" she asked. "Can you keep a level head?"

"Yeah, although if you think I'm in a bad mood now, it's nothing compared to Dodd's. He's ballistic."

She just nodded her acceptance. She hit the intercom, and Herb came to the door.

"Please have one of the interns bring in coffee for two."

"Yes, Ms. Braylin." He closed the door quietly.

"Lark…" Greg paused and looked around the office as if he were seeing it for the first time. "It's been a long time since I've been in here."

They were interrupted while a young man, college age, brought in a coffee tray and placed it on the sideboard.

“Thank you,” she said.

He smiled and left quickly.

As she rose and walked toward the sideboard, she understood this was one of those make-or-break moments for her future. Would Greg stay her ally? “Did Mr. Dodd ever run by you the basic running of the company or ask for your input?” Lark didn’t offer to pour coffee for Greg. She took her cup to the desk and resumed her position. “Within the last weeks, did he tell you I wanted security at the main entrance?”

“No.” It was a definite answer.

“I did, and there still isn’t a guard there. I just met Tom. Impressions?”

“Never had much to do with him,” he told her as he settled into one of the chairs across from her. “Dodd never spoke to me about it, but then again he wouldn’t. He always said he didn’t want to waste our time on incidentals.”

“Incidentals. I’ll remember that one.” She sipped her coffee. “I’ve ordered Tom to put a full-time guard at the main desk in the lobby to keep the press away. They are to monitor all entrances from the control room. He isn’t receptive to the changes. He’s going to ‘run it by Mr. Dodd’ before making any changes.”

“I’d think that should have been the first thing Tom did under the circumstances.” Greg wandered to the coffee and filled a cup. “What made you finally decide to move in here today? I figured you’d have been in here the second day after you got here.”

“Urchins aren’t allowed at the adult table.” She didn’t bother to hide that she was pissed. “I’m going to up our security temporarily with outside hires. Just for a few weeks. They’ll be in the background, and I’d prefer it not become a major topic. It will, of course, but I'd prefer it not come from you."

"Am I allowed to ask why?"

"Basically, because I moved into this office today. To paraphrase an old movie, Baby's out of the corner!" She laughed at her own reference. "And I've pissed off the board. Dodd and his security man too. There were direct threats from Dodd this morning. He acknowledged he planted the press release with the media. As soon as I mentioned his Connecticut address, he dropped the pretense. I want the outside security to make sure they stay veiled threats."

"Are you afraid of him, Lark?"

For the first time since she'd come into the situation, she heard real concern in his voice. Maybe there was hope for them after all.

"What do you need me to do to help?" He put the cup down.

"We stay a united front: Beyond the headlines, we both need to watch our backs, and I mean that in all directions. Even in here and especially in the parking lot. Photos can come from any direction and any cell phone. We are all on the proverbial candid camera."

They went on to discuss the employees, ignoring the media shitstorm. They discussed their impressions of Herb. They decided to trust him until proven he was a Dodd man. For now, he was made aware that Mr. Dodd was not allowed anywhere near her and was not permitted in her new office.

****

That night on her way home, Lark stopped at a large office-supply store and purchased their cheapest laptop computer. She only wanted it for a specific use and didn't care about extra programs. After that, she walked to a café in the same shopping center that boasted free internet. Settled in a back corner with fresh coffee and a blueberry muffin, she plugged in the new machine and popped in the disc Herb had given her from the back of the photo frame.

What came up confused and astonished her. From the time her mother had left the East Coast, Old Adley must have had a private investigator checking on her. The disc held photos of her on the streets of San Francisco, still heavily pregnant, and photos of Lark herself as an infant, toddler, and child. They continued until five years ago when he passed.

The second folder gave him all Maureen's financial information, where she was working and living along with rent costs and photos of the old warehouse where she eventually settled her studio. On screen were snaps of Lark playing outside their small home in the fenced yard, her mother never far away. She also found copies of her transcripts from kindergarten through college along with the scholarships that paid for her education.

She pushed back in her seat, astonished. The old bastard hadn't let her go. He had just given Maureen the illusion of freedom. Going back to the financial records, she noted while finances were tight at times, her mother always managed to make ends meet. Which must have pissed Adley off to no end. She hadn't needed his money to survive.

Lark found photos of her mother from her early art shows to copies of articles about her works. He even had the articles on the pieces that went to the museums. Along with them was a copy of the receipt for the chandelier that was sold for six figures. At first, she thought he might have been the one who purchased it but realized she'd been in the Los Angeles home of the movie producer when it was installed.

She checked online to see if there was any crossover between the producer and her grandfather and couldn't find any. Lark would have loved to know what he thought when he heard about that sale. A photo of the chandelier was published in an architectural magazine years earlier.

Going back to the photos, she studied each one. Her school photos she was familiar with, but she gave special attention to the ones taken from a distance. When she'd gone over each several times, one thing struck her. In each candid, she was smiling or laughing. She sniffed back tears, remembering her childhood and the realization she hadn't embellished the memories in her mind. She truly had been a happy kid. Every photo with her mother and her together seemed the same, both happy and smiling. A few pictures of her mother alone and seemingly deep in thought gave Lark pause. None were what she would consider depressed or unhappy. Had the investigator sent only the happy ones, or had Adley only kept the happy ones? But that didn't sit right. If Adley had photos that proved Maureen was unhappy, she doubted he'd destroy them. Rather, she figured her and her mother prospering annoyed him.

The bit of information that blew her mind was a copy of a DNA test he'd had done on her against him. For a while she wondered how he'd gotten her DNA to test and realized whoever had taken the photos probably grabbed her garbage. The date on the test was three months before the date he changed the will. So Old Adley had covered all his bases in case the board tried to push her out. They wouldn't be able to use that excuse. Now she was glad it had been done and she had the documentation to prove she was the legitimate heir.

She pulled out the disc and carefully put it away. Then she put the thumb drive into the machine. This was a totally different set of files. These were almost too hard to believe. Each folder was marked with a board member's name. When considered carefully, the folders held a treasure trove of information that proved the individual was stealing from the company, embellishing expenses, and writing and sending memos that disparaged the company name and Adley himself.

She had no idea how he garnered the information. Some were downloaded from the office computers and showed the corporate logo. Others were copies of typed correspondence; others were copies of handwritten notes. Lark wanted to know how he went about gathering the information but wouldn't ask just yet. Herb would be her information man, but for now just having the information in the files was enough.

She remembered his comment that Adley wanted someone he could trust at his door. It was a sad statement about his later life. The man had known he was being pushed out of the company he worked all his life to build, and a bunch of greedy men who were supposed to be his friends and confidants only wanted the money they could skim off the top of profits.

She would have to think long and hard about what to do with the information. For now, she had a throbbing headache and just wanted to go home. On the ride, she had to decide how to use this information and whether to share it with Greg and if so, when. One side of her was furious, and the other was emotional.

So Adley had kept an eye on his daughter after all. While he never told her he was proud, or invited her home, he'd been checking on them. The other side of her couldn't reconcile the board members who were biting the hands that fed them. She could only figure he passed too soon and didn't have time to implement changes according to the information. Judging by the dates, he started collecting the information about two years before he passed away. She wondered what his grand plan might have been.

Lark pulled over to the side of the road and was almost sick to her stomach. She turned up the air-conditioning until she was shaking from the cold instead of anger. His will had changed around the same time as he began to collect information. The rest of her drive home was slow and methodical.

Once there, she grabbed the dogs for a walk and let herself feel the gamut of emotions that went with the discoveries. Her lightbulb moment occurred when she accepted no derogatory information would come from Greg's direction. Adley had made a few notes that the boy had wanderlust and no mind for the business, but no proof beyond that he masterminded any coup or was in consort with any of the board members. For that she was sincerely thankful.

She would consider the knowledge carefully and, when her mind was clear, decide how to use it to her fullest advantage. As she'd thought earlier, how she used this information would be key in all directions for her future and the company's.

****

The following night she asked Greg to give her an hour of his time after their meal. He agreed, asked several times what it was about, but she just shook her head. "Please just wait," she told him.

After the meal she went to the library and printed out two copies of the research from Adley's thumb drive. When Greg arrived, she shooed him from the library, folders in hand along with the spy device she'd bought months before.

She stopped at Adley's master bedroom door, the room she'd only breached once. While she wanted to stop to enjoy the opulence, she had more important things to do. She dropped the folders on the table in Adley's seating area and used the device to scan the room. It didn't detect any cameras or microphones. That was when she relaxed just a bit.

"Come and sit, please."

He moved to the seating area and took the chair across from the one she'd all but dropped into. "Now will you tell me what's so important and why we're in Adley's room?"

"Yes. I thought it appropriate to do this in here because Adley was the one who did all the work." She reached to the folders on the table and handed him one. "When I took over Adley's office, I asked Herb if he had any backups of the files from his computer. He showed me a thumb drive that was hidden under Adley's tobacco rack."

"Adley knew his way around a computer, so I'm not surprised he backed up files. I never thought to search for them or ask for them." Greg lifted the folder on his lap. "Do I dare look at these?"

"That's why I brought you in here. It seemed fitting to share the information he had been collecting on his board members here in his private space. I certainly don't trust the office yet, even though the security team says it's clean. You never know who is sneaking in there after hours. And of course, they are all Dodd's men."

"Don't we have cameras running after hours?"

"Yes, we do. But Tom from security knows the system and is in Will Dodd's pocket."

"Okay, so what's here?" he asked, starting to read the pages.

Lark used the time to reread the same files, information she'd never forget.

Greg let out a few cuss words, the occasional grimace, and finally, a loud "Fuck me!"

"That's pretty much what I said too." She shifted in her seat. "I figured we can use this material to remind the board members that they aren't bulletproof and that retirement as opposed to fighting us and our new management style is preferable."

"Why would Adley collect all this?"

"I don't know for sure. When I first met Herb, he mentioned in passing that Adley had hired him because he wanted someone he could trust at his door. At the time I thought it was an odd statement, but now not so much. Two years before he died, Adley knew something wasn't right. He was collecting the information for the same reason we're going to use it. It was his insurance policy."

"He'd have no way of knowing Dodd and the board would circumvent his will and not bring you home."

"Greg, I really don't want to ask this, and I know it's like throwing gasoline on a fire, but how did Old Adley die?"

"He had a heart attack at his desk one day." He closed his eyes and shook his head. "Are you suggesting Dodd or the board helped him die?"

"I'm not suggesting anything. I was never told how he passed, only that it was here at home."

"I was away on business at the time. By the time I got back, the doctors said they had replaced a valve in his heart and sent him home to recover. When he died here, they signed it off as a blood clot or stroke from the surgery." He dropped his head to his hands. "I never thought to question any of it."

"Clots and strokes are common after major surgery. Most likely he did die as stated. I just never knew the circumstances."

"With all this going on in his mind, I don't know how the old guy didn't blow a gasket long before he actually died. This is two years of research, and some of the dates on the documents go back a few years before he started keeping track." Greg tossed the papers on the table and stood, running his fingers through his hair as he paced. "What does this all mean, and where do we go from here?"

"I need a few days to go through all this with Harvey Masters. Then we can decide the best way to leverage the information that will scare the spit out of those old dinosaurs and, hopefully, force Will Dodd's hand. I'm hoping when he sees this list, he'll either make a major scene or just say the wrong thing." Lark pulled several deep breaths. "No matter what, Greg, we need to be a united front. I can't have those old bastards walking the halls every day and using the company like a cash register. I can't stand the sight of any of them."

"Agreed. Let your guy Harvey see all this and make some sense of it and how we can use it to our best advantage."

"I'm surprised you're not questioning my use of

Harvey."

"He's an outsider and doesn't have a dog in the fight. I'd trust him before anyone who had a hand in this…garbage." He dropped back into his chair. "Between you and me, I feel more foolish now than I did when I realized what they were doing behind my back and with you and the will. If I'd had Old Adley's back instead of just enjoying the family name and lifestyle, I might have been some help to the old guy."

"If he didn't talk to you about this, then you'd have no way of knowing. You said yourself some of the documents went back years before he began keeping copies of them. He was fooled, too, until he started looking more closely. This isn't your fault…until you found out about the will."

"We're back to that. I thought we'd gotten past that."

"We have, or at least I have. I'm just saying Adley didn't know who to trust and had to assume you were too young to be drawn into the carnage it became. I think he was trying to protect you in his own way."

"You're just saying that to make me feel better. It doesn't."

"Look, you knew the man. I didn't. I choose to believe he wanted solid evidence before he sat you down and dumped the company and all this trouble in your lap or mine."

"In all these years, I've not set foot in this room since he died. Why did you bring us in here tonight?"

"I wanted to feel close to him. And in some abstract way, if it's possible, to let him know we found this and wouldn't let it die with him."

"You found it," Greg said. "I appreciate you letting

me in on this before dropping it on the board and keeping me looking like a fool."

"I'm going to walk the dogs. I need air." She gathered up the pages and headed to the door. "Do you want to meet with Harvey and me when we go over all this?"

"Yes, please. Where will you settle him? Certainly not at the office."

"No, I've asked him to come here tomorrow. I don't want to change the routine, or the board might ask questions. There are plenty of guest rooms to make him comfortable, and he can use a separate one as a work space. I don't want him to set up in the office or dining room in case we get unexpected company. We'll all be in the same place to go over his findings at night."

"I'll head in to work at the normal time," he said. "When Harvey has answers, we can meet and go over what he's found and his suggestions."

"I just hope what he finds corroborates what Adley has in this file. Then we have leverage." She left him alone in the room. One side of her wanted to take her time and look around, but the other side of her knew to get away from Greg before she said or did something to embarrass herself. Like dropping on his lap and kissing him with abandon.

Chapter Thirteen

By the following Friday, Lark was fired up again. She'd hoped that with a little time the board members would at least look at the reports. They hadn't. They had spent their time sheltered in their offices, refusing to acknowledge her calls or emails. Apparently, they didn't care if she knew they had outside counsel coming in. It wasn't hard to find out. All she did was pull up the file from the main reception desk. Since her changes to policy, all visitors signed in with photo IDs.

During the same week, Steve's private security team arrived and set up recording devices all over the building, offices, and the estate. They set up her and Greg's new phones, courtesy of Steve. The team also set up a bypass on the existing security systems and erased all evidence they had ever existed. They gave her and Greg a crash course in how to monitor the systems.

This second round of company business would be all over the news by day's end. At least it was Friday, so she hoped something drastic would happen that would make their small in-house fight a secondary thought as opposed to a major news story. She didn't need another reason besides the tabloid gossip for their stock numbers to drop. If she was going to start a war with the board members, she wanted to do it before the next quarter's end. "Heaven help me if this all goes south." Her hope was that the new quarter would reflect true numbers with all this crap behind her. Then she'd be able to tell if she was making a difference or not.

Lark had one last saving grace. Alone in her huge office on Thursday, she phoned each of the lawyers that had been in and out of the building. "I'm calling for…" She told each one the name of the member they'd been in to see. "There is a board meeting here Friday morning, and your client will want your counsel." Surprisingly, none of them asked why she was calling and not their client.

She specifically informed each of them of the new security procedures implemented in the building and offices. She told them straight out all meetings would be recorded. Not a single one acknowledged the sentence. But she recorded the calls in case of future issues. Once specifically told, they wouldn't be able to balk. They had been warned their calls and visits were recorded. Harvey had assured her it was legal as long as the recording was revealed before the start of the meetings.

When they arrived Friday morning, they were shown to a separate conference room. She wanted them together, which usually wasn't a good idea, but for today she wanted to know their approach. She heard more than she'd expected. Obviously, some of them knew each other better than others, but it was a reasonably small community of lawyers who served their type of company. She'd had coffee and pastries set out and just watched and listened. By the time the board meeting started, she was ready.

She was thankful she'd called Harvey Masters to come east weeks earlier. He had been invested at the house with access to all the company files. Together with the research he'd helped her with before she came to the

East Coast and what she'd found since arriving, they quietly made arrangements with local legal help to have the subpoenas issued. Along with the new security crew, they were ready to seize all company records and property held by all board members and select employees, including Tom from security.

Either she was totally off base or just wrong or Greg was with her now. Hopefully, he'd be with her in all ways continually, physical included.

Again, she sat at the head of the table with Greg to her right and Herb on her left taking notes. When the board straggled in and took their seats, each one had a large file before them. Their contracts she figured. She noted a plethora of multicolored sticky notes peeking from each file. It didn't matter. Lark had gone back to her usual uniform of jeans and boots. She no longer felt the need to impress anyone with her professional look.

"Gentlemen, has anyone bothered to read or investigate the information I gave you?" All she got were stony glares. "I can only assume you all feel put out. I came along and, in a short time, figured out how you'd all been screwing over the company, even if some of it was in bits and pieces."

"I've gone over my contract and—"

She cut Mr. Dodd off midsentence. "Let's all save some time." She picked up the remote, and the huge television screen on the far wall came to life. The men were outraged when they saw their counsel seated and laughing.

"You have no right to speak to our lawyers." Dodd pounded the table with his fist.

"I haven't spoken to your lawyers. I simply invited them here this morning to save some time. If any of you had questions, they're ready to help you." She gave them an overly sweet smile. "I've been advised, since issues have come to light, this is totally legal in all ways. Each lawyer was specifically notified of the new recording procedures during meetings." She flicked the remote and backtracked to the men entering the room and helping themselves to food and drink. There were introductions and acquaintances renewed. Then she sat and waited until the good stuff started. The conversations about the reasons they were there were enlightening.

When the men felt relaxed and apparently safe, they started talking openly regarding the issues each board member had contacted them about. The lawyers gleaned that none of the board was in the right, especially keeping Lark from knowing she had an inheritance. In the end, the consensus was that the board had not only overstepped their positions but committed fraud in too many directions to count individually and as a unit.

As the conversation went on, Lark didn't care what the board members thought. She glanced from Greg to Dodd. When the lawyers let tidbits of their clients' misinformation come to light, Greg's hands fisted on the table. She gave him a quick look, and he sat back, dropping his hands to his lap.

Dodd's lawyer let out the final blow. "According to Will Dodd, once Old Adley died, that boy had no idea how he was being used. Hell, Dodd's got a second home in Connecticut that the company pays for, and nobody realizes it exists. He put it under a dummy corporate name, and the company just pays the bills. Keeps his ditzy wife up there and only visits on weekends. It was all he could take of her cloying attention."

Another lawyer added, "With all the expensive

education that boy got, you'd think he'd bother to watch the bottom line. It was easier to flit in and out and just smile with clients. He's the one who should be fired for stupidity. All this going on right under his nose, and he didn't bother to even look or listen."

Another added, "This broad is a tough bitch. I'd hire her to watch my back. Man, she must have studied the contracts and pulled each one apart, especially the board members'. I'm afraid she's dug up the corpses from hell. I wouldn't want to be any man in that room. This place is never going to be the same again."

A different man added, "If the board hadn't conveniently forgotten her existence, they might have pulled this off. But all she has to do is demand back pay and expenses. Bringing her in at the beginning would have been cheaper. She probably would have just gone along with Dodd and Greg, not bothering to open her eyes. Hell hath no fury like a woman scorned, and with the money involved here…"

Lark snapped off the television and sat back. She waited through the hollering and threats being tossed at her. Then she looked at Greg. "Did you realize the amount of disdain these twisted men carry for you?"

He didn't say a word. He was the one with the steely-eyed glares at the board. She understood how foolish he was made to look and on a different level, how he might feel. To know he'd trusted these men and thought all the fatherly advice was in his best interests had to make his blood boil.

Just a few months ago, showing the members these videos and conversations would have pleased her. She hadn't created this situation. She'd just uncovered the melee. Now it was a hollow victory. Lark didn't like being the one to tell Greg outright he'd been fucked and hadn't known it. She pitied him. Hollow was not a good sensation. That was her problem. Now she had strong feelings for him. Different than how she'd regarded men in the past but definite stirrings beyond just lust and sex. Not to discount either, but she'd bonded with him. Now it was time to find out if the emotions were reciprocal and if so, to what degree.

"Shall I ask your lawyers to come in and explain each of your positions? Or can we send them on their way before they divulge more secrets?" Pride swept through her when the room went silent. "Their fees are coming out of your private accounts. The company is not paying for their services. Check your contracts." She nodded to Herb and asked him to thank the lawyers in the other conference room and to see them out in person.

She added a quick thank-you to Herb and went back to the steely glares from the men in the room. With a tap on the remote, they watched as their counsel were dismissed. When the outside legal counsel had left, she shut off the television and tossed the remote control on the table before her. Moments later Herb returned and took his place beside her.

"Using the term loosely, gentlemen," she started, "check and mate. The questions are where do we go from here, and how will you handle yourselves? How are the two of us"—she looked at Greg—"supposed to trust your guidance or integrity? Wouldn't you agree since Adley passed away, you've all gone above expectations to defraud not only me and my cousin personally but the entire corporation and stockholders?"

Not one of the members looked directly at her. Lark took the stack of pages from in front of her and handed one to Greg. While he scanned them, she continued to watch the older men.

"All that education wasn't lost on us totally," she told them.

"Son of a bitch," Greg said. "Dodd, you fucked us royally."

"Not just Dodd. Look at the list from each of them." She and Greg spoke in whispers, noting each member and the list of offenses.

"If you're accusing me of something illegal, I deserve the right to know," Dodd told her.

With that, Lark stood and walked around the table, handing each man a detailed list of their offenses. She did not give them the disclosures on the other members.

"The two of us have discussed this and decided to give you all the weekend to make your choices. Financial restitution and retirement will most likely be the best road for each of you. But you have other options. I will remind you of all the nondisclosure agreements you signed. Think carefully. We've spoken about *slander* at a previous meeting. If any of you go to the press or leak any of this information online or in any form to anyone, the stock plummets. So does any retirement packages you're all counting on minus restitution. After Mr. Dodd's social media smear campaign"—she glared at him with total contempt—"which he has acknowledged responsibility for, we don't need any more bad press. It will directly affect your retirement packages.

"Spend the rest of the weekend considering your options carefully. I would prefer not to waste time in court, but I will just fuck with all of you. Don't piss me off again. It will be detrimental to your financial futures. And the television coverage of you all being escorted up the steps of the court building in handcuffs won't bode well for your futures. We'll reconvene on Monday at ten a.m."

Greg stood and stared down the length of the table at each person in turn. "Your decisions will be crucial to your futures. Retirement for most of you seems most logical. Considering how you've treated Lark and me, you will all agree our working situations have changed. Think carefully because one wrong word from any of you publicly and this will go public too." He raised the papers listing their offenses.

"Tit for tat." Lark shook her head. "Such a waste." She whispered to Herb, and he left after acknowledging her words with a nod.

"Before we end this meeting," she added, "you should all be aware that measures have been taken to protect the company assets. We have warrants to search each of your offices, computers, files, and homes. Everything pertaining to your work for this company has been seized this morning while we've been here."

"You have no right" was the consensus.

"Actually, the company had every right because it's all company property. The proper warrants have been signed and served. My cousin and I will make our decisions over the next few days. We'll see you Monday for your answers. You will all be here. If you're not, we will have to assume you've decided to retire." She headed to the door and paused. The first thing that went through her mind was to be thankful she was wearing her comfortable jeans and cowboy boots. The second was to realize Greg was close behind her.

Her parting shot was her finest. "By the way, all accounts have been frozen. None of you will have access to any of them until next week. Company credit cards have been suspended too. We've hired an outside forensic accountant to go over the accounts. All company cell phones are to be collected. Use your own phones over the weekend."

"You bitch, you better watch your back, you illegitimate snot!" Dodd used his arm to wipe the papers off the table before him.

"That, Mr. Dodd, is a threat to my well-being. I'm surprised you made it in front of witnesses. I'm glad we hired private security to watch our backs."

Greg took a step closer to her. "They're the ones that should be watching their backs," he said as they left the room. He closed the door behind him quietly. The two of them walked directly to Lark's new office. By the time they got there, she had turned on the real-time camera and microphone from the conference room. They huddled around the screen, watching and listening to the animosity being strewn around the room.

For supposedly smart men, none considered they were still being recorded, or they just didn't care anymore.

They went from "somebody needs to teach that bitch a lesson," to "maybe they need to have an accident." At that point, two of the men stood and headed out, both telling the others they wanted nothing to do with their suggestions. Both mumbled references to retirement sounding better than this job. The rest ranted a bit longer, but they all left the room. Though they had been notified, none seemed to censor their verbal tirades.

Greg was the one who spoke first. "I'd bet their first calls are to their homes to see if the warrants have been served."

Lark and Greg spent the rest of the day listening to the conversations going on, both in real time and by phone. Their outside security company was worth every penny they'd spent. Using the three monitors and new laptops, they switched between the board member offices.

"I'm speechless in too many ways to admit," Greg told her. "Why the cell phones, just to piss them off?"

"That too, but I figured they probably keep a lot of information in them and will have to go looking for numbers to call in the favors they think they'll get."

"Why didn't you tell me about the rest of this shit?" He paced the length of her office. "After everything we've talked about these last weeks, I figured you'd started to trust me a bit."

"I am starting, but I didn't want you pulled aside for information. Until it was all in motion, it was best to leave you out of the loop. When the hate and repercussion begin, they'll be directed at me."

"You should have told me. You turned yourself into a blatant target."

"Probably, but would you have gone along with my ideas without question?" She didn't wait for an answer. "I don't think you would have, just for old times' sake. I needed us all to know just what they were doing behind our backs and to what degree. We were together at Harvey's briefings. As soon as I found the backup information, I let you in."

"You've been here all this time, and I never realized how much weight of this situation you were carrying alone."

Lark dismissed his concern with a shake of her head. "It's over now. It's all out in the open." She went to her desk and pulled out a stack of paper files, then reached across the desk to hand them to him. "These are the personnel files on some of our people already in-house I think can take over for a while. Can we go through them and see what you think? You know them a bit better than I do."

"Only if we can get food," Greg said.

****

Later that evening, Greg stood at the dining room window, watching Lark swim her laps. He needed to decompress from their day at the office.

"I've never seen those old bastards sweat," he said, refilling his wineglass as he talked to Baby sitting in the doorway. The St. Bernard's tail swung side to side as if she understood.

"I can't believe Dodd threatened her in front of the whole room. After she told them weeks ago about the recording devices in the board room and showed them the cameras in the other conference room, you'd think they would have had better sense." He let out an exasperated sigh. "How did I not know any of this was going on? Was I that stupid or just trusting? Or was it easier not to ask? I didn't want the answers that would upset my daily routine. It was a nice bubble of existence while it lasted." He put his glass down and walked to the door to pet the dog.

"I trusted our advisors. Adley trusted them, and I automatically did too. The more I think of it, the more I realize I saw signs and ignored them. How the hell did she pick up on all this?" He continued to pet the dog.

"She was the outsider. She was the wild card the members didn't count on. And she had an axe to grind. If Dodd hadn't tried to shut her out from the beginning, she might not have dug deep or deeper. The more he shunned her, the more she realized something wasn't right.

"What do we do now, Baby?" The dog just stared up at him for a moment and dropped her head down onto her paws.

"We do what they never expect," Lark said, entering the room in her toweling robe from the pool.

"I thought you were still outside. And I was more confused why Baby was inside and you were outside."

"She didn't want to go out. I was frustrated and needed to swim."

"What did you mean we do what they never expect?"

She gave him a sly grin. "I'm going to change. I'll meet you back here in a few." As she left, Baby stood and ambled out the door after her.

****

Lark let her hair air-dry and pulled on comfortable sweats before returning to Greg. He was in the office, an empty glass in his hand. He turned as she approached, the dogs alerting him to her arrival. She yanked back yet another round of romantic wishes that couldn't come to fruition, at least for now. Maybe in a while, when all the business stuff was settled, but for now they both had to make the company a priority.

She dropped onto the sofa, and Spike jumped up beside her. She noted Greg took his time filling two glasses of sparkling water. He joined her and put one on the table in front of her and sat across from her.

"You seem nervous." She held back a smile.

"If I wasn't… Just tell me what you meant by doing the thing they least expect."

"It is so simple. I can't believe we didn't realize it sooner."

Greg put his glass on the table. He leaned forward, his hands clasped in his lap.

"Relax and breathe," she told him. "Tomorrow morning, you and I are going into Manhattan. I'd like to use the limousine. I want us as visible as possible with limits. A limo always garners attention, and I don't want either of us to have to drive."

"I thought we were laying low?" His confusion showed on his scrunched brow.

"That was the original plan. But after this morning's meeting, I realized we'd be wasting a huge advantage. You and I are going to pretape interviews for the Sunday morning news shows. We'll be a united front. The whole premise is simple. We go on the defensive before the board members take away the opportunity." She reached forward, raised her glass, and sipped.

"I'm missing something. Why would we do interviews?"

"To put out our version of events and guide the coverage in our favor." She gave him the condensed version of her idea. When she was finished, he sat back and smiled.

"Damn. Remind me never to piss you off…or not again," he joked.

"There is an old saying, and I don't know who it is attributed to. It says, 'When the wind is in your favor, capture it in your sails.' I'm paraphrasing, but you get the idea. I believe the wind is in our favor right now. Let's not let it blow by unused."

Greg stared at her. "At times you frighten and astound me, Lark."

"Thank you, Greg. That's the nicest thing you've said to me in…ever!" She smiled, and he laughed.

****

After several rounds of thank-yous and shaking hands, Lark and Greg Braylin left the studio. Their limo was conspicuously parked at the front entrance to the building where their last of three interviews was taped. Several different news and media reporters near the vehicle shouted questions.

"We've made our statements," Greg said. "You can get all your information tomorrow morning." Once in the vehicle, he was glad to be back in the car. When he went to question her, she put her finger to her lips.

"We're not sure about the vehicle being bugged since we left home. Anyone could have dropped down and placed a device under it without the driver noticing."

He nodded. "I'm starving. What are you in the mood for?"

"Actually, I want New York pizza. I had a client who went to school here years back and always talked about a place downtown that in his opinion had the best pizza." She pulled out her phone and scrolled until she found the right information. "Think we can find it, if it's still there?"

"It's still there." He lowered the privacy screen to give the driver the name of the pizza joint downtown. In his mind, it was the best pizza he'd ever had too. He refrained from asking her about the client, realizing whoever the man was had most likely been left behind in California.

Settling back in the seat, he let out several deep breaths. They were quiet during the drive. His mind was still spinning after the day they'd had. He had to admit to himself Lark was an interesting woman in all ways. He never would have thought to get their perspective on the record before Monday when they'd meet the board members. She had very efficiently shut down yet another road for the members to browbeat and threaten them or their futures. Anyone who went against their interview perspectives would be going against their nondisclosure agreements. She was one smart woman, and he sent up a silent prayer she was now on his side.

He dropped his hand on the seat between them, and she reached to cover it with hers. For just a few seconds, they clasped hands, a moment of solidarity.

Then she looked at him and smiled. "This can't happen, at least for a while."

"I know, but we all want what we can't have."

They were silent until they pulled up in front of the pizza place. Greg wondered what might have happened to him and the company if Adley hadn't had the forethought to bring her onboard. Once inside, at a back booth with their order placed, they both looked at their surroundings.

"Not the finest restaurant I've ever taken a woman to, but by far, the best pizza."

"I'll take quality over esthetics. Besides, I'm not dressed to impress."

"For which Will Dodd will twist about for years to come. You impressed me today," Greg told her as the waitress dropped off paper plates and two fountain sodas.

"Do you think the board members will watch them tomorrow?" She savored the first sips of the bubbly drink.

"I'm sure of it. Only one of them needs to see the

promo from one of the channels, and all of them will know. I'd love to be a fly on the wall of Dodd's den tomorrow morning."

"His and the rest of the board members'." She pushed back and glanced around. "I'd bet they'll all be on the phone as soon as the segment is over, comparing stories for their next moves." She sobered and looked directly at Greg. "I almost reached across the table for your hand. We can't let that happen."

"I know, but it is a bitch. We finally got things straight between us, and now we'll have to avoid each other. I hate Will Dodd and the entire board, and myself a bit too."

She nodded. "Let it go. We won in the long run." Glancing around them again, she added, "For a while, we'll keep our distance. But when things smooth out in a bit, it's nobody's business what we do together behind closed doors." She winked at him and rubbed her hands together as the large metal pan was placed between them. "This smells amazing."

They each reached for a slice and pulled them onto their plates.

Greg handed her a paper napkin. "Your first lesson about New York pizza. Fold the top crust slightly and blot the extra oil with the napkin. Then enjoy your meal."

She did as she was told. With the first bite, Lark let out a sigh. "This is my new version of nirvana."

"That, my dear nonblood cousin, is the nicest thing you've ever said to me."

"Giving credit where credit is due," she teased. "I know it's basically the same ingredients, but it just tastes…better." She wound the string of cheese from her first bite around her finger, then ate the cheese before taking a second bite.

"Same ingredients, different water. It's like New York bagels. I've had good bagels in lots of places, but New York bagels always taste the best."

"I'm not going to argue with you. This is great. Since I have no experience with East Coast bagels yet, I'll take your word for it."

"I've heard there are pizza and bagel shops in Florida that truck in water from New York," Greg added between bites. "They have the best reputations for authentic taste."

"I've had great pizza and bagels in California, but this pizza is the best. Maybe it's because I'm not carrying the same amount of angst I moved here with, but in reality, this just tastes amazing."

"Agreed," he said, enjoying the simple meal. For the first time in a long time, he too lost most of the angst he'd been carrying for months.

On the drive home Greg noted Lark had relaxed back against the seat. He followed her lead, letting his head rest on the back of the seat. "This is the first time in the last months I've felt relaxed," he offered.

"Agreed," Lark said. "And sated…by food."

"What do you think will happen tomorrow when the board members watch the interviews?"

She gave him a wide smile. "Most likely they'll scream and rant and rave. But the sweet part is we never lied. We told our version of the truth. Any one of them who tries to change the facts presented will be voiding their NDAs." She settled back and looked out the window. "I wouldn't want to be Mrs. Dodd tomorrow morning, or ever actually."

"You think he'll have the strongest reaction?"

"Don't you? He's got the most to lose. He's been under the impression for the last five years that he'd eventually take over Adley's place. Only I screwed that up royally. He's the one we have to watch carefully."

"Remind me to stay on your good side." He turned to stare out his side of the vehicle. "Most times you scare the hell out of me, Lark. Other times I just want to drop at your feet and ask for attention."

She gave him a sidelong glance. "One thing at a time. Once the business is back on track, we'll both have time for private issues."

He laughed but didn't attempt to push his agenda any further. To touch her right now would be his downfall, and in the last months, he'd spent enough time on the outside.

The ride from the city was quick and quiet. As they were nearing the estate, Lark turned to him. "Are you going to watch the interviews tomorrow morning?"

"The issue is which one to actually view."

"I'm going to DVR all three. I plan to have fresh coffee at hand and enjoy each one. We need to remind Clara and Edward not to answer the house phone and not to let anyone on the property for the next few days. That includes the day staff."

"Do you think we need additional security?"

"I think we'll be okay with the new monitoring systems. I just don't want the press having access to any of the staff, especially the day staff who might offer opinions."

"I'll tell them when we get home," Greg said with a nod.

Once home, they had the same discussion with Clara and Edward and retired to separate quarters.

"I'll meet you in the den at nine a.m. for coffee and viewing."

"It's a date," Greg agreed. As she turned to go to her room, he paused. "Lark, this is the most fun I've had in a long time. Thank you for today."

"Thank you too. It's nice not to have to be on alert twenty-four seven." She hesitated but only added, "Good night, Greg."

****

Sunday morning, Will Dodd paced the office of his Connecticut home. He had the news on, waiting and seething. The local news had previewed an upcoming segment on their national program set to start at nine a.m. He knew the anchor to be tough and unforgiving and prayed the seasoned professional would ask the right questions to upend whatever these two overprivileged people would say. He'd fended off three calls from board members when the preview aired. Then he'd taken the house phone off the hook. He grabbed his wife's cell phone and shut that off too so as not to be disturbed during the interview. Since his phone had been confiscated, that was a nonissue.

"Son of a bitch. How dare they?" He had no idea what they would say, but just the fact he hadn't thought to do an interview before them made him mad, madder than when Lark had figured out what he'd been doing with company funds. One side of him was already making mental notes of defense, and the other was furious she would take the situation public.

His wife came to the doorway with a mug of coffee for him, and he screamed at her to leave him alone. He took a few steps and slammed the door in her face. She was the least of his worries, although she was one.

Taking away her style of living would not be pleasant.

When the news program started, he turned up the volume. There they were, Greg and Lark Braylin. The announcer introduced them and the anchor who was about to do the interview. He sat on the edge of the coffee table before the TV, anxious to hear how the two bastard children would try to take away his company. As soon as he had the thought, he got angrier. It would never be his company. At least, he'd milked what he could over the last years. "You illegitimate bitch," he hissed.

"Slut," he said to the television. He'd expected them to be in full professional attire and was surprised to see Greg in tan slacks and a blue shirt with the sleeves rolled back, sans tie. Lark was in her usual uniform. He let out a snort of derision. Her white shirt and denim pants were on full view along with her cowboy boots, although she'd cleaned them up a bit. She'd skipped the blazer today. Her hair was braided down her back as usual. He figured her one concession was a bit of makeup.

"I was surprised when you called and requested this interview," the anchor started.

"We decided that after the last weeks of misinformation from the tabloid reports, gossip sites, and photographs, it would be simpler to just be honest and let the public make their own informed opinions about us and the company." She stared directly into the camera.

"Ms. Braylin, it's been hinted in some reports and blatantly reported in others that you were left out of the company for years. Can you comment on that report?"

"Of course. While I've only come east the last months, I was involved behind the scenes, learning about Braylin Industries."

She didn't say for how long, just that she was behind

the scenes, which was the truth. Dodd hated her for the misleading information, although she hadn't blatantly lied. "So that's her approach. She had done her research before coming to Long Island." He mumbled under his breath, talking to the television as if they might hear him.

"I was aware of the company all my life, but my mother and I chose to make our own way on the West Coast."

"She was Adley's disinherited daughter, Maureen?"

"While my mother and her father had differences of opinion, I was always aware of the family and the business. My mother was an artist and chose her career path early on. She was never going to be a part of the company."

"She went by Maureen Bray. Was that so Mr. Braylin wouldn't be embarrassed by her choice?"

"Goodness no," Lark said, sounding offended. "Mother wanted her works to be judged on their merit, not her family history. She was an amazing artist, working mainly in glass."

"Some of her pieces are in museums," Greg broke in.

"Yes, I read that last night while doing my research for this interview. I also saw some of her works went for six figures."

"She was rewarded for her hard work with sales, but for her, the actual work was her reward. The pieces on display in the museums were her favorites."

"Your bio is less complete. Can you fill us in on your personal history?"

"Of course. I'm a CPA with a second degree in theoretical mathematics."

"I've never known anyone who can see numbers the

way my cousin does."

"Greg, were you aware your cousin was going to join the company?" the anchor asked.

Dodd hollered at the screen. "You're supposed to be the shark reporter. Where is your snarky attitude you're known for? Hell, don't let them fool you!"

"Of course. In fact, we'd met several times in the past. It was always assumed she'd come to work with the company. The timing was her choice."

Greg seemed to have relaxed with Lark. Something had shifted between them. "They're probably screwing by now," Will mused and had a lightbulb moment. "No, I would have known. Greg has no finesse, and he's always boasting about his sexual conquests." Yet the realization didn't leave his mind. "Fuck me, they are screwing."

The anchor turned to Lark. "I was sorry to hear of your loss."

"Thank you. Staying on the West Coast was my decision, especially when my mother took ill. After her passing, it seemed time to come back east and take my place with the company."

Dodd was seething, pacing before the television. "Garbage, pure garbage and propaganda. I can work with that." He rubbed his hands together, a plan forming in his mind.

"Greg and I have equal say in the business. However, while we were hoping to keep changes to personnel quiet for a bit, the vicious headlines forced us to come forward. Come Monday, there will be a release of information about some board members retiring."

"Can you tell me why these board members are retiring?" the host asked.

“Yes,” Greg answered. “Most of the men are well past retirement age and deserve to relax. They’ve given Braylin Industries the best of their lives, and it’s time they take a respite.”

“I’d like to make it clear that these retirements were not forced. Rather, they stayed on until I was able to come east and take my place beside Greg to run the company. I’d also like it to be known that all the replacements are being promoted from within the company. Each person was personally selected and educated to take over when their superiors retired.”

“So there is no big shake-up at the company?”

“There will be shake-ups, but none that will impact our daily business. We’re all very aware a smooth transition is best for all concerned. Which is why we didn’t blatantly announce my arrival. We both”—Lark glanced at Greg—“wanted the transitions of power to be seamless, and we feel we’ll accomplish just that goal.”

“Surely there has to be some dissent?” the anchor asked.

“Actually, not as much as people would assume. While we appreciate our employees staying the course for the extra time Lark requested to complete her personal career goals, they all knew of her existence and eventual place in the boardroom.”

“Liar,” Dodd yelled at the television. “I’ll show you who can do interviews and how to do them right.”

“There were reports that Ms. Braylin was specifically left out of the business and her inheritance. Would either of you like to comment on that?”

“Again, Lark knew of her eventual place in the company. Whatever lies or fabrications have been spread by unscrupulous persons were done for the shock value.

It's made us believe those rumors were started by competitors to shake our stock values."

"Would you care to comment on who you think spread those lies?"

"There are too many to contemplate," Lark said. "Any of our competitors would like to shake the foundations of Braylin Industries. But it's all just lies for their own benefit. As were the headlines fed to the tabloids. Shock value being what it is in this day of social media, I can only assume they are disappointed their fabrications didn't affect our daily bottom line." She paused and looked directly into the camera. "I especially liked the headline that called me an urchin. Someone had their thesaurus out that day." She laughed.

"Son of a bitch." Dodd realized his error. Calling her an urchin had been his downfall.

"Do you believe your stock will take a hit with these changes, and are you doing this interview to head off any possible damage?"

"We run a strong company with strict values." Greg's tone was authoritative.

"You mentioned competitors spreading rumors. Is there any chance the rumors came from inside the company?"

Lark laughed. "No. Our people all sign strict nondisclosure agreements. None of them would jeopardize their retirement packages with gossip and innuendo." She looked directly into the camera as she said the words.

"So come the open of business on Monday, you expect things to stay the same?"

"No, not completely. While our goal is a smooth transition, we have been working behind the scenes to condense our personnel for efficiency. Granted, there will be retirements, but mainly we've been shifting our personnel into positions where they'll have a chance to use their specific talents."

"What will you say to the people who think this is a huge smoke screen to salvage your corporate name?"

"Anyone who has dealt with Braylin Industries over the years will understand our basic concept hasn't changed. Vicious lies and speculation won't change how we do business each day."

"You little shit," Dodd said as Greg spoke. "You need to watch your back, boy!"

"Are you skeptical the rumors will continue?" the anchor asked.

"We can't control rumors," Lark reiterated. "But we know the truth, and people who work with us do too. Any more rumor or innuendo is just that, borne from jealousy and the hope of destruction. Braylin has a strong history of doing the right thing. We will continue to work each day with Adley Braylin's goals in mind."

"Those goals—do you feel the reputation of the company has been tarnished?"

"No, not at all. If anyone chooses to believe gossip over substance, that's their prerogative. Our clients understand we have their best interests at heart, and our goal is to continue on with Adley's business plan. As the saying goes, if it ain't broke, don't fix it."

"There are rumors you both live in the same home. Do you care to comment on that situation?"

Lark and Greg both laughed.

"If you've ever seen the home, you'd realize it's more of an estate. We each have our own space, and to have separate homes would be a waste. After all, this is our *family* home, and we plan to continue to live there and enjoy it as it was meant to be, a family home." Lark smiled for the camera.

"What about future spouses?" the anchor asked with a sly smile.

"Lark and I can go days without seeing each other at the house. There is more than enough room for our future families to have our own private spaces and share the main living areas. That's the least of our concerns." Greg sat back and crossed one ankle over his other knee.

"Fuck you, Greg. You're an interloper too. You might have the education, but you don't have the blood. As for Lark, you might have the bloodline, but you don't have the breeding." Dodd walked to the bar in the corner and poured himself a large scotch. He drank it down and refilled the glass before going to the television.

"Bringing us back to the salacious headlines one last time, are either of you afraid of the repercussions of this interview and the disbursement of information? There were many headlines that hinted at your personal security."

"You don't have security," Dodd said. "I own the security in that house and that building."

"No," Lark said quickly. "We have an amazing security team in place *now*."

Dodd stood tall. There were things going on behind his back, and he didn't like it. If they had brought in a new security team, why didn't he know? What hadn't Tom told him? As soon as the interview was over, he'd be his first call. After all, Tom owed him his position in the company and the perks that went with it. Had he gone to the other side? "Damn you, Tom."

"All our personal and professional spaces have been

updated. Anybody attempting to breach our security will be surprised by our efficiency." Again, she looked directly into the camera.

"How did you feel when you saw the photograph of you poolside in print?"

"I felt violated," she said. "This is my home, my sanctuary, and everyone should be able to relax and enjoy their privacy. However, we've taken measures to make sure no more photographs are taken through the hedges."

"We're considering turning the west lawn into a helicopter pad to declare it a no-fly zone to keep drones from flying over," Greg teased. "Actually, we're having a screened atrium placed over the pool for privacy."

Dodd stopped listening. He was still seething about the security issues. "What new security team?" he asked the empty room for a second time. He wasn't aware of any new security. They were just talking out of their asses.

"On a different note, you two seem very relaxed in your personal appearance. What would you say to the people who don't think your style of dress is appropriate for the corporate world?"

"That's on me," Lark admitted. "When necessary, I clean up well for the clients. But on a daily basis, our minds and work ethic are what's important, not what I wear for comfort. Remember I'm a West Coast woman at heart. We don't judge people strictly for their attire. We go by their honesty and intelligence." She smiled at the anchor. "I'll admit it took people at the company a bit to get used to my laid-back look, but I feel I've overridden those concerns."

"Laid-back look, my ass," Dodd said as if Lark and

Greg could hear him.

"I have to admit you two seem to have made the transition easily. Can you comment on the changes in your lives?"

"As we've stated, Lark and I knew these changes were in our future."

"For me personally, I feel the impact of the move most with my animals. They're the ones who have had to get used to a new home, routine, and surroundings. Although the staff has gone out of their way to make the dogs feel at home as much as they've made me feel at home."

"And you, Greg?"

"I'll admit I wasn't used to pets, but they are good listeners, and they never talk back." He let out a chuckle, and the anchor laughed with him.

"When the market opens tomorrow, what will you expect?"

"The better question is what to expect when the market closes tomorrow, isn't it?" Lark asked. "But since this new management team has been in place, we don't imagine any drastic changes. We've already proven our ability to run the company without issues."

"Thank you both for taking the time to talk with me." The anchor turned to look into the camera. "After the break…"

Dodd took his empty glass and launched it into the television. The glass and screen splintered into pieces. "Son of a bitch!"

He heard his wife talking to someone at the door and glanced out the front window. A news van from the local station was parked outside. "What the fuck?" He threw open the office door.

"Mr. Dodd, do you have any comment on the interview Greg and Lark Braylin gave?"

"This is private property. Please leave." It was the most restraint he could manage before he slammed the door in the reporter's face. In that moment, he knew he'd been outmaneuvered. To say anything would endanger his retirement. His life had changed dramatically. Since Friday, when subpoenas were served and his records taken, he'd had the sinking feeling he'd be lucky to get by without Lark having him arrested. She still might, but he hoped he had a few days to consider his future. He'd gambled and lost. He couldn't start bad-mouthing either of them or the company without endangering his retirement.

A new realization struck him. He'd lose this home, and the one on Long Island where he lived during the week would probably have to be sold. He wouldn't be able to justify living apart from his wife in retirement. He was screwed. This was the opportunity his wife had longed for. For years, at least the last five, he'd promised her when he retired, they'd sell out and move to Florida. He hated Florida. Even more, he hated the idea of spending more time with his wife. Instantly, he knew a divorce was out of the question. Within a short period of time, he'd have no choice but to become the consummate husband, even if it was just for show.

"You two, wait. If you're going to make my life miserable in all directions, I will make you regret it." He believed what he said. That he would eventually take down both these snotty kids and run Braylin his way one day.

Chapter Fourteen

Over the next months as summer turned into fall, Greg had been amazed how easily Lark slid into her new role. She simply reminded the board members they drafted their contracts. It wasn't her fault their broad strokes canceled out what they assumed would feed their greed for more power and money. There had been bumps along the road, mainly with Will Dodd. She had shut him down quickly, as she had with grumblings from the board members. A swell of pride went through him when she told off Dodd.

"Dodd, you have no power, no extension of power. Your hubris has left you in your current position," Lark reminded him.

"Little bitch," he called her. "You have no lasting power and will be overthrown quickly. I will watch and laugh as you slink away. It will be the best day of my life."

"I don't slink. Before Harvey, Greg, and I are done, you will be gone with none of your ill-gotten gains. Don't piss me off further. Jail is still an option in your future."

"Idle threats," Dodd persisted. "You wouldn't dare to take that threat public. Stock prices will plummet, and mismanagement will be blamed on you."

"The last months proved my viability and staying power, Dodd. You are a dinosaur and have been outmaneuvered by the two people you didn't think smart enough to catch your underhanded dealings."

Dodd stood and leaned across the table, slamming his fist close to Lark. Greg was thankful she didn't shrink back. He and Harvey both stood at the move, but she gave them a look that he interpreted as *don't interfere*. Slowly, he sat back in his seat beside her as Harvey took his seat on the other side of her.

"Walk away, Dodd, before I follow through on my threats. I have the documentation to back up my position."

Dodd sat back down and gave her a cynical laugh. "Just because the rest of the board folded so quickly, don't count on getting rid of me." He gave Lark and Greg a look which from experience was meant to be demeaning. "I can still take both of you out one way or another."

"I'm sick of your idle threats. You have no backing, Dodd. Accept retirement, and you will be the one to slink away. We've already repossessed your Connecticut home."

After several more rounds of threats, Dodd did just that, leaving the board room grumbling under his breath about retribution to come.

"Don't take his threats seriously, Lark. We have the new security team watching our backs. They'll keep an eye on Dodd and his whereabouts and his future moves."

Lark smiled and reached for the phone. "Herb, please alert security Mr. Dodd should be leaving the building…now. Have them make sure he's off the property."

His Connecticut house was turned back to the company and on the market for sale.

From what Greg heard through the grapevine recently, Will did not like being retired, living on Long Island, and being a full-time husband. Greg sat in the backyard of the estate, the dogs sleeping around him. He smiled when he thought about how Dodd had made his own situation and now had to live with no position and no freedoms from his wife. Apparently, she was still totally infatuated with him and making him live up to the years of promises to spend their golden years together. It was poetic justice from Greg's point of view.

Eventually, Dodd walked away with his tail between his legs. With the help of her West Coast lawyer, Harvey, they managed to disengage with the current board members with little fuss. Her tapes of their few board meetings and their lawyers discussing their indiscretions sank most of their arguments. Adley's collection of evidence eventually shut down the rest of their arguments, just like Will Dodd's.

They had installed current employees drawn from each department as intermediary board members until the first of the year. So far, Greg had to admit their new board was much more enthusiastic and willing to work with them on all issues. While they had opinions on each topic, they knew their departments and their employees and were utilizing them to the fullest potential.

Alone in the conference room, Greg admitted to Lark, "Some days you annoy the hell out of me that you managed this transition with ease. Other days, I'm glad to sit back and watch you create."

She pushed off his compliment. "My mind works in different directions than yours. I think we're finding a level where we complement each other's strengths. You still meet with clients and are the face of the company."

"You have surpassed becoming my equal. We balance each other, which isn't lost on employees or clients."

With ease, she replaced Tom and his security team. A new team was installed. They were willing to work with them on all fronts.

"You were right about the extra income for the company brought in by renting out the fourth floor of the building to the computer tech company. When I thought the extra people would complicate our working environment, the reality is I forget they are up there most days."

"Good sound proofing," she teased.

"Yes, but you consolidated several smaller departments, freeing up space for an in-house day-care center. Absentee rates have dropped considerably."

"We had the room, and it just made sense to have onsite childcare."

She was still driving her gently used truck, and he retained one sedan and one SUV for his use. They kept a sedan and SUV for Edward and Clara to use along with the old clunker for the groundskeeper. The rest were sold or turned back to the lease company. They retained one town car for corporate use, and stunning him again, she had left his two sports cars. Lark had sold their corporate plane and now used a time-share system with several other companies when corporate travel was required.

"As to the unused properties, you've turned them into a lucrative side business by renting them as vacation properties. You were right again, which at times still annoys the hell out of me. The employees who oversee each one are no longer a drain on the company, their salaries, and the homes' upkeep coming from the rental income." Greg stood and walked to the sideboard. "Coffee?"

"No thanks. Sparkling water, please." She thanked him as he placed the glass in front of her. "As to the rental income, it was just economics."

His only sticking point was his want to have her in his bed. They had made the agreement months back that they should each date. Being with each other just wasn't wise on too many fronts. Greg was surprised when she brought home her vet for supper. While he wanted to hate the guy, he found he was softening to his occasional presence in the house.

He continued to date but with much more discretion. He had two women he spent time with but not with a sexual component to their relationships. Casual worked for him at this time in his life. Casual because he never wanted Lark to hear he was bedding his dates. In his world, the day would come soon when they could be together behind closed doors.

They still exchanged longing looks and the occasional brush of the hand or shoulder. Since their television interviews, they were becoming much more visible. Thankfully, the headlines became about their work and the company's prosperity, not their personal relationship. With them both being seen in public with other dates, the pressure of the lurid stories soon dropped away.

On Wednesday nights, they met in Adley's master bedroom and relaxed in the seating area, going over the week's activities and business they didn't want to discuss at the office.

"Sometimes I think it's such a waste to let that huge bed be left untouched and unused for any reason," she admitted one evening.

Greg agreed but they gave each other wide berths. Hell, he'd even gotten used to the dogs being underfoot, including Spike.

"If someone had asked you when I first showed up at the house with the dogs, I'd have bet you figured they'd be long gone," she teased.

"Now I couldn't imagine them not being around," he admitted.

On Saturday nights, they would meet in the kitchen after midnight and talk over their dates or evenings. The first few weeks had been complicated to say the least. He didn't want to hear about her time spent with the vet, and he was loath to admit he wasn't bedding his dates regularly.

They were arranging the company's holiday party, letting her assistant Herb and his assistant do most of the plans. It had been decided to use the main floor of their building for the event instead of renting out a high-priced restaurant. She had been right again. They had used the same area in October when their new board members were announced.

Greg admitted, "With a bit of decorating, the marble floor and columns along with specialized lighting give the area an ambience I hadn't been able to imagine."

"Using the reception area and keeping the parties to finger foods and sweets cut down on the costs," she reminded him.

"It gives everyone a much more relaxed tone instead of being stuck at a table with the same people you worked with each day."

"People mingle, and departments merge ideas. Productivity is up and entertainment costs down. I consider that a win-win," she said with a smile.

Occasionally, he let himself wonder what might have happened if they had brought Lark into the company right after Adley passed away. He had no answer. All he knew was she was working miracles from his perspective. As she was fond of saying, "If it ain't broke, don't fix it." Her calmer approach upped productivity. Some days it pissed him off that she was so relaxed and competent. Other days he thanked her silently when she handled issues before they became issues.

She was quick to share the details of problems as they arose, always asking for his opinion. Most times they came to an agreement easily, as soon as he realized her anticipation of disasters cut them out. Some days, it creeped him out that her intuition was so attuned.

He had stopped using her form to masturbate to each morning. After the photos circulated by the media last summer, they'd had a screen cage erected over the entire swimming area. It reminded him of a Florida backyard, but their privacy was more important. It also cut out his viewing of her, unless he joined her for a swim. Occasionally, he did, but most often, he preferred to use the lower-level gym he'd fought with Old Adley to install years earlier. He didn't need to be on display in a public gym any longer.

****

The night of the office holiday party made Lark appreciate how much time had passed. The last months had gone by in a blur.

The last thing Lark wanted to do tonight was get dressed up and go to the office party. She had no choice, but she would have preferred a night of television and snacks with the dogs. As she reviewed her wardrobe choices, she pulled out the simple black sheath. When she was closing the closet door, the peach dress she'd worn to the music school caught her eye. She hadn't worn it since.

Lark looked at herself in the mirror, and her mind raced with the possibilities. Shock value alone would be worth wearing the dress. But she wasn't about to put on a show for the employees and their dates. The photographers would have loved the sheath, but she instantly wondered if any photos of her from the music school performance would surface. That could be detrimental to her and Greg in too many directions.

After all, the Braylin family had finally managed to get off the tabloid lists. Yes, the newspapers and websites still published their photos, but those were staged business pictures. Promotional photos would be taken tonight at the holiday party and circulated. While she slipped into the black dress, her mind didn't stop considering how Greg might react. She hoped to wear the peach dress in front of Greg sometime soon when they were alone.

Arriving at the party, she noted how people looked at her, dressed to impress instead of her casual jeans-and-boots office look. She smiled and nodded and hoped she said all the right things to all the right people. She gravitated toward Harvey.

Her lawyer, Harvey Masters, had handled all the crap with the board members easily.

"You've been a good friend and lawyer to me and my mother for years. I'm thankful you agreed to stay on the East Coast and handle the contract issues as each member fought for the best deal they could arrange."

“The deal was too good to reject,” Harvey admitted. “I like the diversity of the company, and Long Island is an interesting place. I also like the ease of getting into New York City with all the restaurants, theaters, and history.”

“Kind of like being a kid in a new candy store,” she teased him. “You are an asset in all directions, especially taking me out of the line of fire.”

She’d mingled and smiled until her cheeks hurt. Standing to the side with a glass of sparkling water, she couldn’t help but remember how Adley had helped rid the company of Will Dodd.

She’d sat in on those meetings. Tom was fired for cause and his security personnel let go. They hired an entire new team. Dodd tried to be stoic at the beginning of the negotiations. After a few meetings when his arrogance overwhelmed her, she simply reminded him of all the documentation Adley had left her. In the end, he walked away with his retirement package and warnings about nondisclosure agreements.

Her finest day was when she drove to Connecticut and took possession of the home Braylin was paying for. Even better was the look on his wife’s face when they explained in basic facts that she was leaving the home and her personal items would be shipped to Long Island. Lark would have loved to have been a fly on the wall during their drive to Long Island while Dodd explained the issues.

Of course, she had to assume his version would turn him into the golden boy usurped by the younger Braylins, who didn’t appreciate all he did for them. She occasionally wondered how he would justify their lack of savings since almost all his ill-gotten gains were found in hidden accounts and returned to Braylin.

As the party wound down, Lark stood between Greg and Harvey. “Have you heard the rumor Dodd has been shopping himself to television and radio stations as a corporate commentator?”

“Thankfully, none have taken on his overblown ego,” Greg said.

Harvey didn’t hold back his smile. “All it took was that one disastrous radio interview to end his aspirations for a future as on-air talent.”

“We still have security keeping an eye on him,” she reminded both men.

Greg added, “The last I heard, he and his wife were in Florida looking for homes in the same community as his wife’s sister and her family.”

“They have to go somewhere,” Harvey said, not holding back a laugh. “Their Long Island home is currently listed for sale. Nothing against the good people of Florida, but now he’ll be their cross to bear.”

“Goodbye to him and his superior attitude and lies,” Lark toasted in a whisper with the other men. “One side of me knows I’ll ultimately find peace with the situations created by Dodd and the greedy board members. But I’ll never forget or forgive the arrogant man who thought he could keep my inheritance.”

“You’re coming to terms with his underhanded dealings,” Harvey said.

“Not to would allow him to win. I won’t give him the power over me.” She gave them a smile and wandered away, shaking hands with the late arrival to the party.

Lark continued to circulate, checking on the catering and music as well as socializing. She was becoming increasingly uncomfortable using her vet as a beard and hadn't invited him tonight. This was business, not a private event. While she enjoyed his company—and apparently, he hers—she knew keeping him as a friend wasn't going to last much longer. She was slowly withdrawing from him. Dating him had been a show for the public. Greg also dated, although from their weekend conversations, she knew he was doing it for similar reasons. They were seen in public with others. Eventually, the gossip died down, and their stock didn't tank. And thanks to people being human, within a few weeks other people took their places in the headlines of the scandal sheets and sites.

After their late-night snack and confession sessions, as they began to refer to them, she went to her room alone. So did he. She knew he was just down the hall. How many nights did she walk to her door with the intention of going to his room? Too often to count, yet each time she reminded herself of the headlines and the company's bottom line. Her main question was how long did she have to give the company her entire life? Wasn't she due some personal satisfaction? *Of course* was her answer. With any other man it would have been easy. The problem was she didn't want other men. She wanted Greg, which brought around the cycle of reasons they shouldn't be together. Frustration was at a level she'd never experienced in her private life.

That evening she had to avoid standing too close to Greg. A few times she caught his eye across the room and felt that same rush of heat vibrate through her as she had the night at the music school. With a smile plastered on her lips, she carried her glass of champagne or sparkling water and circulated through the guests. By agreement, she told all who might ask or listen that friends were coming from the West Coast to spend their vacation with her. She just didn't want anyone to know she'd be alone on the estate. With Greg going upstate to ski, their holiday plans were set.

By the time she was driving home, she couldn't remember most of the conversations. She was thankful she could remember the employee names and a tidbit about their families or dates. It had been a hacking night in too many ways. All she wanted was a few down days to clear her mind. Then it struck her.

She had a few days coming. The holidays fell on a Saturday, so the company was closed the following Monday. She would oversee the skeleton staff working the week between Christmas and New Year's Day. As she drove up to the house, a wide smile crossed her lips. The rest of the plan fell into place. They had given Edward and Clara the holidays off, reinforcing they could fend for themselves for a bit. Of course, Clara would fill the freezer, and the pantries would be stocked. Neither wanted the time off, but they couldn't disagree when she and Greg bought them round-trip tickets and all expenses paid for their vacations.

In the kitchen with the dogs out for a run, she met Greg for a quick drink. He drank beer, and she had a tall glass of milk with ice cubes keeping it cold.

"I never realized how much I'd miss Edward," Greg said. "Going to Florida with an eye toward finding a retirement community is a good idea, as long as he stays on the other coast from the Dodds."

"He could have retired years ago, but he stayed on to help us." Lark sipped at her milk. "He'll work a few more years, but I wanted him to have some time to relax and enjoy being a senior citizen."

"He's going to find an assistant and train him for a year or two. I can't imagine having to train house staff with all that's going on at work."

"I miss Clara too," she admitted. "She always wanted to see the northern lights. Hopefully, with clear skies, she will this year."

Greg sipped his beer. "She's past retirement age too."

Lark sighed. "I don't want to think about replacing her either."

"Similar to Edward, she'll find and train her replacement to the house ways for a few years before she actually leaves."

"We've discussed the possibility of replacing them with day employees instead of live-ins. That is how the rest of the staff is employed. They work days and live on their own."

"I understand your reluctance to let them go," Greg said. "We'll wait until after the first of the year to decide if we need two new live-ins."

"The change in situation would give us the privacy we crave," Lark said.

Back in her room, she hung up the black dress and fingered the peach dress. A memory from the music school surfaced as she relived the sleeves being slipped off her shoulders and Greg's lips latching onto her nipple.

She was staying home, and Greg was about to go skiing for the long weekend. While she wouldn't sabotage his vacation, she could drop a hint that she'd be alone on New Year's Eve. She wouldn't. If he came back early, it would be his own idea. Lots of wonderful ideas sprang to life as she drew a bath and used her own hands to find a bit of relief.

****

Christmas morning they had an early breakfast together. "Are you sure you don't want to come with me to ski or for me to stay home so you're not alone?" Greg asked several times before he left on his trip.

"I appreciate the offer, but I'll be fine on my own. Besides, since I came east last spring, I've had no real time alone."

"And I haven't taken a vacation."

"I'm not alone. I have three companions that don't talk back."

"We agreed our vacations would be our presents. Are you sure you aren't disappointed with nothing to open this morning?" he asked.

"Being left alone by the press was the only gift I need."

Greg gave her a mock toast with the last of his coffee. He still seemed hesitant but left after their scheduled breakfast together. She was thankful to spend the day with the dogs. Christmas without her mother was difficult, and she didn't want to have to put on a false smile for anyone.

She enjoyed the time alone. She wandered the house endlessly, discovering different items she'd not noticed. She spent a lot of time up in the attic looking through the old photo albums and peeking into trunks of old clothing. She also found time to go through stacks of artwork that were covered and leaned in the eaves of the attic. Some were just ugly; others, she recognized the artists' names. Two she thought she might like to take downstairs and hang in her room or the library. For now, just knowing they were up there was a strange comfort. She wandered the property with the dogs until the cold forced her back inside. She missed swimming, but that would come again with spring. For now, her long walks would suffice as exercise.

Dusk filled the sky the night of New Year's Eve. The alarm told her someone was at the front gate. She pulled up the camera and noted it was Greg's SUV. So he'd come home early. Lark hoped he hadn't come home with a new girlfriend. As soon as she had the thought, she dismissed it. If he'd found a woman, he'd still be on vacation. Her other reason was worse.

What if he was injured? But then would he be driving? Before it all went through her mind a second time, he pulled into the garage. Then he was at the kitchen door. When instinct wanted her to run to meet him, the dogs got to him first. She stood to the side, watching him pet each one in turn. He even gave each a treat from the tin stashed under the counter and waited until they had finished eating them. Spike got an extra ear rub.

"Hi, you're home early. Is everything okay?"

"Yeah." He pulled off his heavy jacket. "It wasn't as much fun as I remember."

"I'm sorry. I was hoping you were enjoying your vacation." She leaned in the kitchen doorway.

"It was okay, but there wasn't as much snow as I'd hoped, and it was beyond crowded."

"Oh, when I saw your truck come in, I was afraid you were injured."

"No, only my pride from a few spills I took. I'm sure there will be photos on social media of my less graceful falls by tomorrow."

"I was about to put up a fresh pot of coffee. Interested in a cup?"

"Definitely. Just let me grab my gear and wash up."

He left her in the kitchen, a room so familiar it sent a chill through her. She put the coffee in the filter and added the water, as a warmth chased through her. Similar to how it warmed her so many nights when they shared a snack and their evening events.

He was back sooner than she'd imagined, or had she been daydreaming? She busied herself feeding the dogs, taking down mugs, and pulling milk from the refrigerator. They took their usual seats across from each other, and she asked him for details about his trip. After a second refill and stories about long lines at the lifts and his impatience being at a new level, he asked her what she had planned for the evening.

"Out to supper with the vet to ring in the new year?"

She smiled and shook her head. "Actually, we decided we're going in different directions on different time frames."

"You broke up with him?" His voice cracked when he asked the question.

"It was more of a mutual agreement. He was looking for something permanent, and I wasn't. It seemed only fair to cut him loose to find a woman who wanted to marry."

Greg studied her for long moments. "Don't you want to get married?" He stood and went to the pot. He lifted it by way of asking if she wanted a refill.

She shook her head. "I couldn't imagine myself married to him. Marriage will come in time when it's the right person. For now, I know myself well enough to know it wasn't fair to string him along just to have a date for public functions."

"That I understand. So, what did you have planned for the evening?"

"Not much. Chinese takeout and a good bottle of wine before the television. And if I'm still awake, I'll watch the ball drop in Times Square."

"Would company spoil your plans?"

"Not at all. Besides, this is your house too." She stood and went about cleaning out the coffeepot. "I was going to head out soon to pick the takeout up before it got too late to be driving."

He was at the counter, seeming on edge. "Want company?"

"Sure. I'll grab my coat and put the dogs in the run while we're out."

When she returned, he was in the kitchen with his jacket on.

"You want to drive, or should I? Are you tired from traveling?"

"I'll drive. My truck is already warmed up."

After the dogs were securely locked in the run, they walked to his truck. He drove, and they listened to the radio on the way to the Chinese restaurant they frequented. The parking lot was crowded, so she ran in while he circled.

She returned carrying a large carton. As she placed it in the back, he laughed.

"Seems like a lot of food," he joked.

"Leftovers," she said and smiled. "My mom and I always treated ourselves to takeout on New Year's Eve. It became a tradition."

As he waited his turn to exit the lot, he asked, "No dates?"

"No, the eve was always so much of a forced party. Places were crowded, and service was never great. Even when I was grown up, I'd go home for the eve. It always felt natural to be safe at home to start the new year."

"This year I couldn't begin to think about being at the resort for the evening. Too much drinking and too many loud people. I must be getting old, Lark. It just didn't appeal to me either."

"Does that mean you've grown up or that I've spoiled partying for you?"

"Not you. But while I was away, I realized that a partying type of vacation wasn't my style anymore. I suppose the last year forced me to reevaluate my life and style of living and realize I had long gotten bored but didn't make changes. If I did make changes, I'd have to accept I was getting older."

"Welcome to my world," she joked. A light layer of snow flurries covered the truck and windshield. "You brought the snow with you."

"Sure, now it snows. I'd still rather be home with you, snow or no snow."

Back at the house, they set out the food before the television in the den and flipped between holiday programs, forgoing the wine for sparkling water. When they'd eaten their fill, they put the leftovers in the refrigerator, and she had her first real uncomfortable moment.

"It's still early. I think I'm going to take a hot bath. Meet you back here around eleven?"

"Sounds like a plan. I could use a shower and a few minutes to go through my email."

"See you later." She headed upstairs, the dogs automatically following her.

Once there, Lark had a decision to make. She would take her bath and do all the things she promised herself. While soaking, she used the washcloth to fend off the sensual feelings that were running rampant through her mind and body. With freshly shaven legs and moisturizer slathered all over her body, she let her hair air-dry and stood before her closet. Her original plan was comfortable sweats and a T-shirt. Now, not so much.

"Oh hell, the worst thing that can happen is he'll make fun of me." She pulled out the peach dress and matching shoes. She skipped the full makeup, using just a bit of tinted moisturizer, a tad of mascara, and a colored lip gloss. Then she pulled her hair up in a loose twist off her neck. As she slid into the dress, a new feeling washed over her.

"It's do or die," she said to the dogs. "If he isn't interested, I'll be embarrassed, but I'll live." She debated forgoing the heels but slipped into them, for herself and the full illusion more than for Greg. Then she pushed back the sleeves and tucked a condom under the band.

When she entered the room, Greg was opening a bottle of wine. He was a handsome man, she thought yet again. He had pulled on worn jeans and a button-down shirt sans tie. The sleeves were rolled back, and he was barefoot. The dogs ran in before her, alerting him to her presence.

"Wow, you look amazing," he said. "I figured we'd ring in the year with a glass of wine."

She watched a blush run up his throat and land on his cheeks, feeling a similar heat on her cheeks. "Sounds good to me." She slowly walked toward him and took the glass he offered. He stared at her, and she had to force herself not to turn away from his gaze.

"I never thought I'd see you in that dress again." He cleared his throat. "A toast to the new year and the future."

"To the future." But she only wet her lips with the fruity liquid. Then she put it aside and reached for him. With her hand wrapped around his neck, she leaned in and whispered, "Happy New Year, Greg."

"Happy New Year, Lark." His hand with the glass encircled her waist and the other behind her head.

What was supposed to be a quick kiss turned into something totally different. Sensual, sexual, and full of need. When he pulled away, she was almost afraid she'd been wrong. But he put the glass down and went back to her lips, kissing her as he never had.

She all but swooned from the attention. It had been too long, and she'd been aching for him since she first walked into this house almost a year ago. She didn't know how long they stayed there, kissing with hands fondling, until the television noise became intrusive. They separated. The program had changed to the last hour before the ball dropped.

"Come with me, Lark." He reached for the wine bottle.

She took her full glass and his empty one and followed. While she thought they might make love before the television, he apparently had a different idea.

She walked beside him up the stairs and stalled when they got to the top. "Your room or mine?"

"How about ours?" He drew her forward toward Adley's master bedroom.

He pushed open the door, and she saw he'd been in here at some point. The curtains were drawn and the bedspread pulled back. Candles were ready to be lit on the side tables and on top of the bureaus.

"Was I that much of a sure thing?" she asked.

"I figured if I was wrong, I could come in here tomorrow and take away the evidence."

"You weren't wrong. I've wanted you since the day I walked into this house and realized who you were."

He put the wine on the bedside table and took the glasses from her hands. She began to get a serious case of nerves. Her hands shook when she handed him the glasses. Greg put them next to the wine bottle and turned to her. He pushed one strap of her dress off her shoulder and dipped down to her nipple.

"You have no idea how long I've thought about doing this…again." He licked and sucked and palmed her other breast with his free hand.

She moved against him, feeling him surge when her hip grazed his penis. He switched breasts, and she let out a groan of approval.

"These are perfect breasts, with amazing raspberry nipples."

"I remember how your erection stretched me like I'd never felt before."

"I remember how you felt like hot velvet wrapping around me." He pulled her tighter, his hands on her butt. She hiked up her skirt, wrapping her leg around his thigh. Instantly, his lips were back against her nipple.

"That is amazing," she whispered and used her hand to hold his lips tighter to her breast. From that moment, they became caught in a haze of kisses and licks, of jutting hips and roaming hands. When he dropped his hand, he groaned. She knew he felt her heat. He kissed her full out until she had to pull back to breathe.

"No panties this time." Smiling, he dropped to his

knees before her and used both hands to push her skirt up around her thighs, baring her to him. His lips instantly encompassed her, and he held her to his mouth. “So sweet,” he mumbled against her.

Lark felt the orgasm build inside her and pinched her own nipples as he continued to lick her. Greg added his fingers into the mix, and she let the moment happen, relishing the pinpoint flecks of colored light that flooded her closed eyes. As the moment passed, he licked her through the orgasm and began again. As a second moment flashed through her, she wanted more.

Greg seemed confused when she stepped back. She took the condom from her sleeve and pulled the material down. Then she tossed the package on the nightstand. She did the same with the other sleeve. She shimmied her hips just a bit and let the silk flow over her and down her legs, landing in a puddle of color on the floor. His jaw dropped open, and his fingers flexed at his sides.

“Beautiful, stunning,” he muttered.

Reaching for her hand, he stood before her. Slowly, she unbuttoned his shirt and pushed it off his shoulders. Then she reached up to kiss him while stroking his back through the material. When that wasn’t enough, she dropped before him and carefully unbuttoned his jeans, going even slower with the zipper so as not to catch him in it. He sprang to life before her, full and thick, hot to her touch as she stroked him and licked her lips.

“I’ve wanted to do this since the night we met at the concert and then at the music school.” Level with his erect penis, she started slowly with licks and kisses all around him. With the tip of her tongue, she wiped away the droplet that formed on his tip. From that moment, all restraint was gone. She took him in all ways, keeping him off-kilter with licks and kisses until she was comfortable with his size. Then she'd nip at his underside and take him deeper on each pass. When she had her nose buried against his belly, she used her tongue to tease the underside, letting her teeth scrape lightly as she moved back, only to engulf him in one smooth motion. He groaned above her, and she tasted more of his essence. She let her fingers trace down his belly and follow the light layer of hair that encompassed his cock like a halo.

Greg reached down and drew her up to stand before him. Then he lifted her and placed her on the bed. He grabbed the condom from the side table and handed it to her. "I want this to go slow, but you sucking me has me on edge. The second time will be slower, but for now, I've got to be inside you."

"Agreed," she whispered as she opened the package and slid the covering over his length.

He placed his hands on the bed on either side of her shoulders and slowly lowered himself over her. Lark used her hand to guide him inside her. He teased at her opening, but she wasn't in the mood to go slow. She grasped his butt cheeks and tugged him. With one smooth pull, she had him deep inside her. Her inner self pulsed around him, and he gritted his teeth above her.

"Slow down, Lark. I want us to enjoy this. To remember this."

"I'll remember it, and slow can be next time. For now, just let me feel you stretch me." She heard the pleading in her own tone and refused to look at his features to see if he was gloating. At that moment, she didn't care. She let her body take over and pulse around him, drawing him deeper until he hit the perfect spot inside her where the world ended and only a kaleidoscope of colors lived.

As the moment passed, she used her hands to keep him there, even though his breathing was off-kilter and his arms shook to hold his weight. She gave a small twitch of her hips, and a second round of color flashed through her. His groan was all she heard. Or was it her groan? It didn't matter. When her body finally released him, he slowly withdrew and slid onto the bed beside her. Then he reached for her hand.

"Damn," he whispered. "Thank you."

"Thank you, several times," she teased.

They lay side by side until their breathing returned to something close to normal. They stayed there for a long time, their fingers interlaced. Lark had no idea what he was thinking, but she knew if he looked, she wore a sly grin on her lips.

When the situation might have gotten uncomfortable, Greg sat up, reaching to the side table. He couldn't grab the wineglasses, so he pushed himself off the bed and stood beside it. He grabbed a tissue from the box and got rid of the used condom. Then he laughed.

"How did we manage to do this with my jeans still on?" He shoved them down his legs and kicked them off.

"We managed to do it with your pants on at the music school," she teased. "Help me up."

"Maybe not. I think I like you just where you are, spread wide for me." He offered his hand to help her stand.

She drew her hair back from her face and stood beside him as he filled the glasses. She ran her fingernails across his back and shoulders, making patterns while she teased his skin with light nips to his neck.

He took his time topping off both glasses and handed one to her. She slid down on the bed on her side, the hand with the glass resting on her hip.

“What a sight. It will be burned into my memory forever. Promise me you’ll never get rid of those shoes. They are the perfect finish to your spectacular body.”

Her cheeks heated and not from the wine. “I’ll save them for special occasions.”

“Thank you. I know how you hate wearing heels. But I do appreciate it, especially when they’re displayed so efficiently.”

“Thank you, too. You’re not too hard to look at either. But I want to feel all of you, all over.”

He lay beside her, tugging a pillow behind his neck to raise himself up as he sipped. “Happy New Year, Lark.”

“Happy New Year, Greg.” She pushed up to check the time. It was a few minutes before midnight. She scooted to the edge of the bed and stood before walking to the television in the seating area. She couldn’t see the screen but turned up the volume so they could hear the crowds and the countdown. She went back to the bed and tossed the remote on the side table. Then she paused to pull the few remaining pins from her hair, letting it fall around her shoulders. She kicked off her shoes before lying tucked against him. They were silent as they listened to the countdown, and then the crowds went wild. Their kiss was intense. Her free hand dropped to his chest and began stroking him, lightly pinching his nipples and dipping lower to cup his growing interest.

Greg shifted her to find the remote and silence the television but left it on for light. While the candles were all around, they never did get a chance to light them. Their second round of loving was intense in a different direction. Slow and easy, learning and experimenting. When she couldn't take the intensity any longer, she reached to put her glass aside and took his too. He had dropped a few packages on the bedside table. He must have left them there when he set out the candles. She grabbed another condom, tore open the package, and then quickly covered his erection. Lark shifted to straddle him.

His hands went to her waist to guide her, but she didn't take her time. Again, she engulfed him with her body in one smooth motion, taking him as deep as she could. With a bit of shifting, she had him in the right spot. She moved subtly from side to side, forward and back. His groans and whispers to slow down or stay there weren't lost on her, but she knew what she needed to find her release.

Lark slowly let her head fall back and drew his hands to her breasts. "Pinch them," she told him, and he obliged. She dropped her hand to their joining and stroked them both. That pushed her over the edge into the abyss, and from his surge inside her, she knew he'd gone with her.

She let her weight drop to the side, and he instantly reached to pull her against him.

"Thank you," she said.

"Thank you too. Do you think we'll ever get to a time when slow is included in the process?"

"We'll go slow when we're old." She paused until he agreed. "Can I tell you something without you taking it as an insult?"

His body stiffened beside her.

"Yes," he said tentatively.

"I'm starved. You have to feed me before you get seconds."

"Feed you before I get seconds? I thought we were well beyond seconds."

"Forget the numbers. I need food."

"If I must." He stretched and sat up on the side of the bed. He turned his jeans right side out and slid his legs into them. He handed her his shirt. "Is that okay, or do you want to go to your room for something else?"

"This will work." She pulled on the oversized shirt. After buttoning it, she folded back the sleeves a few more times from where he'd folded them when he was wearing it. They left Adley's bedroom and found all three dogs lying in the hall before the door. "At least they left us alone," she teased.

"I had a talk with them earlier," he told her as they headed downstairs. "I promised them a walk and treats if they left us alone for a while."

"It worked." She paused to pet each dog. When they reached the kitchen, she let the dogs out to run and met Greg at the refrigerator door. She leaned over his shoulder as they surveyed their options. "Chinese?"

"How about a ham sandwich?"

"That will work," she said and helped him take out the makings and set about assembling their sandwiches. They sat at the table in their usual places, a gallon of milk between them. They began to eat in relative silence, but it wasn't an uncomfortable quiet. He finished the milk in his glass and nodded when she went to refill it.

After the first few bites, she finally asked what she wanted to know. "Why Adley's bedroom?"

"I figured it would be our bedroom eventually. I

wanted us to start out where we'd eventually spend the rest of our days and nights."

"Really? The rest of our days and nights? How do you think that will work?"

"Don't know, don't care. All I know is that is my goal. For us to be together and a united front in all directions."

"Don't you think we've given the public enough scandals in past months?"

"We didn't make those scandals. They were thrust upon us. Besides, we'll take our time and work in our own time frame. I guess I just wanted to seal the room as ours…forever."

"I can live with that," she told him.

Their sandwiches were forgotten to long, soul-searching kisses until the dogs' barking interrupted them.

Greg went to the back door and gasped. "Lark, come here."

She moved to his side and wrapped her arm around his waist as he dropped his over her shoulders. The snow had begun to stick, and the whole yard looked like a winter wonderland. "It's beautiful."

"You're beautiful, and you're mine. Do we have an understanding?"

"Yes, we have an understanding, as long as you think you can live with the urchin as your partner."

"I'll take you as my urchin partner and wife or any way I can keep you. As long as I have you."

"Agreed," she told him.

When the dogs finally had enough of waiting, she let them in and dried them off. Each was given a treat by Greg along with a pat on the head and a quick ear rub.

“I’m getting cold,” she told him.

They cleaned the kitchen and walked up the stairs, directly into Adley’s master suite. The dogs were promptly shut out in the hallway for the night. Greg found the television remote and turned it off while Lark lit the waiting candles.

She watched him kick off his jeans and sprawl out on the bed. She joined him after unbuttoning his shirt and dropping it beside his jeans. “What would you like?”

“Everything. Everything and anything. I want it all with you.”

“Agreed.” She dropped a kiss on his lips. “I was hoping the dress tonight was a hint or icebreaker.”

“It worked in all ways,” he said before reaching to her breasts, his kiss intense.

That one kiss led to others, and if the dogs hadn’t started whining outside the bedroom door the following morning, she might have tried to entice him to stay there all day or at least until they wanted food.

Epilogue

New Year's Eve, One Year Later

Greg stood before the fireplace in the living room, waiting for Lark to join him. Baby and Princess lay in their usual places, and Spike sat on the sofa at attention.

She entered wearing his favorite dress, the peach one he'd had the privilege of taking off her twice. She'd twisted her hair up off her neck, and she wore the diamond earrings she had worn the night at the music school. She looked at him and winked. Heat chased up his neck and cheeks, and he just didn't care.

In the last year, they'd learned to trust each other in all aspects of their lives. Their private relationship was kept behind closed doors, except for Edward and Clara. Both were respectfully thrilled that they had worked past the issues that brought Lark to the East Coast.

For the first months Lark and Greg slept and had sex in Adley's room but kept their clothes in their old rooms to dress. Six months later, they ordered new linens and moved their personal belongings into the master bedroom, making it theirs.

Greg still wasn't sure how he'd gotten so lucky to have Lark become his partner in all aspects of life. In reality, they'd become partners in all ways a year ago. Life still amazed him that they'd managed to come so far in such a short time.

If anyone had told him when she first arrived that Lark would become his most prized person, he wouldn't have believed them. Now he only saw a bright future for them.

While the year had its ups and downs, there were more ups than anything else. With Lark beside him, he'd learned how to reason through an argument and what caring for a person truly meant. Eventually, they'd marry, but for now, this was a comfortable arrangement. They'd proved themselves as stable and vibrant leaders of the company. Now it was time to enjoy their private lives.

He insisted on a relationship agreement, a sort of prenuptial agreement, so she would never feel he was with her or ultimately marrying her just for a larger portion of the company. She didn't argue with him. The move was sensible for their futures. At work, they kept to separate offices unless there were business issues. At home, they came together each night, leaving the company outside the gates.

Marriage was never a word he associated with himself, yet with Lark it was the word that bonded them. Tonight, this step was the first toward their future.

She met him before the fireplace, and he handed her a glass of wine. His toast was simple.

"Will you marry me? Will you be my wife and partner for the rest of our days?"

She gave him a smile he now knew meant more than just yes. "Yes, I'll marry you…in a few years. I accept you as my partner for the rest of our days. I'll marry you in a few years when we've had more time together. I feel that's rational for both of us. We're committed to each other. That's all I need for now. Can you live with that solution?"

"While I'd rather us just get married right away, I

understand your need for time."

She laughed at him. "Did you ever consider you'd marry anyone?"

"Never, but I hadn't met you. Let's take our time and enjoy each other and our accomplishments. Your commitment to me is what I truly want. A piece of paper announcing it to the world can come later."

"Thank you for understanding. In the last years, life for both of us has been a whirlwind. I just want to enjoy our time together without more scrutiny."

"Agreed. We do things in our time."

He leaned forward and dropped a kiss on her lips. One led to another, and he pulled away reluctantly. They toasted and sipped the wine. He put his glass on the mantel, and she followed suit. Then he reached in his pocket and took out a velvet box. He opened it, and they both surveyed the contents.

Of course, they knew what was inside. They'd designed them and gone to the jeweler together to have them made. After their New Year's Eve together last year, they had both dropped the pretense of animosity and began to trust and love.

While they often talked about their relationship being permanent, it was too soon for a wedding, and they both understood it would undermine their authority at work. But by summer, he had made it clear he wanted her permanently by his side. He'd mentioned family jewelry in the safe, which technically belonged to her. And he offered to buy her any engagement ring she desired. Lark was the one who made the decision. She wanted her ring to reflect the family. So she started sketching a version of the company logo, a hexagon with the *B* in the center.

Her version was constructed in platinum with the *B* in diamonds, inlaid on a base of brushed gold. It was similar to the logo, but just a bit different. She'd chosen a slim band to his wider band, but the design was the same.

She took the larger one from the box, and he the smaller one. Then he put the box on the mantel too.

"To our futures." He slipped the ring on her third left finger.

"To our futures." She slipped the ring on his third left finger.

This kiss was different. It was sensual, sexual, and it held a promise of the future. If people noticed the rings, their answer would be simple. Each felt married to the corporation. Reluctantly, he pulled back again and reached for her hand. She went willingly up the stairs.

Upstairs, Greg swept her off her feet as they entered what had been Adley's old bedroom. After they had redecorated the room to their liking, it had become their sanctuary. He placed her down in the reading area where a bottle of champagne on ice waited. With a little flourish, he opened the bottle, and she held the glasses while he filled them.

"To my future wife, my private urchin heiress," he said with a smile.

"To my future husband…" She gave him a sly smile he'd come to know meant intimacy and loving.

www.ingramcontent.com/pod-product-compliance
Lightning Source LLC
Chambersburg PA
CBHW070101030726
47506CB00002B/552
9781509249718